HEAR AND FORGIVE

Emyr Humphreys

HEAR AND FORGIVE

MACDONALD · LONDON

First published in Great Britain in 1952

This edition published in 1971 by
Macdonald and Company (Publishers) Ltd
49/50 Poland Street, London W.1

Copyright © Emyr Humphreys, 1952

SBN 356 03798 3X

Reproduced and printed in Great Britain by
Redwood Press Limited, Trowbridge & London

"Then hear thou in heaven thy dwelling place,
and forgive, and do, and give to every man
according to his ways, whose heart thou knowest
(for thou, even thou only, knowest the hearts
of all the children of men) . . . "

I
GRIFFITH JONES
GYDA PHARCH AC EDMYGEDD

I

"CALL ME ROGER," he said, waving his glass generously, as if he had given me something. He had a good appearance; tall, long streaks of grey in his well groomed hair; fit and forty. His nose, though twisted possibly in some childish escapade, occupied a dignified position in his long face. His voice was agreeably nasal. His large dark eyes suggested wide experience with women. When he smiled he displayed long teeth in perfect condition. "Writing a novel is easy."

Someone passed, pushing me against him uncomfortably close. His breath was wine-warm, wine-friendly.

"I met Charles de Visor once. In a hotel in the Rockies of all places. Fly-away Creek it was called. We spent quite an evening together. He gave me the low-down, and after all I should say he made more out of the game than anyone you could mention. He said, take a bunch of unlikely individuals and string 'em together as best you can, and keep going as long as you can keep the reader guessing. He told me it was easy. Can't think why I never tried it myself."

Regaining my proper distance I began to like him again. He had an engaging way of letting you know he believed what he was saying was a lot of nonsense. I was wondering when I should tell him that I knew his brother well and how I should put it with the most amusing effect. He seemed a lighter version of his brother, and I liked his brother a lot.

"Politics is my line," he said to my surprise. It seemed too solemn a subject for him. "Politics and foreign affairs." He peered at my glass with polite concern. "Your glass is empty. Let me get you a drink."

He wove his way expertly among the press of people to the buffet where the drinks were being served. I was enjoying the party. It was being given by an American magazine to celebrate the opening of their London office, and the catering was lavish. I never reckoned to write anything for the magazine, but I saw no reason why I should not make the best of the

9

invitation. It was an interesting occasion. Helen was away and I felt like a night out. I leaned against the wall as unobtrusively as I could, waiting for Roger to return.

He was some sort of journalist. He had been introduced to me as Roger Allenside. I saw the resemblance at once. He was obviously Edward Allenside's brother. They were both tall with long distinguished if not exactly handsome faces. But Edward's nose was long and straight and he kept his hair close-cropped. I suspected the difference meant something: a roundhead and a cavalier perhaps, or was I being fortuitously romantic? Obviously Roger hadn't read any of my books. He seemed to imagine that I was able to live by writing. Was it some absurd pride that restrained me from telling him I was a teacher at the Bilateral school of which his brother Edward was the headmaster?

One of our hosts, the English fiction editor I think he was called, came up to me and said he wanted me to know about a feature he intended to run in the English Edition. It was to be called "The most curious character I have ever known." As he earnestly expounded his idea I amused myself by wondering whether Roger would do. The magazine would pay half a dollar a word. It was the kind of thing that Roger could do most probably far better than I.

Sure enough, when he came back, Roger stood listening to the executive expounding the kind of thing he wanted. He waited patiently until the executive had finished, when he handed me my glass, his eyes twinkled delightedly and he began to speak. He had met a man in Patagonia who claimed to be the rightful king of England. He was a half-caste and his name was Domenico Plantagenet Jones. The executive listened carefully at first, but something in Roger's eloquence put him off. He became suspicious. He murmured something about the story not being authentic enough. "Our readers want 'real life'," he added and moved away. For a moment Roger looked a little disappointed. Then he began to laugh. "There goes a man," he said, "with very little imagination. You can tell by the way he walks. He carries his head as if it were a portable strong box."

By this I had become eager for an opportunity to tell Roger how well I knew his brother. But Roger had decided there were one or two people he would like me to meet. "Real people, you know," he added with a smile. "Real life, real people. Oh dear yes."

We climbed a wide staircase to a quieter room where nearly everyone was able to sit down. I saw my publisher away in a corner and I was anxious to catch his eye, but Roger was unwilling to let me go. I waved across the room but the publisher just wasn't looking. He was deeply engaged in conversation with two eminent members of my profession. It would have been a chance to meet them. *This is David Flint one of our most promising young authors.* . . .

I found Roger's friends dull. There was a fat girl, thickly made up, who wrote on interior decoration for an expensive women's magazine. A jolly type with a handle-bar moustache who was introduced to me as the sports editor of a national daily. A morose dyspeptic man of incredible thinness who drank only lemonade, was a Canadian journalist of some kind who seemed to know no one except Roger and every now and then made half-hearted attempts to win his attention. But Roger was engaged in holding the attention of all of us at once. Finally a bald-headed beak-nosed man, who, inexplicably, was a house agent. He listened with a fixed smile to everything Roger had to say. Roger apparently had got him in. In his own subdued manner he was obviously tingling with excitement at having arrived at a literary party in a Knightsbridge hotel. Every now and then his glance shot across the room in search of celebrities and then returned to settle dutifully on Roger's face. Roger seemed to have aimed at collecting a bunch of good listeners. I began to consider how best to get away. It was all very well to be studying my headmaster's brother, but there might be more important contacts within easy reach that I was missing. Roger was talking now about South Africa.

"So I took him home in the office car. He was absolutely blotto, poor chap. The farm was an incredible place. I can't tell you too much about it though. Maybe I'll put it into a novel." He grinned happily at me.

"You really ought to write a novel, Roger darling," the fat girl said.

"But there is such a thing as the law of libel, isn't there?" The house agent looked knowingly at his hero.

"Not if you keep your mouth shut, my dear Rufus."

The house agent laughed.

"Don't worry Roger. I know how to keep a secret."

The strains of dance music floated faintly up from the ground floor. I saw a chance of escape.

"I want to dance." I meant it to sound firm but no one seemed to have noticed I had spoken.

"Between ourselves, in strict confidence," Roger said, "I don't mind you knowing. He was the only son of Lord Whiteway. You've heard of Lord Whiteway?"

Rufus Wod slapped his knees delightedly. The others did not seem to see the joke. But I forgot I wanted to dance and listened eagerly.

"Oh a very big noise indeed isn't he, Rufus?"

Rufus sniggered ecstatically.

This was absurd. Lord Whiteway *was* a very big noise. Chairman of Brown Properties and member of endless boards of directors but most important of all to me, Chairman of the County Education Committee, and, this was really too much, Chairman of our School Governors. The Bilateral was in the heart of the South London suburb that was Whiteway's little Empire. And there was more than that in it too. He was Helen's uncle. My Helen's uncle!

"What did you say his name was?" the fat girl exclaimed. "Horace! I didn't know people still used that name."

"He *was* a very good poet." The Canadian journalist winced to restrain a dyspeptic belch. I glanced at him sympathetically. He was obviously a man of decent culture. If only I wasn't intent now on every word that passed Roger's lips, I would make an effort to detach him from this company and enjoy his conversation.

"Horace Walker-Brown. Highly respectable name I should say." Something about Roger's grin suggested that wine had lubricated his tongue rather more than he could control. He was on the brink of the mood in which a man gives away valuable secrets just to win laughter and approval from his admiring companions. "The Honourable Horace Walker-Brown. His papa sends him a substantial cheque once a month, and little Horace waddles down to Durban to collect it, and spend it. A darkie writes home to acknowledge receipt of same with a pro forma sort of letter saying how well the farm is doing."

And this was Helen's second cousin. I had heard of him. Some passing reference to a latter day empire builder. There was a certain coolness between Helen and her uncle. Her father, Whiteway's first cousin, had been senior partner in the firm. From what Helen had told me, it seemed her father had no real taste for business. He had an eccentric interest in religion. Certainly there were plenty of books on religion in Helen's maisonette in Kensington, in which I was living alone since Helen was away in Switzerland. Lord Whiteway, or Harold Walker-Brown as he was then, had gained complete control. Helen still derived most of her considerable income from "Brown Properties", but I fancied the slight resentment in Helen's attitude towards her uncle was due to his having made her father less of a man than she would have wished him to be. Helen had a most practical nature. Her religious impulses seemed to obtain their outlet more in a personal sort of philanthropy than in any refinements of dogma or comparative religion.

"Two!" said the fat girl in a voice of shocked yet intrigued amazement.

"Two cape-coloureds," Roger repeated solemnly. "Mother and daughter, competing for Horace's attentions, quarrelling about him all day, and more or less running the place."

"No. I can't believe it," the fat girl said; as if incredibility lent additional enchantment to the story.

"True every word," Roger protested. Rufus Wod nodded knowingly. Now Roger seemed to regret having said so much about Horace. He began a new story about a war correspondent who had flown home from Belgrade via Cairo, Durban, Cape Town, Casablanca and Marseilles.

I thought of Lord Whiteway on the day I was interviewed for my present job. He sat behind a long table, a large mountain, with two normal sized men on his right and a middle-aged woman and a small man on his left. He asked me leading questions. A domed head crowned the mountain and he spoke with a rich clerical voice. He asked me whether I was prepared to share the responsibility for Religious Instruction in the school. He said he attached great importance to the work. Rather inanely and a little too anxious to please I had added so did I. The headmaster had smiled at me encouragingly. I liked him at sight. I got the job. I don't know whether Helen had told her uncle I was trying; but in any case they usually took the man the headmaster wanted. Allenside had taken to me just as I had taken to him. Outside school we often shared each other's company. We had been on a walking tour in Cornwall together. We were so friendly we tacitly agreed that it was wiser to conceal the extent of our friendship from the rest of the staff.

I was glad now I had not told Roger that I knew his brother when we were first introduced. It helped me now not to call out inviting the company to share my inane amazement that I lived in a flat that belonged to this very Horace Walker-Brown's second cousin, my friend, Helen Brown. Something about Roger's appearance must have compelled me to hesitate in spite of the name and the physical resemblance: something out of keeping. His manner was so different from Edward Allenside's: and the headmaster had never mentioned a brother. Perhaps their paths separated long ago and I would find myself in the embarrassing position of linking two men who wished to remain apart. Roger was saloon bars, clubs, the odour of good-time decay; a social climbing journalist deliberately operating his charm. Edward was clean shoes on a classroom floor, a time table and steady work.

"Roger! Will you give me a dance?" The fat girl had got up and it was impossible to refuse her. He glanced at me as if it was convenient now to remember that I had just expressed a wish to go dancing, but I moved away to give them more than ample room to pass. I followed them down stairs and I found Rufus Wod the house agent walking alongside me. He wore evening dress and his thin stooping figure might have belonged to a scholar. Only his face, I thought since I disliked the man, gave away at once what kind of books he poured over.

"Isn't that V—— P—— over there?" He nodded eagerly in the direction of the overcrowded first floor where most of the guests were still congregating. "And there's S—surely? Very like his photographs don't you think?"

He did not seem to mind my not answering.

"I'm afraid I haven't read any of your novels, Mr. Flint. I get so little time for reading. I'm really quite ignorant. When I do get a moment to spare I like to turn to the old favourites, you know. Dickens, I mean, and Miss Austen. Have you written many? Forgive the question. I had heard of your name, of course."

It was going to be difficult to get rid of him. He stood firmly by my side watching the dancers. Roger and the fat girl gyrated past. Tall as she was, we caught Roger's wink over her head.

"Did you know Roger before?"

His eye was fixed on me now with real interest, bright with dissembling some little jealous calculation. I shook my head.

"I suppose you could call us quite old friends." How proud he was of the fact. I wondered for a moment what obscure suburb he had crawled out of. "We used to work in the same office before the war. Roger was going to be an architect then. I was on the business side. He still takes quite a keen interest in houses and motor cars."

Wod giggled inexplicably. The last remark must have been a private joke.

I gazed around impatiently in the hope of catching a glimpse of someone I knew. I felt myself rapidly sinking to Wod's level. It was one thing to be alone, morose and intense, standing enveloped in contemptuous anti-sociability, striking an interesting pose; quite another to be amalgamated in mediocrity with Mr. Wod. With sudden panic I began to think we appeared the most drab couple in the entire building; even the cloakroom attendants were more deserving of notice. I wished I could vaguely detach myself with some eccentric absent-minded look, and I damned my bourgeois inhibitions for not allowing me to do so.

Roger and the fat girl stopped in front of us. That the music had stopped I realised a moment later.

"You wanted to dance with Sylvia, Flint?"

The passive monument stood waiting for me to steer her round. The music started again and my arm lay along her waist as if along the back of a well-padded arm-chair. Her armpits had been shaved and scented but our exertions—absurdly the dance was a polka—had begun to make her sweat gently. Beads of sweat forced their way out through the smooth layers of make up, but Sylvia continued to maintain a small fixed smile. For my part I could feel the long drips rolling down my nose, and my vest, I knew, when we stopped would be soaked with spine-chilling sweat. The prospect was

15

even more distressing than having to keep smiling on. I told myself I was out of training. Teaching and writing involved too much standing still and sitting down. We swirled past where Rufus Wod was still standing, alone. Roger had not taken long to get away. Coming round again I caught a glimpse of him in animated conversation with an attractive literary agent whom I knew quite well. I vowed to accost her as soon as the music was over. Sweat or no sweat, I would ask her to dance.

She looked a little surprised to see me.

"You look a little harassed, David," she said as we took the floor. "Not running away from the police, I hope?"

"I think I must be." I push the hair off my forehead. "My dear Rosalind, how nice to see you. You've no idea."

"How's your school? Still teaching Scripture?"

"Fine. Absolutely fine." All my friends knew I taught scripture in a Bilateral School. After Rufus Wod and Sylvia I felt the attractive literary agent was a very old friend indeed.

"That chap you were talking to—Roger Allenside."

"He's one of our authors."

"What kind of books does he write?"

"He's written one or two travel books. He says he's writing one now, about South Africa. He just said he was thinking of calling it 'In Black and White.' Do you like it?"

I shook my head.

"His articles sell well. Especially in America."

We passed Rufus Wod again. He nodded at me benevolently.

"He's my headmaster's brother."

"Who? That beaky man?"

"No. Allenside."

She expressed polite surprise. Naturally she didn't find the knowledge as interesting as I did. No one disbelieves coincidences however improbable; but no one is interested in them either unless they are personally relevant.

"They're not a bit alike."

I must have sounded puzzled, because she smiled at me and said:

"That's quite often the case, David. I have a sister in a convent."

"I didn't know you were a Catholic."

"I'm not. I'm just an unthinking Anglican."

16

When we sat down she asked me how my new book was progressing. She really seemed interested so I told her it was about the first Duke of Somerset who executed his brother Sir Thomas Seymour for the good of the country and ultimately got executed himself by the Earl of Warwick.

"Is that why you are so interested in brothers?"

I hadn't realised it myself until then. Two brothers, one serious, thoughtful, high-minded; the other, gay and irresponsible. Did the Allenside brothers fit into the pattern?

I became anxious to get into conversation with Roger again. My curiosity was roused. In the course of duty, I didn't mind any longer if it meant hob-nobbing with Rufus Wod again. He said he had worked with Roger in the same office. Perhaps Sylvia even had something to tell me that I wanted to know. Quite suddenly they ceased to be dull nonentities that I wished to avoid. My professional interest was roused. *The counterfeit presentment of two brothers*. . . . Wasn't that exactly what I was after? Roger and Edward. Two continents to explore. Already my blood was racing with the impulse of creative excitement. Or was it the wine, the place and the music? I was tempted to ask the attractive literary agent to come out for a walk in the Park. Across the street it would be dark and quiet. But this was nobody else's business except mine. The sharing would come later with the anonymous dear reader who took my book down from the Public Library shelf. It was a secretive process, like keeping an intimate diary that one day everyone could read. Not a noble profession at all; but like watching spiders, an obsession half way between a hobby and a science.

Now I had attached myself to the literary agent I found it difficult to cast off again in order to go voyaging through the rooms in search of Roger. Not that I imagined that I owed her the boon of my company. I feared only that she might imagine I wished to rid myself of hers. Had I any of the perspicacity that novelists are supposed to employ, I could have foreseen that someone else would not be long in spotting so attractive a dancing partner. I found myself alone again rather sooner than I would have wished. Could it be that, all the time, she was wondering how to shed me?

I circulated the hired rooms in search of Roger until I wearied of the pursuit and consoled myself with the amusingly fuddled reflections of a B.B.C. poet. When he expressed the

17

wish to go downstairs and dance with me, a rapid calculation
of the effect such an escapade would have upon my reputation
allowed me to follow my natural inclination and refuse: that
sort of thing was all right for poets. Instead we stood in the
foyer (the right word, I insist, for this was a house devoted to
entertainment) and enjoyed a heated discussion on the Holy
Spirit, he being a recently converted High Anglican and
myself a Dissenter of the Independent Persuasion. We argued
with heat but with enough of the fashionable detachment
affected by our Byzantine generation who have declined from
messianic political leftism to speculative religion.

About midnight, when most of the guests were gone, Roger
appeared again, on his arm a statuesque darkly handsome
woman, most strikingly draped, with the traditionally dazzling
white shoulders, and about her throat a velvet band of deep
purple. When he saw me there was a tell-tale hesitation before
he smiled that suggested it had been an effort to remember my
name.

"David!" They advanced towards me. "Lydia, I'd like you
to meet David Flint, the novelist."

"Hello!" She was American: and much younger than I
had imagined. Possibly not yet twenty.

"I don't suppose you've read any of his books, any more
than I have."

"I guess not." She must have been born in an envelope of
self-possession. "But I will now."

After all it was exactly the right thing to say.

"We're looking for a taxi. Can we give you a lift?"

A commissionaire took care of us. The street light nestled
into the dark tree-tops of the Park across the road. I looked
up and breathed deeply. It was a mild yet starlit night. The
balm of summer stealing through a night in early May. Roger
gave the commissionaire half a crown. I also intended to, but
the taxi moved off while my hand was still in my pocket. I sat
with my back to the driver. I saw Roger take confident
possession of the American girl's hand. I felt envious and
wondered whether I had been invited to witness the triumph
of his skill; whether my jealousy was to be his applause.

"Lydia has come to England to complete her education."
Roger laughed pleasantly. "She's here for six months, David.
Now what advice have you to give her, David?"

I was tempted to say that I could leave all that safely to him, but instead I talked at such length that Roger was obviously very pleased at the way Lydia leaned forward, with her hair hanging on either side of her head like the ears of an eager spaniel. Roger treated her with the serious consideration of an affectionate uncle. When the taxi stopped to drop me off at South Kensington Station I was on the verge of rebuking myself for my unworthy suspicions. Roger gave me his telephone number and I promised to ring. I gave him mine. But as the taxi swung round the square I caught a glimpse of them. She was being taken with a perfectly judged degree of passive willingness into Roger's arms.

I walked down the Fulham Road to the flat in which I was living alone now Helen was away, lonely, a little sorry for myself, a little regretful I had not made more profitable use of the party, and grudgingly envious of the obvious success that Roger Allenside had with women. There was no reason why some personable young woman should not be accompanying me homeward now except a certain negative kind of conscience, and a lack of the requisite skills in pseudo-wooing.

II

Before the bell had stopped ringing the headmaster
entered the staff-room.

"Good morning, gentlemen."

He sounded cheerful. The sunlight pierced the dingy room
from the top corner of one window, like a spotlight. Edward
Allenside was habitually even-tempered, but morning sunshine, as he told me himself, always made him feel exceptionally energetic, cheerful and optimistic. This morning I watched
him with particular interest. His face was rounder than
Roger's; his hair, close-clipped, did not appear so grey. The
long straight nose seemed more sober and restrained. He
stood at the head of the table with legs apart, at once more
purposeful and more reposeful than his brother. Not that
Roger was aimless or jumpy. Roger was altogether more self-
conscious. He used his person as if he were an actor producing
his own play.

Conversations subsided and from where we stood or sat we
listened with respectful care to his résumé of the day's an-
nouncements. One or two modifications of time-table were
discussed. I noticed Mr. Briarman had quietly placed himself
on the headmaster's right and simultaneously almost Mr. Dell
had moved to a corresponding position on his left. Contenders
for a vacant throne. The position of Deputy Head was vacant.
An appointment would have to be made in the near future. It
diverted me to observe the progress of manœuvres. There was
also impending, the award of a special responsibility allowance. Only yesterday Bill Hawkes, teacher of building geometry
(who was not in the running) assured me that atmosphere of
the staff room was "as bad as the ruddy Security Council."
Bill Hawkes had come to teaching after many years in the
building industry. It was his habit to take what he humorously referred to as "The wider view." Briarman, a lean,
pale-faced man with untidy hair and small eyes, had also made
teaching his second career after ten years abroad. But he never

made too much of the fact since Dell liked to remind us that he had spent "over twenty years in the profession," and that length of active teaching service was regarded by the Union as a vital factor in the composition of promotion lists. It was all rather difficult for Allenside, since everyone knew the Governors would accept his recommendation without question: difficult, unpleasant even, since I knew he was not the kind of man who enjoyed this aspect of the exercise of power.

"The hymn this morning, Mr. Flint?" He smiled at me. I stepped forward with my hymn book open.

"Number thirteen, Mr. Allenside. '*Now thank we all our God.*'"

"Is there anything I've forgotten?" He prepared to lead the way into the Assembly Hall.

Unexpectedly Brunt, the engineering master, spoke from the corner in which he had been sitting in morose silence, stroking the corner of his clipped moustache with a knuckle or biting the corner of a finger nail.

"There is one thing."

He arose and advanced towards the table holding before him a copy of *The Daily Worker*, torn into three long strips.

"There's this Mr. Allenside." Brunt laid the three strips carefully on the table. He appeared to have decided beforehand what to say. "When I got here this morning, I found my paper on this table torn. I would like to draw the staff's attention to this piece of wilful and malicious damage to my property. I demand to know who is responsible for this."

The headmaster pressed his lips together regretfully. He did not immediately notice that Brunt was staring very pointedly across the table at Eglinton, who sat, staring back at Brunt and smoking with studied unconcern.

Eglinton was a Catholic. He had a narrow nose and a refined accent. He specialised in being a gentleman. It was obvious that anything he said would upset Brunt's temper. Bill Hawkes, who was standing at my side, muttered in my ear: "Ain't they just like a pack of bloody kids?"

Exhaling smoke with calculated calm, Eglinton said:

"I must say I applaud the action."

As if stuck with a pin, Mr. Brunt exploded.

"Did you hear that, colleagues! Out of his own mouth. . . ."

"Gentlemen!" The headmaster's voice rose slightly. In silence everyone waited for him to speak. "Will you deal with this yourselves please, as a staff-room matter? I would prefer not to consider regulating standards of behaviour in the Staff-room as part of my duties."

Without another word he led the way to the hall. When the headmaster took his place on the dais at the centre of a semi-circle of members of staff, the whole school, from Form One, still in short trousers, to the tallest Prefects in the back, was completely silent. I took my seat at the piano. Allenside gave out the hymn and the boys began to sing. It was not melodious, but reasonably cheerful. I kept my mind on my playing so as not to strike up a chord for a fourth verse when there wasn't one. I did that once, and a wave of titters swept the assembled school.

Mr. Visot stepped forward to read the lesson. The boys called him Visotski. Like Brunt he was a Communist Party member. Certainly he did look as if he had just shuffled out of the British Museum. His feet were unusually big, his thin legs were always encased in baggy trousers and his jackets were always buttoned tight across his narrow chest. I fancied his suits (I estimated that he must have possessed three) were all stained with ink and gravy in the same places. A bulging forehead protruded above thick-lensed spectacles which concealed red-rimmed, blood-shot, yet absolutely warm and friendly eyes. His lips were curved like a duck's beak as he read with gusto. It wasn't often he could be so sure of a quiet hearing.

Seated with my back now to the piano I had a good view of my colleagues. Mr. Dell, inclined to plumpness with bald head and large moustache, a vicar's warden, was stirring uncomfortably in his chair. It was always the same when Visot read the lesson. "Where's the man's conscience?" Dell would say; and sometimes gaze accusingly at me as if I were an accomplice in a flagrant act of sacrilege. I selected the passages and the readers for the morning assemblies.

At the moment Visot was declaiming vigorously:

"*But I say unto you, love your enemies, bless them that curse you, do good to them that hate you, and pray for them which despitefully use you and persecute you* . . .

There was more than one way of catching the conscience of

the king. I bowed my head a little to conceal a self-congratulatory smile. But I became apprehensive of my own smugness again. The words flew up, the thoughts remained below. It was happening with me and it could happen with him. We wore armour of different metal but both designed to keep the Holy Spirit out. Before Visot had finished reading I disliked myself so much I would have welcomed a public humiliation.

The headmaster stood up and closed his eyes. "*Our* Father . . ." he began. Other mornings with half opened eyes I have slyly observed the attitudes adopted by the other men on the platform: Brunt with his blue eyes wide open, at attention, like a soldier about to be decorated, usually stood opposite me: but this morning I was too intent on my own supplication to notice anyone else. I had acquired the habit of talking to God as if he were listening. This was strange because half my time I failed to succeed in persuading myself He existed. A nervous traveller I suppose, who chatted to an imaginary father-figure to keep up his spirits in the frightening dark. And yet in the staff-room I was the Defender of the Faith. I flattered myself that I could argue Brunt and Visot under the table. I loved to provoke them by talking of *The Unconditional* and *The Absolute*. Few things gave me quite as much exultation as the effort to tear some thesis of Brunt or Visot or Briarman, our respectable agnostic, to shreds.

The Headmaster stepped forward to read the day's notices. Although the Bilateral was housed now in a shabby building, there were promises and plans for spacious new buildings, and Allenside exerted himself to inspire the whole of the school with something of his own enthusiasm for the Bilateral experiment. There were changes in time-tables, and I put my hand in my breast-pocket to make suitable notes in my diary. (I do so not to display my keenness but to relieve my memory of any superfluous burdens.) As I did so the back of my hand rubbed the envelope of the letter I had received that morning from my wife. I had still not read it properly. But I knew with bitter certainty that she refused.

Later in my class-room, while a junior form were answering questions I had written on the roller-blackboard concerning the prophet Elijah, I was able to glance at it, the letter hidden by the up-turned lid of my attache case. It was short enough.

Dear Davie, (Is there anything more sour than a discarded name of endearment?) *I was sorry to get your letter even though we were longing to hear from you. as for what you ask I would like to please you Davie, but honestly I can't do it for little Stanley's sake. I have not shown your letter to Father because as you know he would not understand and it would upset him. I have made up my own mind about this so dont blame Father or anyone else.*

Your wife
Phyllis

As inarticulate as ever. I could not work up any indignation against her as I gazed at her neat but sparsely punctuated writing. Cursing her would be like kicking a docile cow. It was foolish, unrealistic, of me to have expected anything else. Not that she really was docile. That was merely the impression her brief letters gave. She could be as stubborn as a mule; the martinet of a semi-detached home.

Phyllis Rayment. Rayment the ironmonger's daughter. I married her in a hurry in August 1939. I was twenty-two then and I had just collected my degree. I was going to be a conchie if war broke out. My name was down for a Pacifist Service Unit. Like so many others I imagined a war would be the end. It was just my luck that I imagined myself to be in love with Phyllis at the time.

I still think she was personable enough. Her body might still excite me if only it did not belong to Phyllis. I don't mind admitting when I first went away early in 1940 to clean ditches in the Fen Country I was disconsolate without her. An enlarged photograph in a celluloid case balanced precariously on the mantelpiece of the bedroom in the damp cottage I shared with four other chaps. All earnest young men like myself. A week-end at home (I still called it "*at home*" then, but in fact it was my father-in-law's house) was a heavenly interlude of bliss and comfort. Phyllis protected me from her parents' disapproval. The door of our room was closed and there was too little time for anyone to open it and intrude upon our brief privacy.

I date the beginning of the end of our love long before any breach appeared on the surface. There was one week-end I remember I had particularly been looking forward to. Phyllis was five months pregnant and I was full of self-indulgent concern about her. She wrote one of her brief notes asking me not to come home that week-end since her brother Stanley would be home on leave. Stanley was an assertive articled clerk who fancied his prospects and knew all the answers. We never liked each other. He tried his best to dissuade his sister from marrying me—"*He's not your type Phyl, definitely not*"—and although at the wedding breakfast he was the life and soul of the party, he was the first to pronounce— truthfully enough—that the marriage was a mistake. In asking me not to come home Phyllis was concerned to avoid placing me in what she feared would be an awkward and unpleasant situation. But I was hurt. I spent that week-end in London at Max Hepple's flat in Tavistock Square with Max and his brother Derek who worked alongside me in the ditches. There was a party. Mostly intellectuals in the N.F.S., girl ambulance drivers and a soldier or two. No one bothered about me being a conchie. Plenty to drink and a gramophone. I enjoyed myself immensely. I felt I had been a moderate success in a kind of society I had not moved in before. On Sunday morning I showed Max some of my stories and poems, and we sat on the floor listening to Bach on the gramophone. I needed a way of living very different from that of Elmscot, Warrington Avenue. I felt I had found my true *ambiente*. I was accepted without question among persons of my own kind. I had begun to work on my first novel. Some of my poems were published in the little reviews. I began to acquire the faint aura of being a promising young writer; but I became increasingly aware of how little ice that would cut in Warrington Avenue. There I was Mr. Rayment the ironmonger's misfortune, an unprofitable if not disreputable son-in-law, and little more.

Our son was born. Not without irony I myself suggested he should be called Stanley after his uncle and Herbert after my father-in-law. He was christened Herbert Stanley David Flint. I was present at the christening. The minister was a little uncertain how to handle me: Mr. Rayment was a senior deacon in his church.

When the blitz began we were established as a Service Unit in Bethnal Green. How ridiculously enjoyable it all seems in retrospect. One forgets the moments of agonising fright and remembers only the delight of a heightened awareness of living, the strange freedom in the daytime, after a night of fire, of walking whole among the smouldering streets. There were times when one felt like a neutral spectator who has stumbled across the field of battle of Waterloo.

Between the raids we worked in London hospitals. I didn't enjoy hospital work so much. I preferred to come across a corpse among debris than on the cold slab of the mortuary. Knowing the circumstances of death always makes it a little less terrifying and stark. But it was in hospital I met Marian. She couldn't have been more than eighteen. I loved her at once. She walked through the wards like Primavera in starched white cap and apron. Flowers sprang up where her feet had been. The bunch of safety pins fastened to her belt made music for me. We spent unforgettable hours together in Max's flat. The first time she was so shy she undressed in the dark and her whole body trembled when I touched her. There was a day and a night and another day in November, and on the second day we came out into the chill air, deliriously happy and ravenously hungry to see that the sun was already setting. Once she came from Night Duty and I woke up to see her standing in the centre of the room. I was surprised I remember at how little she wore beneath her uniform. It was the earthly Paradise. A loveliness one does not expect to know again. For a short time I was something I can still look back upon and admire. Love gave me dignity. Marian found an absurd animal of ink and paper and for a short while made him a man.

Marian is dead. It was only a temporary rehabilitation.

While I was in Egypt, waiting for transport to Yugoslavia with a War Relief Team, the hospital was struck by a flying bomb. In June Nineteen forty-four, Marian was killed.

Do not think I am making a romantic mountain out of a war-time mole-hill. She was only a girl of course and we had little time together. I am not pretending I can even remember exactly now what she looked like. I lost my wallet containing photographs of her when I was perched on the back of a lorry, trying to guide a food convoy to a Bailey bridge to cross the Po just east of Piacenza in May, nineteen forty-five. When I wasn't working I drank as heavily as I could. All I really remember of Marian now represents a path of moonlight on dark shifting water. I came that way, I walked that water. It was a miracle. But I cannot go back. It will not happen again.

In the Middle East and in Yugoslavia there were consolations. A man of my kind cannot live for long without the company of women. I sometimes wonder where they are now. I even toy with the notion of returning to those women and those places, but I know I never will. As each year passes they grow more remote. Time past has its own way of dying. It is a period of my life I would not wish to disinter; unless, of course, at some future time there is material there I might need for some new novel.

I returned to England in nineteen forty-six. I hung about London until being short of money drove me home. When I rang the front door bell a fair-haired freckled boy of six opened the door. This was Stanley. I lifted my arm to pat his head. He fled to the kitchen. I heard him say in a deplorable accent, "Mummy, there's a man I don't know at the front door." Phyllis appeared; uncertain; glad to see me, but with reservations. The old man was hostile from the start. I had no right in his view to be alive when Stanley so much more worthwhile a person was irretrievably dead. The old man no longer went to the shop, he was about the house all day walking woodenly about, crippled with arthritis. In bed Phyllis declared we would not make love until she had satisfactory explanations for several matters outstanding I had not seen fit to explain to her. She cried. It was all very absurd. I stuck it for a week. Stanley and his grandfather were in league against me; Phyllis swept silently around the house in a snivelling huff. Physically she was attractive enough still, although fatter, but her character had congealed it seemed to me into the unlovely shape of a battling housewife who used her tongue like a duster. Then someone suggested there were teaching posts in London. The old man had begun rumbling complaints about how long I was intending to live on his money. It seemed a heaven sent excuse.

I became a teacher. "On Supply" at first. Moved from one school to another, over-crowded three deckers mostly, dusty, dingy, smelly, incredibly depressing. More for the change than anything else I went on one or two courses. In order to get in a better type of school, and because I am religious enough by nature, I began to specialise in Religious Instruction. Teachers of Scripture were scarce. So much for my teaching career.

A hand was raised in the centre of the class-room.

"Yes, Goodbody?"

"I've finished, sir."

I pushed the letter in my pocket. The little interlude was over. I closed the door quickly on my private life and became a public figure.

"Very well. Bring your book out here."

I made corrections in his book. He was one of the few boys in the class who had any previous knowledge of the contents of the Old Testament. He attended a Baptist Sunday School. I circulated the room, glancing at the grubby books in which the boys were scrawling their sparse scratches of knowledge on the great white map of their ignorance. I took my job seriously. I conducted my classes on the edge of the suburban forest, where the children were young rabbits in warrens of materialistic complacency. I fancied I was sympathetic towards them since I myself was little more than a rabbit of larger size.

III

I HAD INTENDED TO sit next to Allenside at lunch in the school canteen, in the hope of an opportunity of telling him that I had met his brother. But Briarman was already seated alongside him. The pale face was turned with intent possessiveness upon Allenside as if ready to extract significance even from the way in which the headmaster chewed his food.

In general, members of staff tended to favour Dell's claims to the deputy headship. Chiefly, I suspect, because Briarman was one of those men who succeed in pleasing their superiors only by alienating their colleagues. When I first joined the staff of the Bilateral I was asked to accompany Briarman to the games field, a ten minutes walk away, to assist him in supervising games. There were to be two games of cricket in progress and the rest were to practise in the nets. The game I was supervising ended at five minutes to four. I told the boys they could change and go home. Briarman turned them out of the Pavilion. It was the rule he said that no one was to leave the field until he had given them permission to do so. The boys wandered sheepishly back to where I was standing. Furious with injured dignity I stalked back to school. The only person in the staff-room was Bill Hawkes. I told him my story, edited by now with exaggerated coolness. Hawkes nodded approvingly. "You want to watch Briarman," he said. "He's a bloody rattle-snake. He's spent too much time pushing Wogs about in Persia. If he gets the job he'll know how to chuck his weight about." Briarman had been some kind of policeman employed by Anglo-Iranian. Probably a spy Hawkes said. We found it easy to run him down.

The headmaster, however, held Briarman in very high esteem, although I doubt whether he liked him personally. It was enough for Allenside that Briarman was a keen and efficient school teacher, a man who took infinite pains with his work and who sacrificed many leisure hours for the good of the school. It was Allenside's custom to think of each member of his staff as highly as he could. It was part of the fairmindedness of the man that made me admire him.

He was, in part, the model for my portrait of Edward Seymour, Duke of Somerset and Lord Protector of England. It seemed to me that only a man obsessed with justice and righteousness could have done all that Somerset did; and it seemed to me that even the execution of his brother, for whom he had a true affection, resembled in spirit Abraham's willingness to sacrifice his son in obedience to God's commandment. Allenside possessed, to a greater degree than any other man I had known, qualities of moral passion and a concern for justice that, only less powerfully than love, can make one true Christian more formidable than a regiment of devils. But of course Allenside did not profess to be a Christian in any strict legitimate sense and there were cardinal differences between creating a new kind of school and a new kind of State.

I know of course that it is awareness of my own lack of such qualities that makes my admiration for Allenside the more intense. The trivial moral stands I have made have been due as much to cowardice as to conviction. There is in all weak men who are intelligent enough not to hanker after worldly power a timid yearning towards martyrdom, a green underwater plant in a cold still pond that aspires to but will never breathe the burning air.

It was a difficult choice Allenside had to make. Dell had good degrees and he was, by common consent, an excellent class teacher. Briarman's academic qualifications did not include a University degree. At forty-nine, the man was still sensitive about it. It acted as a spur to his efficiency; it made him for ever anxious to assert his correctness and too ready to point out other men's lapses.

Dell was popular enough in the staff-room. His shining bald head, flourishing moustache and large pipe with the great bowl perpetually overfull like a crow's nest alight; his ample form filling a battered easy-chair; his warm expressive manner: they helped to give the room a club-like atmosphere when he was there. There was a certain boyishness about him, an innocence, that I found at once attractive and annoying. He would not condescend to push his claim for the deputy headship in any way, yet he would be unforgivingly bitter if he were overlooked. Already he was hurt that Allenside should have hesitated so long. He had moved to sit at the other end of the Refectory table, alongside Mr. Downs (nicknamed "Dodger" by the boys) the Art Master, whose antediluvian inefficiency got on Allenside's nerves. Downs protected himself against a hostile world by ardent support of the Teachers' Union and devoted membership of the Freemasons. His loose lips were fleshy and yet bloodless. He created a protective covering of pale fat for himself that was still as vulnerable as a snail without a shell. Eglinton reported his wife was the same. Downs, who saw something to be afraid of in everything, was an easy butt for Eglinton's wit.

After lunch the staff drank coffee in the staff-room. Two prefects were responsible for bringing down the jugs and cups from the canteen. We met them coming out of the staff-room. They were whispering and smiling at each other. When we went inside we discovered Eglinton's copy of the *Times* torn into three long strips and neatly laid on the table.

I glanced at Allenside. It was easy to see that he was very annoyed. It was his custom to join us for coffee after lunch; part of the business of maintaining good relations with all his staff. Today, however, he turned abruptly, and without making any comment, left the room.

For a while the staff-room was silent, as if waiting until Allenside was out of earshot. Eglinton slowly picked up the pieces and deposited them quietly in the waste-paper basket under the table. He sat down without saying anything and lit a cigarette. As I poured out the coffee, I thought Eglinton's silence meant he was studying what move to make next. If he treated all this like a game, a game of chess, he stood a better chance to win.

Dell made himself comfortable in his customary chair. Briarman leaned against the wall by the door, his arm outstretched, his hand resting on the door-knob. He was the first to speak.

"The Old Man's annoyed, good and proper." Briarman liked us to remember that he had spent some years at sea. He always referred to Allenside, nine years his junior, as the Old Man.

Unwilling to appear less impartial, Dell said, between puffs at the pipe he was lighting, "I must say . . . I think . . . all this is getting . . . childish." He tossed the spent match expertly across the room into the empty grate.

Then everyone talked at once, as if Dell's remark had detonated comment in every corner of the room. Visot told Thorpe, history, there was a principle involved. Mitchley, plumbing and metal work, pointed out to Robinson, Latin, that after all the *Times* cost twice as much, while at the same time Robinson was saying, "Good God, to think grown men can act in this way." Dell declared that we should settle this among ourselves. Downs repeated, with a deeply worried look on his fat pale face: "After all we don't want to quarrel do we." The chorus of comment had far from spent itself when Brunt pushed open the door.

"Any coffee left?"

I pointed to his cup. The room fell silent.

"What's up?"

Brunt settled himself tailorwise upon a side table.

Bill Hawkes pointed towards the waste-paper basket. "The Hidden Hand has struck again."

We laughed at this. The tension eased, but only for a moment. Brunt shrugged his shoulders and said nothing. His gaze roved round the room as he lifted the cup with both hands to his lips.

Hawkes tried again. "Come on fellows. Who done it? Any offers? Who done it?"

Then with more wit than I would have credited him Brunt said solemnly,

"I must say I applaud the action."

"Can we be sure," Downs said anxiously, "it wasn't one of the boys?"

"That's the sinister part about it," Eglinton exclaimed. "It might well have been."

Brunt pounced upon this remark before most of us had realised its implication.

"You're not suggesting, I hope, that any member of staff might have influenced any boy to do such a thing?"

"Isn't it a fact," Eglinton said, "that communist literature circulates among certain senior boys. Where, I wonder, do they obtain the filthy stuff?"

Visot leaned forward his face crimson with anger.

"If you are trying to insinuate that they get it from either Brunt or myself, you know damn well it's an absolute lie."

Visot said *damn* with a quaint emphasis that made Bill

Hawkes smile. Visot usually spoke with the bookish eloquence of a self-taught lay preacher.

"Tibbot in VI R always has a *Daily Worker* in his locker," Downs said helpfully. Eglinton teased him cruelly, yet he always supported anything Eglinton said: as if he were attempting to propitiate an angry deity. "And what about those lads you take camping at week-ends, Bert?"

"You keep your nose out of this. And for God's sake don't call me Bert." Brunt glared at Downs. "This is the kind of thing that can lead to serious trouble."

Eglinton said coolly: "It might help to clean things up a bit."

"What exactly do you mean by that?" Visot stretched his neck in Eglinton's direction threateningly. "Would you tell us please?"

Eglinton drew on his cigarette and did not answer. He had no quarrel with Visot. Not disliking Visot was the excuse Eglinton always offered for his intense dislike of Brunt. But of course Visot was not in the running for the post of special responsibility. Eglinton fancied the choice lay between himself and Brunt. Mitchley was also in the running but he was not inclined to take Mitchley seriously.

Visot said, "I happen to know it wasn't Bert Brunt that tore up Eglinton's *Times*, or any of the boys."

"The question at issue surely is this." Briarman stepped forward and laid both hands on the table. "Everyone has a right to bring any paper he chooses into this staff-room and all of us have the right to expect our private property should be respected. That's the question as I see it."

"Quite." Mr. Glide's voice was an unexpected intrusion. He liked to spend the lunch hour playing chess with Briarman or Robinson. "I agree absolutely."

Several of us made approving noises.

"Well I don't," said Eglinton.

"Neither do I," said Downs gazing obediently at Eglinton's face, willing to agree at once with anything Eglinton said on the subject, and hoping Eglinton would not make one of those quick switches of mood and topic that he feared and detested.

"I don't see why I should have the *Daily Worker* thrust under my nose day after day. These Communists are out to wreck this country and everything this country stands for."

I watched him closely. It wasn't a game any longer. This was what he really felt passionately. These were the pent up feelings accumulated on the daily journey to and from Purley as he quietly imbibed his daily paper. Perhaps deeper than that. I don't believe he was an exceptionally pious Catholic, but he had a certain arrogance that may well have been born of some obscure boyhood shame. He would be more English than the English and yet loyal to his side as well.

He got up, ostensibly to stub his cigarette in the ash tray on the table.

"And while they are at their dirty work," he said, "they will hide behind things like professional conduct and trade unions, and claim the sanctuary of our free institutions. And people like us will stand aside and let them get on with their wrecking, doing nothing about it; nothing at all."

"Except for tearing up an occasional *Daily Worker*," Visot said quite good-humouredly. But his remark was eclipsed by Brunt's blazing anger. He had jumped down from his table perch.

"You suburban fascist! Wouldn't you like to get me into trouble! I know that's what you are after. I'm not going to deny myself the pleasure of giving you a damn good hiding much longer."

"Steady Bert." Bill Hawkes held him by the arm. "Steady now. Steady."

Eglinton had become very pale. The hate let loose between them appalled me. Quite cheerfully I knew one would have plunged a bayonet deep into the other's neck. And beneath my distaste I was disturbingly aware of the exultant sensation of the spectator at a cockfight.

"This can be taken to a higher authority," Eglinton said as quietly as he could, regaining control of himself and yet still eager to strike the most telling blow.

"It would be easy for you to start a smear campaign against me, wouldn't it? You've got plenty of crypto-Fascists around here who would be glad enough to help you to do it. I'd like you all to witness what Eglinton has just said. If anything starts, you'll know just exactly who has started it."

"Nobody's going to start anything," Bill Hawkes said cheerfully. "Come and sit down Bert. Come and sit down."

Brunt shook his arm free and without another word, as if not trusting himself to say more, marched out of the room.

34

Dell took out his pipe and rapped his hand on the table for silence. "This can be settled quite easily. I propose that no daily paper of any kind be left on this table. There isn't really any room for them anyway. Only learned journals bought by the staff-room committee. Will someone second that?"

"I'll second it." Mitchley raised his hand. There were murmurs of approval and amusement.

Dell, warm and jovial with success, said, "All those in favour, gentlemen."

Everyone raised a hand, except Visot. He shrugged his shoulders ruefully, as if uncertain what to do next. Then with a sudden smile, he lifted his case, placed it on his knees, took out a copy of the *Daily Worker* and shook it out with a flourish, ready to read.

Now that Brunt had left the staff-room, Downs felt a little bolder. Like the boys, he knew there was no reason to be afraid of Visot.

"Isn't it a fact, Vizzy," Downs leaned forward and wagged his finger, "that Tibbot of VI R has Bolshy books that belong to you?"

"Cut it out, Downs." Bill Hawkes had opened the *Illustrated Weekly News*. "We've had enough for one afternoon."

Visot had lowered his paper. He said. "It would be interesting to know how you obtained that little piece of information."

Downs was a little flustered by Visot's calmness. He had hoped his remark would have had the opposite effect.

"I happened to go into his locker for some books he had borrowed from the Library, that's why."

"Distributing communist literature?" Eglinton murmured. His voice sounded perfectly friendly. He had no quarrel with Visot. Visot was not in the running for the Special Responsibility Allowance. Eglinton viewed Visot as a harmless sort of crank.

Visot was upset. Perhaps he was angry with himself for giving way to a species of guilty discomfort.

"Not at all," he said loudly. "The lad is a friend of mine; so are his parents. He comes to my home and I lend him books. . . ."

"Which he returns to you in school?" Downs was as pleased as if he had made a smart interpolation.

"Which he has returned to me in school. So what?" The Americanism sounded odd in Visot's emphatic suburban voice.

Dell put down his paper and drummed his fingers heavily on the table. "It isn't really wise you know," he said, looking at Visot over the top of the spectacles he wore only for reading, "to hob-nob with the boys. I've often seen it lead to trouble."

The advice annoyed Visot intensely. "That's just the difference between your ideas of education and mine. I refuse to consider the schoolboy as my natural enemy."

Dell took his pipe out of his mouth and said dryly:

"He often seems to consider you as his."

This amused the staff-room. I was sorry for Visot. He blushed deeply, and then smiled as widely as he could. The laughter was not unfriendly, but it was difficult to estimate exactly how deeply it upset Visot's self-esteem. He probably concealed from himself how agonisingly bad a teacher he was, and would have preferred physical assault than this public revelation of ineptitude.

"Mind your p's and q's Dell." Downs grinned widely in anticipation of his own joke. His teeth were uniformly rotten but no one had succeeded in persuading him to have them out. "You're talking to a future Commissar of Education. 'E'll have your pension sliced in 'alf."

"P's, q's and h's," Eglinton murmured. Downs looked at him imploringly. Things were back to normal. He hadn't escaped. Robinson and Glide had begun their game of chess on the small table in the corner. There was still a quarter of an hour until the bell went for afternoon school.

IV

THE CLEANERS WERE IN the class-room when I got away from school. The dust rose in clouds. Dust of the arena. The shadow of a bird moved across the sunlit wall, making me for a moment as I locked my desk resentful of the uncreative waste of time this working day had been. I was trapped in an oppressive sternly ugly building among disgruntled teachers and undeveloped boys. I was too tired to think sympathetically of Allenside's enthusiasm for "the creative experiment"; a school to combine the virtues (if any) of a State Secondary School, Grammar and Technical Type, and those of a public school.

I took a bus up to the Common. It was the long way round to Helen's flat but the shadow of a bird, I imagine, and the warm sunlight enticed me into the trees. It was unspectacular heath, coarse, with too many ragged assemblies of anaemic silver birches. But it was wide and open to the sky. I lay down by an isolated beech tree and through its branches on which the buds were gradually breaking, I gazed at the high clouds that drifted across the limitless sky. I tasted young grass and put my nose to the earth in the hope that I would be sensitive enough to catch the odour of growing.

It was necessary to come to such a place as this, away from people. The breeze would rinse my head of the distasteful lees of an unprofitable day. Under the surface of my discontent a deeper trouble was stirring. I had not felt so strongly about her for years. It was hateful. Phyllis had refused to do as I asked. And Helen would have to be informed. I felt already the guilt of causing her displeasure, of not complying with Helen's clearly expressed desire which was also my own.

Helen had been away six weeks now. Her postcards arrived regularly from Switzerland. She never wrote letters. If one postcard could not contain all she had to say she would write on two or three and send them together in an envelope. This arrangement suited me well enough. I sent postcards in return,

37

out of my collection of Edwardian views of seaside resorts. I would let her know the progress of my work. I imagine they made plaintive reading; although I could not complain too much since she was still prepared to pay me the equivalent of my teacher's salary and provide me with a private studio. I would not agree to this on grounds of individualist dignity and a superstition that I should maintain myself by honest labour in order to succeed in my art. In the same way I had said once, making excuses as she sat watching me from her armchair by the fire, in the same way as St. Paul stitched tents. But my strongest reason was a fear of coming completely under Helen's domination. Her will was stronger than mine; my teaching job was my refuge and protection.

There is no limit to the complications we can create by making our own way, which at any given moment seems a clear and simple path through the undergrowth of living. I cannot conceal from myself how much my conscience nags me on behalf of my deserted wife. It succeeds in doing so however much I try to smother it with considering my obligations to Helen Brown.

The position between Helen and myself is not altogether satisfactory and therefore not easy to explain. We met casually enough. One day in the Christmas holidays soon after I began teaching we met at a lunch with mutual friends, Max Hepple and a school friend of Helen's named Julia Humphriss. Max and I had not seen each other for some time. He was getting on in his career as an architect and I had not long since published my first novel. We made a great fuss of each other. Now and again stealing a glance at Helen, who was very quiet, I fancied she had a poor opinion of me. She was nothing to look at: a round serious unexpressive face, straight hair, plainly dressed. She did not speak enough for me to form any opinion of her qualities. When Max and Julia departed cheerfully together at three o'clock, Helen and I were left alone. Neither of us had any plans for the rest of the afternoon, but we both prepared to depart our separate ways as if we had somewhere in particular to go. It was cold in the street. The grass in Saint James's Square, although green, scarcely covered the bald black earth. We must have talked quite intimately, as people sometimes do with strangers on a long train journey, because I had confessed to her I had nowhere to go except my lodging house on Christmas Day. She invited me to her flat in Kensington for Christmas dinner.

I slept late that Christmas morning after rather a dull party with acquaintances (I can no longer remember their names) of petty bourgeois habits in Notting Hill Gate. I seem to have got invited on the strength of having written a book. Someone slapped my back when I went in and cried happily: "Here he is, the famous author." It was too ridiculous. They played games that would have been dull at a children's party; the drink was cheap and vile, but in order to be thought of as 'a jolly decent fellow' I joined in the 'fun.'

I arrived at Helen's without having eaten any breakfast. Helen opened the door. After the party of the night before she seemed incredibly civilised. The table was already laid for two. In a short time Helen served the meal. It was excellent. She watched me do full justice to the food and drink with quiet pleasure and also perhaps quiet curiosity. Afterwards when we had cleared away together, we sat in great comfort before the blazing coal fire. Needless to say, with very little prompting needed, she listened quietly to the story of my life. I kept nothing back. Her quietness demanded honesty. I tried to be honest. I described the stagnant market town in Shropshire where I had been born. My father's saddler's shop. My mother's early death. The housekeeper who became my step-mother. How my father had nothing to do with his poor relations most of whom, as far as I could discover, belonged to the labouring classes. The Congregational Chapel I attended as a boy. My father's hopes that I would enter the Ministry. My County School career in a large neighbouring town. My first attempts to write. Phyllis. My early marriage. Myself as a conscientious objector, in the Fen Country, in London, abroad. My writing. My teaching. By five o'clock she knew all about me; even, by a vague romantic reference, about Marian as well.

I did not learn so much that day about her. She only told me that she had divorced her husband earlier in the year. That she had three adopted children, all girls. She was deeply concerned about one of them, Nicola, a refugee child aged six, whose health was delicate. I gathered at once she must have been fairly wealthy. But I honestly do not believe that influenced our subsequent relations in any direct way.

39

I also guessed correctly that she was five years older than I.

I was enthusiastic about our new friendship. I became a frequent visitor at the flat. Not a day passed without at least my telephoning Helen. I began to take it for granted that she was at least as interested in my career and my general welfare as I was myself. In a month's time I was ready to believe that I was in love with her. Almost as soon as the idea crossed my mind I rushed out to see her. To my disappointment when I arrived I found her busy helping a trained nurse of formidably ugly face put two of her adopted children, Nicola and Maureen, to bed. When after what seemed to me a great deal of fuss the bedroom doors were finally shut I was commanded to talk quietly. When we began to talk Helen did not give me her usual sympathetic attention. She did not tell me to go, but she expressed no regret when I announced I would have to be going. Before shutting the door after me, she was calling the nurse from the kitchen.

I decided to absent myself from the felicity of her company for some time. In a few days' time I became aware how lonely I was. I had never been so acutely aware of my solitude. Before I had called it my freedom. Not that I have ever lacked friends, but the nature of my work demands not only a continuous detachment, but sudden unexplainable withdrawals from the scheduled obligations of social living, which are not always so easy to resume. This awareness of solitude began to interfere with my work. I began to resent my digs intensely, in particular the landlady's wireless and the monumental sauce bottle that for ever seemed to be on my table either in memory of one indigestible meal or in preparation for another. I abandoned a novel of which I had already completed thirty thousand words and took to eking out my evenings in cinemas and the uncongenial saloon bars of depressing pubs. I spent hours lounging about the Embankment having 'ideas' which, like fireworks, seemed brilliant while they lasted, but afterwards left the sky more solidly black than before. I suffered moods of depression that I had never known before and which frightened me like physical danger.

In February I fell ill. I went to bed in my nauseating attic bedroom; and contemplating the faded flowers in the wallpaper's pattern, I had ample time to consider the vanity of my talent and the undistinguished futility of my existence. As much reading as I could manage without being caught by my red-beaked landlady was devoted to the Metaphysical Poets. Even they did not alleviate the sickening depression that comes as a man imagines himself to be on the brink of nothingness.

In such a state Helen found me. I must have been asleep when she entered. I opened my eyes, and there she stood rotund and warmly dressed, her cheeks glowing from the cold outside. Immediately, delighted as I was to see her, I sulked.

"Visiting one of your waifs and strays?" I said.

She nodded and sat down on the edge of my bed. It appeared she had been aware of my condition for some days. She had been in conversation with the doctor, a sour Scotchman who had given me the impression that I was one of the least favourable aspects of his duties. The next day a car would call for me and remove me to convalescence in Helen's flat. I said I could not possibly dream of it. Helen smiled. I summoned my energy to make a great refusal. But the misery of my surroundings was too much for me. I gave in. Before she left I found myself thanking her profusely for all that she had done.

I enjoyed my convalescence. Helen left me a great deal to myself since she had bought a house near Boscombe. I learnt that she was a woman who knew how to deploy her abilities. Like her uncle, Lord Whiteway, she had a gift for business and administration. The instinct to arrange and decide and drive was much stronger than the intellectual curiosity which she wished to be accepted as her characteristic trait. She could handle people and things without understanding them; so that although in fact she had no taste of her own in any branch of art, because fundamentally music, painting, literature, made no genuine emotional impression upon her, yet she found no difficulty in pressing aesthetically qualified persons into her service whenever she needed them. Although she knew nothing of art, she could pick upon a good artist, judging him not from his work, but from some quality in his personality that she was strangely swift to perceive.

On the walls of the maisonette were three Euston Road Pasmores and a Hitchens, and good pictures by artists of whom I had not heard before. Evidently she had a flair for being well-advised. The bookshelves were stocked with excellent complete editions few of which appeared to have been read. The only books showing signs of frequent perusal were of a religious, psychological or philosophical nature. But they might have belonged to her father.

I also glanced through her desk: a tidy business-like affair. From a legal correspondence I learnt that the name of her former husband was Major Peter de Wit Theodore George Bayly. She seemed to have cleared the flat completely of all other evidence of Major Bayly's existence. There was a snapshot album in one of the bookshelves but most of the photographs reflected her youth and childhood. Buckets and spades figured prominently and the usual glimpses of an unchanging summer sea. I also gathered that her income could not be much less than eight thousand a year.

I did not bother to examine the room she called the nursery. It was the largest room in the maisonette, containing three small beds. In the silence and emptiness the chintzy cheerfulness seemed rather sad. Altogether it was the kind of large flat that could have belonged to anyone with means and access to canons of contemporary taste. Each individual feature was of sufficient excellence, but they failed to cohere. It was as if some warmth was lacking that could fuse the parts into an identifiable and significant whole. I flattered myself that my presence and the unobtrusive alterations I made went a long way to giving the place the organic unity it needed. The flat was Helen's property but in many ways it seemed made for me.

Our first physical encounter was made in complete darkness. Helen had arrived back from Boscombe full of enthusiasm for her new house. I had never seen her so talkative or so human for that matter: 'human' in the sense that I felt myself tolerating her weakness, and not she mine. She was delighted about my improvement in health. She was agreeable to my starting work the next day. We shared a bottle of Chianti over supper. Her vivacity was so unusual I became sensitive to the subtlest nuances of her mood. Passing my chair for a moment only she laid her hand on my forehead, ostensibly to see how I was progressing, and allowed her fingers to travel lightly through my hair. My old notion that we could be lovers revived. We both became silent and excited. We were alone in the flat. We went to our bedrooms without bidding each other good night. For nearly an hour I lay awake in the darkness, uncertain what to do because I was uncertain what it was exactly she desired me to do. I must have dropped off to sleep because when I awoke again she was lying quietly beside me.

She would not allow me to switch on the light. As I raised my hand she covered it with hers and with surprising strength, forced it down again. There was a satanic power in her love-making. She never once spoke, and as she clutched my body it was as though she had forgotten who I was. It was a challenge I had to meet. I had no time to enjoy the exercise of power and in the end some odd anger in me prevented my sharing her ecstasy. In the morning when I awoke, she had gone.

The daily woman had prepared my breakfast. As usual she brought it in on a tray. I ate hurriedly, anxious to be on time for school. I did not see Helen again for almost a week. When she did return, on the first Saturday in March as I remember she had new plans for us both. We were to go to Italy for three months together. 'To learn to love each other,' she said, turning her face to the fire. And that was the first mention of the word 'love,' between us. Even then as I declared my love for her with unnecessary ardour and made my excuses, I knew I did not want to go. It would have been too unconditional a surrender. (That was the night I made my remark about St. Paul stitching tents.)

Helen went abroad alone. It gave me time to breathe and to think. I liked the comfort of living in her flat, especially the room set aside for me to write in. It was a castle in the clouds from which I sallied forth to my mundane labours and to which I returned, over a bridge that was drawn up after me, to the privacy where my imagination, a rare plant in a guarded glass-house, could flourish undisturbed. I liked the arrangements she made to see I was well looked after. I liked Helen herself, chiefly because I believed she was in love with me and all I did was the least I could do in return. I formed the theory that she was a woman anxious to have children. That accounted for the three adoptions more than the phil-anthropic designs that concealed her true impulse. It might also, I imagined, account for her divorce. They had been

43

married three years. They had no children. It accounted too for the impersonal abandon of her love making which I learnt to share. Helen was a young matriarch. I was to provide her with children. While she was away my imagination ran riot and I was doubly anxious that she should return; so that I could obtain some proper understanding of her, and the motives behind her behaviour; so that I could come to some arrangement with her that would allow me to get my mind back properly on my work.

When she returned she was accompanied by the same grim faced Nurse Jones, and Nicola, who was unaccountably ill. Helen assumed at once that I shared her anxiety. For most of the first evening I listened to a detailed account of the Nicola's health not only during the last six weeks abroad but since Helen had adopted her. Helen had discovered that the child's mother had died of tuberculosis. She had not been told of this at the time of the adoption. She was indignant about that and at the same time guilty, worried that she herself was not giving the child the attention and affection that it needed. Before saying good night she said, "Of course we can't possibly make love while Nicola is ill. I am sure, David, you understand."

I nodded as if I understood. I lay awake a long time that night thinking of the strange household I had wandered into. By my own presence I suppose I made it appear decoratively stranger. To sum up I repeated to myself on the verge of falling asleep: a saddler's son, who writes novels, and teaches Scripture in a Bilateral School having deserted his wife and son and living in surprising comfort with an eccentric wealthy woman of thirty-six as her companion and bed steward in a ménage of adopted children. Pease blossom, Moth, Mustard Seed: Nicola, Maureen, Sigrid. Bottom in Titania's bower, sleeping on a mattress of foam rubber between apple-green sheets.

It was not easy to escape, chiefly because I did not want to. There were features in the arrangement that suited me very well. The room set aside for me was something far superior to anything I had had before. It was redecorated according to my instructions in grey and white. Helen had presented me with a Nicholson for which she had heard me express enthusiastic admiration. I gave it one wall to itself so that it hung

44

in the centre of the smallest of three rectangles of deepening shades of grey.

The window gave an exciting view of broad streets that led towards the park; and of a surprisingly luxuriant back garden where in April and May blossoms of almond, cherry, peach, and apple glowed in the daylight for my refreshment. It was a room in which I felt my art would flourish.

When Helen was away, I was able to give small parties in the flat to which I invited congenial spirits, many of whom exercised some influence in the literary world. These parties, I believed, embellished my reputation and broadened it. They helped to make known that I possessed the right degree of unostentatious eccentricity in morals, manners and opinions. The paragraph beneath the name 'David Flint' in that *Who's Who* which circulated as it were in manuscript among the cognoscenti was agreeably lengthened.

Newlace, a theatre critic, dangled his short legs on either side of Nicola's large rocking horse.

"I didn't realise you had children David?" he said sipping his sherry.

"They're not mine Colin. They're adopted, like me."

I was gratified to observe that he was suitably puzzled. But he smiled back at me respectfully and thoughtfully enough. As if he had decided I was a man to be reckoned with.

While Helen was away I divided my time after school between writing reviews, attending other people's parties, and giving my own. My school-slavery from nine to four, I imagined, was fair penance for any undue pleasure gained in these evening and week-end pursuits. It was a way of living I enjoyed very much and could have gone on enjoying indefinitely. One postcard a day was little enough in return for such good fortune.

Nicola was taken down to Boscombe by ambulance. A doctor in whom Helen had rather more faith than I wished, gave orders the child should be confined to bed for six weeks. During those six weeks Helen came to and fro at unpredictable and frequent intervals. She would telephone too, unexpectedly, and send me flying off to Harley Street, to her solicitors or to her bankers on some errand she considered urgent.

One evening she arrived in London in modest but unmistakable evening dress. She had ordered two seats for the Ballet

45

and I was to accompany her. I had actually promised to call on Frances Edmunds, a woman novelist whose work I admired. But there was nothing for it but to make hurried apologies over the telephone from the theatre. In the taxi Helen explained that she was exhausted from over-work and the doctor (this time a Boscombe man) had ordered her to relax and to leave the care of Nicola, who thank God was much better, and Sigrid and Maureen to the capable Nurse Jones. I did my best to be sympathetic.

The ballet was a poor effort. Helen who had been expecting something better, was outraged. I had not seen her so intense about a theatrical performance before. She seemed to take the whole thing as a personal insult.

At dinner, in a Greek restaurant we favoured at the time, after a lengthy silence in which I amused myself by an unobtrusive study of other diners, Helen unexpectedly launched a discussion, on an academic level, on the subject of divorce. Unaware that what we said would have any personal implications, I declared in the emphatic rather heated manner I employ in theoretic matters, that divorce as a general rule should be regarded by Christians with disapproval. Only when Helen smiled did I recollect that she herself was divorced and that I had deserted my legal wife, and that our cohabitation could only be described in terms of Christian morality as adultery. Helen made no attempt to defend her position or even to excuse it. She said she was quite prepared to believe that what she had done was wrong. She let me understand that nothing would give her greater peace than to be convinced about the rights and wrongs of the matter. It was clear enough to her that what she herself most dearly wanted might very easily have been the only criterion of her past actions. She told me, for the first time, something of her upbringing. Her mother had left her father when she was six and subsequently she had been subjected to a muddled upbringing in the course of which she spent one holiday in Bournemouth with her mother and the next in Perrinport or London with her father who seemed to change his religious beliefs from one year to the other with bewildering regularity.

We left the restaurant feeling warmer and more sympathetic towards each other than at any time since my illness. The fortnight we spent together was on the verge of idyllic. During the Whitsun holiday the car took us to the Cotswolds. We both strove to please each other and we came so near to falling in love that the holiday was almost a honeymoon.

But on either side, it is clear enough to me now in retrospect as I lie staring at the fragile branches of the thin silver birches beginning to bud, against the blue sky, there were fatal reservations. Helen had her business responsibilities that I did not share; her preoccupation with the welfare of the three children; and what I in my more touchy moments considered a lack of complete trust and confidence in me. On my side there was the guilt that disturbed me whenever I remembered Phyllis my wife; and uneasiness and uncertainty about my own behaviour and my own motives that could spring up like fertile weeds to choke the happiest hour or the briefest moment of rapture. At the time I began seriously to reconsider my views about divorce. I re-examined the arguments in favour. Gradually I began to believe that perhaps only in divorce would we ever find a decent solution to our problem. (Our living together had now attained the proportions of a problem.) Like an experienced campaigner, I made a doctrinal retreat on all fronts to soften the blow reality had dealt to the sector held by divorce. My neo-Calvinism was modified a little more. I granted a fresh degree of freedom to the human will and adjusted the balance with a new depth of complication, a barbed wire entanglement laid before my interpretation of the doctrine of the Incarnation. There were conditions, I concluded, under which divorce was not only permissible but desirable.

Later in the year I communicated my new standpoint to Helen with care and moderation. I was pleased to observe that she inclined to agree with me more enthusiastically, more sincerely, than ever before. I felt that she was ready to abandon her detached attitude to matters of doctrine and belief. I even entertained the notion that I was perhaps a chosen instrument that had some significant part to play in her salvation.

During the summer vacation I began work on my book about the Seymour brothers. I gave up reviewing, and Helen arranged for me to use a spacious room above the stables of the House near Boscombe. Half the week I would spend in London at the British Museum reading and making notes; the rest down at Boscombe. Helen took a keener interest in my work than ever before. Each evening I would read to her what had been written during the day. I would wait eagerly on her comments. An adverse opinion would be enough to make me throw the condemned sheet on the fire, there and then. Helen acquired a taste for dispersing blame and commendation, praise and consolation. She would give the closest attention to every word I read in order that her criticism should be valid enough to penetrate my self-possession and have the maximum effect upon me. Being a critic became a new hobby with her.

Then Nicola's health took a turn for the worse. It wasn't often that I saw her; occasionally I would have a cheery word with her through her window—a brief cheery word. The large bright eyes and ready smile depressed me, deepened my feeling of guilt. I am always a little appalled when I find being a Christian so difficult. If only it could all be a little easier and a little more reasonable.

I began to respect Helen's concern for the children more than ever before. Unquestionably Helen had far more potentialities for being good than I had. She had a concern for persons: I only had the ill-natured interest in possible characters for more books. Helen, however naïve or selfish her motives, sought for opportunities of doing good: I badgered and nagged my God in between collecting useful copy.

In September Helen took Nicola to a Swiss sanatorium. She came back for the other two children, removed them from their Boscombe school, and settled them in a school run by two English maiden ladies near Montreux. The ladies, she told me, had been most kind and helpful with Nicola. I did not see Helen again until the New Year. She said I would be left in peace to concentrate on my Seymour book. Between school work and writing, and occasional outings and parties I kept myself very busy.

There were, however, nights when I could not settle down to work, and a perverse restlessness drove me out to wander the streets until my legs ached and I was glad to get home again.

There was one cold clear night in December I walked down the Bayswater Road, undecided whether or not to call on a painter friend. I pondered whether I should ring him up to warn him I was coming. I saw a call-box on the Park side of the road and I hesitated. A figure emerged from the dark of a gateway murmuring 'good night' as she glided behind me. I looked over my shoulder. I saw a still grave Syrian face, large black eyes, strong well-dressed hair. There seemed nothing meretricious about her. We gazed at each other with open and yet dignified curiosity, like two animals in unprepared encounter. Her lips moved again, and her voice, although no more than a whisper, reached me clearly. I imagined nodding my head and walking alongside her. Her room would be small, human, cosy, warm. Her bed. She offered love. Why should I not take it? I needed it. Perhaps some significant experience could be bought. Mortify the spirit by degrading the flesh. If she seemed unhealthy, a cautious thought, or ridiculous, I could give her money and go away. I hesitated too long. She had stepped across the road to where a man in a Trilby had and belted mackintosh stood smoking a cigarette between the lamplight and the shadow of the trees. I suppose my relief was greater than my regret. It happened this way many times, and always in the end I turned away. I am not at all the type to sin my way to Jesus. I am among the pious crowd whose constant torment is trying to convince themselves that somehow they could be good if only some adjustment were made in their spiritual hygiene and sanitation.

It was I who suggested to Helen on the first night of her return in the New Year, that I should ask my wife to divorce me.

"I think," I said, with the raw forcefulness of a youth making a declaration of independence before his parents, "I think, Helen, you and I ought to get married."

To my surprise, Helen laughed. She was not given to hilarity and this was an occasion I would have expected her to take very seriously.

"You will have to get your wife's permission first," she said.

All evening she was inclined to tease me. But when we went to bed she was more tender than I had ever seen her before and when we made love for the first time I heard her murmur my name.

Helen remained with me in the flat throughout February. My Seymour novel had reached a state of impasse which worried me a lot. When I confessed to Helen how badly it was going, with surprising lightheartedness—I somehow fancied the news would upset her—she advised me to take a holiday. With a great feeling of relief, I agreed. Symbolically we locked the door of the room in which I worked. We began to live together with a kind of gay domesticity we had not tried before. When I came home from school, Helen made a point of having tea ready on a trolley, and she never missed presiding over the teacups. She began to make a cult of my comfort. She bought me expensive fur-lined slippers which she insisted on putting on my feet, pushing me back in my arm-chair and thrusting an unopened *Times* into my lap. She installed a reading desk and flexible reading lamp over my bed and presented me with a luxurious dressing gown. She herself now prepared my breakfast and saw me off every morning on my way to school. I developed the habit of looking up to wave at her, standing in the window, before I rushed off to catch my bus.

One evening in March I arrived home armed with some flowers, a bottle of wine and the evening paper. Tea wasn't ready and Helen wasn't in. I suppressed a sulky feeling of disappointment that for a moment made me think of turning and walking out again. On the mantelpiece I found a pencilled note from Helen and a letter with a Swiss stamp addressed in a German hand. Nicola had had a relapse. Helen had left for Switzerland at once. I learnt later that she had flown to Geneva that afternoon.

It was the middle of May and Helen had not returned. There was nothing in her postcards to suggest when that might be. On a postcard there is always something to say, but never room to say anything of consequence. I am not grumbling at the arrangement. It is true that during the first week of her absence, with much labour and much redrafting to the point of filling my waste-paper basket, I wrote my letter to Phyllis asking her to divorce me. I can remember the cold sensation of the iron mouth of the letter box against my naked fingers: an iron Rubicon. But I was able to begin my novel again from the beginning. And now especially with the Allenside brothers as interesting and suggestive models my taste for the work had revived, and I was able to use all the solitude that came my way. Because I felt my book was going well, at school I was lighthearted. I made the children laugh during the lessons and in the staff-room I was always cheerful. I thought Visot and myself were the only two men with any deep measure of content on the staff, apart from the Headmaster. We were living to some purpose.

I was happy as I could ever reasonably expect to be until this letter came from Phyllis. It seemed to threaten everything in a way I could not understand. I must have realised it was possible she would refuse to do as I asked, but men of my selfish temperament never take the alternative to what they want at all seriously until it is thrust before them; and then they are wildly angry with the people who will not do as they ask, or if that is impossible, they go under a beech tree out on the Common and indulge themselves in self-pity.

What had I done to deserve the intolerable mess I found myself in? I had never asked to be born. It was all God's fault. Then frightened at my own blasphemy, I kneeled on the grass and repeated 'Our Father' until I felt calm again. I decided not to be selfish. Walking to the bus, I considered what Helen would say. I worried about her disappointment. Through the thicker trees that lined the roadside I could see a red bus approaching. I had to catch it. I flung myself in, out of breath, just as it started up again. I climbed to the top, which was almost empty, and sat in the front recovering my breath, and ready to sink into deep thought about my novel, so that when I got to the flat I would have some material to begin as quickly as possible on the evening's work. The novel was not only a pleasurable activity, it was a quick escape from myself.

V

THE FRONT DOOR BELL rang. I put down my pen, lifted
the window and looked down into the street. The light was
beginning to fade—it was about nine o'clock—and I could
just make out Roger Allenside and another man whom I did
not know. Roger waved up at me.

"Are you busy?" he called up, smiling. The other man
looked down. He seemed a little embarrassed. "We want you
to come out and have a drink."

"Right ho." This was a chance to study my Thomas
Seymour. Gay Tom, who ran the dowager Queen and the
young Elizabeth in the same house. It was the kind of thing
Roger Allenside could do, and still beam in honest comradely
fashion around the bar of *The Dog and Fox*. "I'll be down in a
moment."

I wondered why he had gone to the trouble of finding out
where I lived. He had given me his telephone number, but
there hadn't been time, the other night, for me to give him
mine. Not merely for the pleasure of my company. Perhaps
he wanted to show this stranger he was in touch with promising
young writers. That had happened to me before. For my own
reasons, I was interested enough in him, but I could see no
real reason why he should be interested in me. Perhaps it was
the impulse of the moment that brought him here: in any
case, I would make the best use of the opportunity.

It was disappointing to discover they had both been drinking: I did not feel in the mood for shepherding them around.
Roger had a car. I doubted at once whether he was fit to
drive it. I began to regret having agreed so readily to come
down: but he had been too far away for me to smell his breath.

"How do you like my new car?"

Roger was not going to wait for the tokens of admiration
we expect from those we hope covet our possessions. A little
drunk, he seemed more anxious than usual to convince his

acquaintances that he lived fully and colourfully, to a degree that they should envy. Since we had met at the American Magazine's party, I had noticed an article of his in a popular Sunday newspaper. *Black and White* glared the headline and in smaller print, *Roger Allenside, Foreign Expert and Author of many Travel Books.*

I sat in the front alongside Roger. The other man had bundled himself in the back just before the car started. He didn't seem very anxious to meet me. I wondered why, but my curiosity was overpowered by a pressing concern for my personal safety. Roger talked too much and laughed too much and braked the car too sharply at traffic lights. Each brief remark I made was meant to act like a finger drawing Roger's attention to the road ahead, and my leg was for ever pressing against an imaginary footbrake.

The length of the journey began to get on my nerves and just as I was about to suggest we stopped for a drink. Roger swerved in and pulled up on the ample gravel space before a new-looking pub called *The Green Huntsman*. We were somewhere west of Hounslow. I could see fields and hedges on one side of the road and on the other lines of semi-detached houses with television aerials at rakish angles black against the violet sky.

"Are you there, Peter?" Roger glanced over his shoulder. "I thought perhaps you'd gone to sleep."

His companion grinned sheepishly.

"You two haven't been properly introduced you know. We must go through the ceremony before we go any further. Mr. David Flint, Major Peter Bayly. I'm sure you've both heard of each other before."

Roger laughed delightedly, as if he had made a joke. As a matter of fact I had never heard Bayly's name in full before. It was only an accident that a document in Helen's desk had given me that much information. She had never told me about him, and I had never asked. Helen wasn't the kind of woman who made complaint against her first lover a major part of her relationship with the next. Perhaps she wished me to consider her a woman of no previous experience; perhaps she felt it would jar too much upon my sensibilities to mention him. She knew I was a man who cherished his illusions. For my part I may have believed she did not want me to pry into

53

her past. She was a woman who told you as much as she wanted you to know. I was content to leave it so.

"I believe you have something in common." Roger laughed again, even more loudly than before. I cursed him to myself for a hulking bloody fool. This was really a dastardly trick, but it was difficult for me to know what to do. How could I strike an attitude of high dudgeon on the ground outside *The Green Huntsman*? I thought of the slow journey by bus back to Kensington. It would take over an hour. Before I had decided my attitude Roger shoved me by the shoulder.

"Come on, old boy. Let's get out and have a drink."

What else could I do?

Roger said it was on him and left Bayly and myself opposite each other in chairs of red leather and oak, miserably ill at ease. Neither of us had the courage to be frank. A quick agreement before Roger came back might have turned the tables on him. But we were too uncertain of each other.

"It's a small world," said Roger cheerfully dumping three pints on the low table.

"Much too small," I said with less bitterness than I felt. This started Roger laughing again. Bayly and I smiled weakly to keep up appearances since several people had turned to look at us.

"I know you chaps will forgive me," Roger said; his confidence made me want to hit him over the head. "Such a series of remarkable coincidences I just couldn't resist it. Peter and I were at school together. Peter fagged for me, didn't you, Peter old boy. I met Peter's cousin at Cambridge, Horace Walker-Brown. He used to come to my parties before I was sent down. During the war Peter married Helen Brown, Horace's second cousin on his father's side. And now you David occupy the flat where my old pal Peter used to dwell. I dossed down there once or twice during the war as a matter of fact, didn't I, Pete old boy?"

Bayly nodded miserably.

"The same old flat. Now isn't that remarkable?" Roger gazed at me with triumphant frankness. "If you shoved all that in a novel, nobody would believe it."

This was my opportunity and I took it.

"Especially if you added," said I, "that I teach in a school

54

where your brother Edward is headmaster; and Lord White-way, Chairman of the Governors.''

"Good God!" Roger thumped the low table with the palm of his hand. "That can't be true."

Bayly lifted his eyebrows in polite amazement. I nodded good-humouredly. Their surprise went some way to restore my spirits. Roger drank deeply and when he put down his glass I was pleased to see he had lost a little of his assured bounce.

"Well, well," he said, "so you're in the same school as dear old Edward the Confessor. How can you stand it? It must be like a monastery. What a job for an artist. How can you stand it?"

I smiled to show my satisfaction.

"Has he told you anything about me?"

"As a matter of fact," I said, "I haven't mentioned that I know you. But I'm sorry now it didn't occur to me to invite you both to the flat the same evening."

Laughter put us on an equal level of good humour. We knew each other now just well enough to share to the full the saloon bar bonhomie on which Roger throve and grew. We were joined by the proprietor, George, an old friend, apparently, of Roger's. Roger made him listen to the story of marvellous coincidences, but to our relief leaving out any suggestion of my relationship with Helen. George was so impressed I suspected the story would find an honoured place in the house's repertoire. No doubt when Roger returned here without us in the near future he would fill in the gaps. George declared it was better than a story he had heard the night before about two men who had taken a taxi from Wimbledon to Windsor. One had got out at Hampton Court. When the taxi arrived at Windsor outside the *Star and Garter*, the driver discovered his fare was dead. Our story was better, George pointed out, because it was more authentic. Truth, he added dogmatically, was stranger than fiction.

By closing time, I was feeling recklessly merry but I behaved with exaggerated restraint. Even Bayly had become less morose. Once or twice he attempted a story about the war in Sicily but he never concluded it; and when he and I visited the lavatory together he clasped me by the arm solemnly and said,

55

"I'm not saying a word against Helen. She was too good for me, that's all. I'm not saying a word against her."

He eyed me silently and when I nodded he seemed satisfied.

Outside it was a brilliant moonlit night. Roger was already at the wheel of his car. He called to me a little impatiently, since not without affection I had moved apart from the others and was staring up at the congregation of stars. It was the sky visible to my naked eye, I was thinking rather irrelevantly, that allowed me to shrug my shoulders at the second law of thermo-dynamics.

As we drove off, it was Peter Bayly who did the talking. He leaned forward from his seat in the back to insert his head in the gap between our shoulders and went on steadily about the war in Sicily although neither of us was listening. Roger had become silent and thoughtful. Even the most convivial of men, I reflected, are at some time or other forced back upon their own thoughts. I did not know what route Roger was taking. We seemed to be going towards North-West London. As we drove on Bayly completed his story, and leaned back and soon fell asleep. I felt myself pleasantly on the verge of slumber. When Roger turned left into a narrow road it occurred to me to ask him where we were going.

"To see a grave," he said.

He appeared to be serious. We stopped on gravel again, but this time before the lych-gate of a churchyard on either side of which two powerful yew trees stood, black shapes against the moonlit sky.

"Leave him there," Roger said softly. "Pity to wake him."

Now the engine was shut off we could hear him snoring gently.

The graveyard was beautifully kept: a smooth undulating lawn was broken by neat rectangular graves. In the centre stood a small chapel, flint-faced, whose walls and windows glittered in the moonlight.

Roger had stopped alongside a particular grave. He was silent for some time, scouring the edges of the stone with his shoe. At last he spoke.

"This is my son's grave," he said.

His face was shadowed since he stood with his back to the moon. I was divided between embarrassment and pity.

56

I stepped back softly on the grass, as if I was moving away from a glimpse of the great ocean bed of human misery.

"I don't often come here," Roger said. "There doesn't seem much point somehow. . . . This is the first time I've been since I got back from Africa."

We walked back to the car, Roger first. He was stooping and it seemed to me how much older he appeared. Old age can visit a man over forty quite suddenly and perch like a grey cat on his shoulder. Roger did not wear a hat and in the moonlight his head bent, how much older he seemed than his broad and vigorous brother. Yet he was barely two years older. Bayly was still asleep, sprawled over the back seat. The pointless little visit was over. Had he made it to win my sympathy?

An illuminated clock in the Edgware Road showed it was ten to eleven. Roger drove first down to Dolphin Square where Peter lived. Peter was still standing on the pavement waving sleepily as we drove away in the direction of Chelsea. Roger's flat overlooked Chelsea Reach where the moored house-boats rocked gently on the moonlit high tide.

"Come up for a drink?"

"It's getting late. . . ."

"Never mind, I'll run you home afterwards."

We stood side by side in the narrow lift. Roger's face still wore a solemn look. It occurred to me how much I was taking for granted, how little I knew about this man. For all I knew he might be a homosexual, a maniac of some kind, a vampire even. I was bred in a small country town. I suppose that is why these thoughts sometimes assail me. Something of the mediaeval imagination that still lingers in the provincial English mind?

Roger offered me a gin and tonic.

"What is it you teach at my brother's school?" he asked.

I was tempted not to say 'Scripture.' Not because I was ashamed, but because it would take me too long to explain to someone like a Roger, someone so aggressively secular.

"Scripture," I said it.

Roger was less surprised than I expected.

"Do you believe in it?" He genuinely wanted to know.

"In what?" I asked carefully.

"In God . . . and all that sort of thing."

With Roger's type it was no use making reservations. It was up to me to make the best showing possible for my side.

"Yes. Don't you?"

He shook his head sadly.

"There isn't much point in it is there? That boy of mine; I'll never see him again."

He stared at me. I thought of quoting Paul on bodies terrestrial and bodies celestial. But this was hardly the time, and in any case he wouldn't have understood. I wasn't sure that I understood myself.

"My step-father was a parson. He and I didn't get on. He used to talk about God as if he had been in school with him. It's not surprising I'm unreligious. I've been inoculated against it. Does Eddie take morning prayers at school?"

I said 'Yes' eagerly, glad to be able to say something.

"I thought he'd be like Uncle James in the end." Roger smiled. "We used to call our step-father Uncle James."

I was curious enough, but it would have been indelicate for me to ask questions. I said it was time I went home. Roger took no notice.

"He'll probably tell you it was my fault, about the boy. I like old Eddie, mind you, but he was always jealous of me. He wanted to marry the boy's mother himself. He met her first. He brought her down to the Rectory from London for the day. That was the first time I saw her. She lives in a bungalow now near Shanklin. I'm told she keeps swarms of cats. I expect she blames me for lots of things too. Do you know whom I am inclined to blame? I'd blame God if I thought he existed."

He leaned forward and looked at me intently. He had drunk gin and an occasional beer all evening, all day as far as I knew, but now his eyes were as clear as if he were speaking of something he had thought about in cold blood for a long time.

"We had the boy at boarding-school. A good boarding-school. I'm a feckless type myself I know, one of nature's beach-combers, but I wanted to give the boy a decent start. I'm not wildly rich, but I know how to get money when I

58

need it. He was getting on very well. You teach. I could show you his school reports. I've still got them. Then in the middle of that hard winter of forty-seven, that awful January, when the school was snowed up, he had meningitis. Before they could get him away to hospital he was dead. Whose fault was that? Not mine any more than anybody else's. If anybody's to blame it's your friend God."

I wasn't going to argue. It was none of my business anyway. I had a right not to be dragged into other people's miseries. I had enough problems of my own. Again I said it was time I went home.

Going down in the lift Roger became more cheerful. He asked me what I thought of Peter. He said Peter was a damned good sort and well worth knowing. He was a car salesman. If ever I wanted a new car Peter was the man to see. He and Roger shared an interest in a garage in Shepherd's Bush.

"One needs one's friends," he said, grinning, "under this Labour Government."

I made no noise of agreement and he was quick to notice it.

"I expect you're some kind of a socialist too. A pink type like my brother Edward. Intellectuals who go for a ride on the Communist tiger. Did you see my article in the *Sunday Mirror* three weeks ago? I called it *They went for a ride on a tiger*. Rather a good title I thought."

He didn't take any notice of my disapproving silence.

"Whiteway liked it. Do you know Whiteway?"

"Not socially." I meant it as a joke but Roger didn't seem to notice.

"I'll take you along to his place next time they have an At Home if you like. I've become quite a friend of the family. Lady Whiteway likes to hear me talking about Horace. And my Lord Whiteway thinks my politics are very sound. He and I are thinking of making a trip together to the States. It was my idea but he seems very taken with it. How would you like to come. Make a team of it?"

I did not take the suggestion seriously.

"Hardly in my line," I said.

"But you'll line up in the end. There is such a thing as the *Reality of Power*. I'm thinking of doing an article

59

on the subject for one of the better Sunday papers. Facing the Facts I thought of calling it. I don't suppose you agree?"

"It's a bit late for me to think about politics." I yawned without putting my hand over my mouth.

"I thought you didn't."

The car drew up outside our terrace.

"I hope you didn't mind my bringing Peter along." Roger smiled in a friendly way. "I thought it might be a situation that would interest you."

"Not at all," I mumbled untruthfully. I quietly decided I could do without a model for Sir Thomas Seymour and I could also afford to give Lady Whiteway's At Home a miss. I only hoped I wasn't too deeply committed to having to see the man again. I had been sorry for him in the graveyard; but he was someone whom, from now on, I would take some trouble to avoid. He was among those people whose mould of toughness was so hard nothing could divert them from the direct route they were taking to damnation.

"Good night, David."

I wished he would not make so free with my Christian name.

"Good night," I answered, fumbling among my pockets for the door-key.

"Oh, David!" He was leaning along the seat to unwind the left-hand window. I came back.

"You couldn't possibly lend me two pounds, could you? I've run dry and I won't be able to get to my bank until tomorrow afternoon."

"Why, of course." I brought out my wallet at once. I handed him the notes.

"Thanks. You'll have them back tomorrow."

"No hurry," I said. "Any time will do."

"Good night."

He waved as the car moved off in rapid acceleration. I opened the front door. It occurred to me that Roger had been more successful in understanding my character than I his. He knew I was the type when touched who was too weak to refuse. It wasn't that he needed the money. Either it was some deep-set habit or he was trying me on; or was it a fee for the evening's entertainment. Garages, journalism, cultivating the Whiteways. What did he tell the poor woman about her

60

worthless son? Did Whiteway realise he was Edward's brother?
Had he wormed his way into the Whiteway's home by means
of some polite blackmail? He was a bad type, and I was very
sorry that he was Edward's brother.

I swallowed half a bottle of milk and went to bed tired,
hungry, and in a bad temper.

VI

"**Y**OU ARE QUITE SURE?"

"Positive, sir." Bansdale nodded his head vigorously. He was small for his age; the only boy in my form who still wore short trousers—if you could call them short, since they came well over his knees. He was known as *Inky Billy*. He invented the name himself. He specialised in ink pellets. More than once I had observed inkspots on Visot's neck and collar. He also specialised in tormenting Visot. *Incorrigibly untidy* Visot had written on his last report. Bansdale's reports managed to damn him with faintest praise imaginable. Mark 26%. Position 23. *He could do better than this if only he tried. P. B. S. Dell.* But we all agreed he was a nice lad. 'No real harm in him,' said Robinson sucking wisely at his pipe. A ready toothy smile, friendly manner, cheerful self-possession: the generally accepted meaning of nice lad: Bansdale, John William Xavier.

Allenside and I sat one side of the desk; Bansdale stood facing us. Allenside was asking the questions, with his customary patient fairness.

"Penge told you he picked them up on the playing fields?"

"Yes sir."

"Then you took them to the Post Office, changed them and bought five shillings worth of sweets?"

"Yes sir."

"What did you do with the rest of the money?"

"Penge kept it."

"How much, do you know?"

"About fifteen bob, I mean shillings sir."

Not much guilt about young Bansdale. A bright-eyed boy clown well satisfied with the laughter of his form mates. He had not yet reached adolescence. I was merry enough as a child myself: always on the brink of laughter. At adolescence we change trains. Bansdale's family was Catholic. In a year or two he would make many choices: and in five or six years' time he would be something as different from this tousle-headed ink-spotted boy as one generation from another. Boyhood is a backward nation, a tropical dependency governed by a handful of uncomprehending adults.

"Send Penge in now will you? You can go back to your class."

When the door closed we leaned back in our chairs.

"No time for a smoke I'm afraid." Allenside smiled. "I'm sorry to use up your free period like this. What about Penge's record card?"

Momentary sunlight pierced the clouds and illuminated a segment of the headmaster's office. Allenside never referred to the room as his study. It was cold and efficient; steel filing cabinets, tidy desks, a typewriter, an iron safe, wooden cupboard, a glass case containing sports trophies, a scrubbed block floor: no carpet, no flowers, no pictures, not even bookshelves. Miss Symond's red coat-hanger hung like the last leaf on a December tree of a coat-stand in the corner.

I still hadn't told him about his brother. There never seemed enough time.

"When are we going to see you again? Can you manage next Saturday?"

"Thank you." I nodded. Although I grudged the time I could spend on my book, it would be a chance to talk about Roger. Besides I always enjoyed Allenside's company. He had the creative touch and he was a man of wide culture. I had no particular liking for his wife: I found her patronising and cold, a social climber; and I suspected that she disliked me. But for her I think Allenside and I would have spent much more time together. We had planned another walking tour in Cornwall during the Easter vacation but Allenside found in the last week of term he had committees to attend during that week. Privately I feared his wife had made such a fuss, he had called off the trip for the sake of domestic peace.

There was a quiet knock at the door. Penge came in, closing the door carefully after him.

"Well Penge. What have you to tell us?"

Flat face, large ears; eyes with sticky corners: a procession of pimples from cheek to cheek across the flat nose, large blackheads nestled at the base of his nostrils. He had no mother to squeeze them. But his clothes were tidy enough. His puzzled stupid bovine eyes were fixed at something invisible above the headmaster's head. *Sheep's head* Eglinton called him. He was the kind of boy who brought out the worst in teachers. *Stupid and unattentive. P. B. S. Dell.* Allenside asked him to change the remark. The report had to be circulated again. Twenty-sixth out of twenty-six. Poor old Penge. Both his parents had been killed in the blitz. He had been reared by a surly grandmother who was passionately attached to cigarettes and whist drives. From time to time she had passed him off on institutions. Now he was fostered, but the foster parents were beginning to regret their choice. Brunt pitied him systematically, defended him at staff meetings against all comers. Visot had taken him home to tea, several times. So had Allenside. I always took pains to be nice with the lad. I knew exactly what he needed: love on a lavish scale, an iron lung of love. I couldn't give it him. All Penge could get was pity or revulsion. Mitchley said, *I've done all I could for that lad. No one could do more. And now he goes and does this.* Mitchley was always eager to impress the head with his educational endeavour. He pinned his hopes on the post of special responsibility. *I damn well ought to get it,* he told me a day or so ago when we were alone in the staff-room together. *No one's done more for the school than I have. I've been on this staff now for fifteen years. It's time I got a little recognition.*

No one called Penge a nice lad. Obviously he stole the savings stamps to buy enough sweets to buy the notice of his form mates. Who knows with what wistful longing he gazed at Bansdale the other side of the room, clowning on top of his desk? He seemed unaware that he had done anything wrong. I could sympathise with him. My own moral sense was equally vague and uncertain. I was glad that Allenside had relieved me of dealing with the problem. If God were a headmaster and I was in Form Two what would I do what would I do?

"I take it you are sorry?"

Penge nodded. His lips began to bend. Of course he was sorry. Sorry for what? Sorry to trouble you sirs. Sorry to be caught. A sorry story. Whatever was to be done with the boy? It was perfectly clear he had taken the stamps from Graham's coat in the cloak-room. Penge had a fondness for asking to be excused: a loophole to freedom that while it lasted had become a clear field. Briarman had suspected Penge long ago. He had suggested laying a trap with marked coins. Brunt, Visot and myself were deeply indignant at the suggestion and Allenside turned it down. But in a way it was a sensible plan. Now we knew he was guilty, how were we to punish him?

"You can go back to your class now, Penge."

Allenside's voice was still fair and kindly.

When Penge had gone he said to me,

"The question now is, shall we recommend that he be sent back to an institution; or shall we take on the responsibility of having him here? It's a question the whole staff ought to decide. Would you agree David?"

I nodded. It warmed me to hear him call me David. And last night I had resented the same address from his brother.

"I suspect you are inclined to favour our keeping him here?"

I said, "Yes, except for the foster parents. I'm not happy about that part of the arrangement. Would it be possible for him to live in an institution and still come here to school?"

Allenside nodded. "That would be worth considering."

Miss Symonds, the headmaster's secretary, brought in coffee and biscuits on a tray. She was small, thin, efficient, unattractive and unadorned to the point of being neuter: or so I thought. But about such matters private judgement is grossly fallible. Once standing with Bill Hawkes in the corridor, Miss Symonds had passed, and Bill, whom I took to be a ladies' man of the widest experience whispered in my ear, "That's a little piece of goods I'd like to handle, so small, so delicate, so fragile, so petite." Bill Hawkes was burly and handsome in a negroid flat-footed manner. As Miss Symonds placed the tray on the desk I had a view of the ivory line that parted her pale hair; it was fringed with dandruff. It puzzled me what Bill Hawkes found so attractive about her. I knew he wasn't joking.

To my relief Miss Symonds went out again. I think she suspected that Allenside and I were rather friendly. She probably warned some of the staff that I was the headmaster's stooge. Allenside walked up and down the room to stretch his legs. He paused by the window to light his pipe. As much of the sky as we saw through his window was dull with the promise of rain.

"How is your new novel going?"

"Rather slowly. Perhaps the story would respond better to being played out on a stage."

"Would that be in prose or in verse?"

"Verse I should think." Abruptly I changed the subject. "I've been meaning to tell you. I met your brother in a party the other night."

Allenside could not prevent himself blushing. My meeting Roger was something he would prefer not to have happened.

"Roger? Is he back again?"

He stood with legs apart, head forward a little, his strong figure apparent within the well cut grey suit. I wondered how much my affection for him stemmed from my pride at being treated as an equal by my superior. No. I liked him because I admired and respected him. He seemed to me to exemplify the qualities of the good man more clearly and uncompromisingly than anyone else I had known: and I was resolved to admire goodness. His management of the school was firm, just, generous. He believed the welfare of each boy was his business and yet he treated them with the respect due to individuals; he was aware of their faults but always prepared to think the best it was possible to think even of the worst of them. I knew enough about schools to realise that he was an exceptionally good headmaster.

"What did you think of him?"

He awaited my answer eagerly. Normally I was always pleased when he consulted my opinion and I always summed up my entire resources of wit and wisdom to give a reply that would win his admiration and approval. Nothing delighted and warmed me more than the knowledge that he valued my advice and my friendship. But now I did not know what to say. After all, Roger was his brother.

I said, "He was very affable. We got on rather well."

Allenside glanced at the clock.

"I must tell you about Roger. He's interesting enough. What they call a colourful character. It seems he has also become an intimate of Lord Whiteway. When I saw Whiteway at County Hall the day before yesterday he chided me for not telling him I had such an interesting and intelligent brother. He does get around."

He paused, as if he was undecided what to say next.

At last he said, "There isn't time now to do justice to Roger. I expect you've guessed that I don't have much to

66

do with him. I'll tell you about him again, at a more suitable time than this."

He bent to unlock a drawer in his desk and extracted a letter. Handing it to me, he said,

"I wanted to show you this. From Bansdale's father to Lord Whiteway. Lord Whiteway passed it on to me. I haven't mentioned it to anyone else."

My Lord, the letter began.

I feel it my duty as a British citizen to bring to your notice that Communist propaganda is being carried on inside the Bilateral School. This evening I have found in my son's satchel a bundle of papers, two dozen copies of the "Daily Worker". My son states that they were given to him by Mr. Visot, one of the masters. Mr. Visot had asked my son to distribute them through letter boxes in our street at night. I am writing to you and not to the headmaster as my son states it would be no use saying anything to the headmaster since he is a Communist as well.

I do not wish to make public scandal so have not yet taken steps to write to the Press.

Hoping your Lordship will take the necessary steps to rectify the matter.

> *I remain,*
> *Your Lordship's faithful servant,*
> *John Aloysius Bansdale.*
> *(Railway Clerk*
>
> *L. P. T. B.*)

I laughed as I handed the letter back.

"Whiteway tends to take it more seriously than I expected. He wasn't satisfied when I explained that Bansdale probably pinched the papers out of Visot's case for a lark; and probably told his father a cock and bull story to get out of a wigging. Whiteway wanted to know why in the first place Visot should have so many copies of the *Worker* with him in school." He paused when Miss Symonds knocked and entered. "It's a stupid business." He came with me to the door. We stood outside in the corridor. The bell went and boys began to hurry past on their way to their class-rooms.

"A stupid business," he repeated, "but also rather delicate. Naturally I must put the whole business before Visot, without too much delay. But first I would like to know what exactly happened and how Visot would be likely to react to a letter of this kind. There is a danger he might too readily welcome persecution. You know him better than I do David. What do you think of the whole business, and how do you think he will react?"

The bell went for the third lesson of the morning.

"Think about it will you and we'll talk it over again some time tomorrow, shall we?"

I had to call in the staff-room to collect some books I had been marking. Dell and Dodger Downs were there preparing to enjoy a free period.

"Come on, Holy Moses, don't keep your class waiting." Downs spoke with heavy affability.

"Just you relax and go to sleep." Automatic staff-room badinage.

"Been having a *tête-à-tête* with our respected headmaster?" Downs enquired grinning. I noticed Dell waiting for my reply. Did he think that the deputy headship had been under discussion, or did he imagine Allenside had asked my opinion of him? There was a sort of respectful dislike in the way he looked at me that suggested that such thoughts had passed through his mind. Miss Symonds must have been talking. She had heard nothing. All she had to go by was the manner in which Allenside and I addressed each other; but that would be just the kind of thing a woman would go by. I would need to be more circumspect. For obvious reasons it would not be good for the staff-room to understand that a friendship existed between the headmaster and a junior member of staff. It pleased me to realise that I would need to be more careful. It is a more subtle and mature pleasure to conceal what one considers to be one's triumphs, than to boast of them openly. Certainly it is the only way to maintain popularity along with success.

VII

"In other words," I said, "you are not prepared to admit that there is such a thing as sin?"

Visot shook his head patiently. "What I am saying is that the term 'sin' has no meaning for me at all."

We sat towards the centre of the trolley-bus on the lower deck. Visot rested his wrists on his attaché case so that he made gestures to accompany his argument by opening and closing his fingers. He seemed more assured of his point of view than I was of mine, and often he would smile broadly at what I said, his large mouth revealing part of his gums which glistened with the saliva that made his talking so relentless and formidable.

"I suppose you would call it anti-social behaviour?" I tried not to sound sarcastic.

"Yes. To a certain extent, I would call it that."

"What about bad-temper, nastiness and malice?"

"They are usually the outcome of some conflict or some maladjustment. They can always be explained, diagnosed like any other illness."

"You believe a Communist state would get round to doing all that in time; after fixing up little details like production, distribution and consumption?"

Visot lifted his eyebrows tolerantly and nodded again.

"All in good time. When we've had half the two thousand years of authority and influence your Christianity has had . . ."

"We just won't know the old place," I finished jovially.

"Quite."

"I can't wait to have my conflicts ironed out."

Visot looked at me solemnly.

"Well you are a bit self-conscious, aren't you?" he said. His innocent directness came out like this from time to time, like a blow in the stomach. Indignation burst through my nostrils like a second wind. Well I'm damned, I said to myself, what

69

cheek. Visot's arm passed my nose as he handed his ticket to the conductor. If there was anything I tended to pride myself on it was my modest and restrained bearing among my colleagues.

It really was a bit too much, from Visot of all people. That very afternoon the devil's own row came out of Room Six where Visot was taking IIIb. Somebody was shouting, "*When did you wash your shirt last, sir?*" Several boys were standing on their desks. Two or three were hanging out of the window (the class-room was on the third floor) shying chalk at passers-by, while Visot red in the face, was standing to attention and crying monotonously, "*Now then IIIb! I will not have this noise! Do you hear?*" (To address a form by its collective name; an abysmal psychological error! When discipline hangs in the balance to acknowledge and underline their collective strength, to encourage each boy to lose his individuality in a riot of herd destructiveness!) Also there was someone sitting on the floor quietly playing a mouth-organ. Then Allenside came in. It was like a transformation scene: the beasts became beautiful, orderly, desk-decorating, soft and silent-mouthed schoolboys. The head deprived them of games for the rest of the term.

It would have been cruel to ask Visot whether he blamed himself for the devils in his class-room. Who was maladjusted there, the boys or the teacher? He would probably blame himself. He would take all the blame belonging to thirty barbarous boys and add it to his own in order not to upset the sweet balance of his soul-sustaining theory. My anger had vanished when we got off the bus to cross Mitcham Common: I had re-established my superiority to my own complete satisfaction. Crossing the Common we resumed our argument about the perfectability of man.

Visot's home was 116, Godolphin Road, one of an endless row of cheaply built semi-detached pebble-dashed dwellings designed to harbour the lower middle classes outside office hours.

"Is that you Gerald?" An old man's voice came from the direction of the kitchen.

"Yes, Dad. Hang your coat here, Flint."

"The kettle's boiling Gerald." I had never heard anyone call Visot Gerald before. In the staff-room he was Vizzy to everyone except Brunt who called him 'Jack'. The boys called him 'Visotski'. Here he was someone else. "Have you brought a friend along?"

He appeared with surprising suddenness in the kitchen doorway an old man with the scraggy features of an ageing eagle and long white hair, seated in a narrow wheel-chair. His eyes were brilliant with the pathetic benevolence of the aged and infirm.

"This is Mr. Flint, Dad, from school. You've heard me speak of him. He's come to hear some of my records."

I shook the long thin hand that was extended eagerly towards me.

"Now that will be really nice. We'll have quite a concert. An audience is so important, isn't it?"

Visot was already preparing tea with surprising speed and neatness. He did not apologise for laying it on the kitchen table, but his father said they always had it there because it was so much less trouble. The old man talked a great deal. He was lonely, no doubt, spending so much of the day by himself. He described in detail an argument he had had with Mr. Speller next door over the garden fence. Mr. Speller, it appeared, was a printer, a keen trade-unionist and a deacon in a Spiritualist Church.

"I pulled his leg a bit you know Gerald. I offered to lend him my copy of the *Rationalist Review* so that he could read A. J. S. Tuck's article on *Spiritualism: the Evidence Examined*. He declined the offer. Do you know what he said, Gerald? He said '*Reading gives me a headache*'."

The old man chuckled in his chair, heaving his head up and down. He was allowed his rationalism although Visot considered it outmoded and undynamic. The old man was grateful. Visot was the hero, head, shield and defender of this household; the provider, the breadwinner, to whom father and brother submitted everything they said and did for confirmation and approval.

At tea, Mr. Visot described how he had lost his legs in the blitz. He had been trapped by a falling beam and suspended head downwards over a hole in the floor. He had not realised at first that anything had happened to his legs. He attributed his discomfort to his position. A fireman had parted the long hair that hung like a curtain in front of his face and Mr. Visot

71

said he heard him say quite distinctly *'Blimey Jim, look 'ere!'* And then he had fainted.

When we had finished tea, Visot's younger brother, Bertie, came in. Bertie worked in a radio shop. Alongside his brother Visot seemed a tower of virility. Bertie's body was thin to the point of being brittle. Only an unusually developed Adam's apple seemed to contain enough strength to save the large head from toppling to the floor. He was painfully shy. When I shook hands with him he kept his gaze upon the floor. I gathered Bertie had a shed in the garden where he spent long happy hours dispatching and picking up signals on his short wave set. His father told me that yesterday evening Bertie had exchanged dignals with enthusiasts in California, Brisbane and Rio de Janeiro. I glanced at Bertie who chewed slowly and seemed to be examining in detail the patterns on his plate; and I wondered how he survived the rigours of the journey all the way down Godolphin Road and into the heart of Streatham. I noticed when he came in it was raining outside and Bertie was wearing goloshes.

We settled down in the overcrowded and dusty drawing-room (I wondered how often the daily woman, who came from nine to twelve except Sundays, was allowed in the room). Piles of magazines and papers were moved off chairs. The table was cleared for laying out the records and Visot grinning said he was now prepared to officiate at the gramophone. We were to hear the first act of *Don Giovanni*.

The old man leaned back in his chair and closed his eyes. There was a certain emaciated beauty about him as he listened. Perhaps, as a young man, he had been as unprepossessing as his sons; perhaps beauty visits everyone at some time between birth and death. Thoughts of this family wove fitfully through the music like cigarette smoke in the still air. Bertie sat near the door watching his father and brother and doing his best to catch from them something of their enjoyment of the music.

I wondered what kind of woman Visot's mother had been and when she had died. It must have been several years ago. This room had the untidy comfortless appearance of a place occupied solely by men. Visot and I were on good terms—we had made two or three visits together to the theatre, and I planned to ask him to the flat when next I gave a sherry party

—but we were not intimate enough for me to ask him any questions about his mother and I doubted if we ever would be. He was too implacably devoted to his party. Friendship with Visot would only follow by conversion to his point of view: something not so entirely improbable as might appear. Did not my own vacillations increase my admiration for his single-minded strength and absolute devotion? When I thought of Roger and his *Realities of Power* and of Lord Whiteway, and of Brown Properties and of American magazines with circulations in tens of millions paying half-a-dollar a worthless word, I was almost driven into Visotski's uncompromising arms.

He listened to the music with his eyes closed, without any movement of his body. He had none of the amateur listener's wandering thoughts and wavering attention. Ridiculous in the class-room, the butt of every scruffy schoolboy's spurting wit, he was one of those happy few among men who would face a firing line coolly for his faith, even though that very faith laid down that in a matter of seconds his whole being would become a carcase rapidly decomposing in a lime pit. Perhaps being certain of that was some assistance to him? I envied the firm simplicity of his faith, in spite of my knowledge that it was based on half-truths and heresy.

The front door bell rang. Bertie went to answer it. There was a murmur of voices, and then Bertie ushered in Tibbot; Tibbot of VIR. He had no cap and his black curly hair glistened from a slight shower of rain which had also speckled the shoulders of the light mackintosh he wore. His corduroy trousers were held above his ankles by bicycle clips. A rectangular bump under his mac betrayed that he was carrying books under his coat. With one hand he shaded his eyes from the bright electric light, with the other he kept the books from slipping down. He was perfectly at ease until he saw me and then he became shy and perhaps a little anxious.

Visot had got up and switched off the gramophone.

"You gentlemen know each other I take it," he said humorously. As a matter of fact I hardly knew Tibbot except as a reliable prefect, who greeted me cheerfully in the corridor every morning when I came into school. "Take your coat off, Richard."

Reassured, the boy extracted the books and handed them

to Visot who placed them on the mantelpiece. I was unable to see their titles. Then the boy unbuttoned his mac and removed it. I could tell that my presence puzzled him. He had never seen me at Visot's before and he had no reason to believe that I was even a fellow-traveller. I longed to make amusing remarks to reveal that although I was not a Party member, I was a socially-conscious Christian of wide sympathies and utter toleration, and that there were many aspects of their party's work that I approved of to the point of fellow-travellership. But I knew that my sympathy was not wanted. These people were sufficient unto themselves. In the untidy drawing-room, drinking cups of tea and discussing music I could sense the solidarity between these four people: Bertie, the cripple in a wheel-chair, Visot whom schoolboys persecuted, the quiet school prefect Tibbot; individually they were weak to the point of being objects of my large capacity for pity. Together they shared a power whose mystical quality was wholly denied to me. It had something of the pacific radiance the early church enjoyed; the resting in righteousness that sustained the tiny Hebrew prophets between the clanking empires and terrifying cohorts of Egypt and Assyria.

When I said it was time for me to go, Tibbot also rose to his feet. We put on our macs in the narrow corridor. I was hoping to have a word in private with Visot about the Bansdale letter before leaving. I was about to suggest that he should accompany me to the end of Godolphin Road, when Visot said to Tibbot,

"Richard, can I have a word with you before you go about the Club?"

The boy went back into the drawing-room. Visot stood on the door-step waiting for me to say 'good night', so obviously intent to speed the parting guest, that I felt it would be useless to mention the Bansdale letter; far better for him to be unaware that I knew anything about it.

I did not enjoy the journey home. It peeved me to think I had involved myself in an hour's journey by tram and by tube on a wet night, to spend a few cheerless hours among uncongenial company. My vague intention had been to help Visot: but the fact was he didn't want any help. He would welcome any kind of fuss with open arms. It amazed me to reflect that seated in their drawing-room drinking their abominable tea and nibbling damp digestive biscuits I had been romantically moved to compare them with the early church. They were in fact more like mesmerised ants pursuing with blind diligence the fruitless industry that was to hasten their own insignificant destruction. If I were to have an illusion, I told myself with some self-satisfaction, heaving up my feet on to the seat in front of me, let it at least be something big. Better the Ruler of Suns and Interstellar Spaces, the King of the Universe, than a grinning Russian totem pole.

All the way home I continued to worry the problem, ragging and nagging not so much facts, figures and arguments as the emotional state behind them. Nothing in life I concluded, in sight of the flat, glad to be back among the broad streets and heavy porticoes of Kensington, nothing in life could possibly compare in importance with gaining experimental knowledge of the existence of God. And nothing was more certain that at any moment in time the light of Grace would fall upon the virtuous soul and the gates of Heaven could open and the shadow of death vanish. But I was not a virtuous soul and I would not be visited by the Comforter. I was one more among the millions of the lost, floundering among the crumbling cities of time; where the ashes gave way before my aimless advancing foot. I had no illusions, and no comfort.

VIII

ALLENSIDE HAD A PLEASANT house between Shirley and West Wickham. When I arrived there on Saturday afternoon I found him putting a new lock on his garage door. I offered to help, but there was nothing I could do except stand and watch patiently until he had finished. Someone was mowing the grass on the front lawn. The trees across the road and the expanse of garden about the house gave one the illusion of being well in the country. The day was cloudy, but warm enough to give a foretaste of summer. To be in a garden after the desert of streets was to reach an oasis. The blooms of flowering shrubs held their place with neat smooth certainty; the young leaves of the copper beech at the bottom of the garden had the pallor of new birth; the linden leaves were still with expectancy, almost ready for the revelations of transforming sunlight.

The car wasn't in the garage, so we would not be able to go out in the country as I had hoped. I was a little disappointed. Still it probably meant Janet his wife was out so we would have the place to ourselves. Janet pursued a career of her own as the author and producer of occasional radio programmes; she took her career very seriously. Certainly it did supplement the family income. Her attitude to me was one of patronising tolerance. As a novelist I was not successful enough; as a teacher I was her husband's subordinate. She expected me to treat her with respectful regard, while allowing her to be as familiar as she fancied with me. For Allenside's sake I endured this arrangement. He was a sensitive man and constantly embarrassed by his wife's attitude, doing everything he could to mitigate it. She was a formidable woman and although I tried hard enough I found it impossible to like her.

A door at the back of the garage led into the back kitchen. A shopping basket on wheels propelled by a walking stick was parked in the corner. A narrow work-bench ran almost the whole length of the left hand wall. Above it from the rafters a child's red tricycle was suspended, a relic of Howard's childhood. Howard, their only child, was fourteen now, a boarder at a progressive school in Bucks. Bearings the place was called. Perhaps they had kept the tricycle for another child? But Janet seemed beyond child bearing. Pursuing her own career had given her the solid square shape of a well-tailored business spinster on the brink of middle-age.

When he had finished and was putting his screwdriver and hammer away, Allenside said, "Janet is out I'm afraid, David. She asked me to apologise for her absence. She has some committee or other this afternoon and she'd promised to have tea with Lady Muriel afterwards."

Lady Muriel was Lord Whiteway's wife. I had a vague idea Helen disliked her. She had been Helen's father's secretary and Helen suspected that she had given Whiteway (or Walker-Brown as he was then) too much help in gaining outright control of the firm. I am hazy about the facts. As often happens, an impression gained from information to which one did not properly listen remains to tantalise when, after months or years, interest has at last been quickened. The impression remains, like a guess, but the details cannot be remembered.

The conscientious novelist should be an undiscriminating listener. His memory should be vast enough for the even distribution of lumber on either side of the narrow aisles of time. Nothing should be thrown away: merely set aside and lightly covered with dust that a flick of words will easily remove. A dull profession: caretakers of a collection of ruins, who stand at the mouth of the past, blinking, unfamiliar with sunlight.

We placed deck chairs against a bare patch of the brick fruit-wall. Allenside offered me his tobacco pouch.

"You were telling me about Roger," he said. He gave me the impression of being cautious, which disappointed me. It meant he would tell me no more than he considered absolutely necessary for me to know. But it would have been uncharacteristic of him to speak too freely. In complete contrast to Roger, and for that matter to me, he used words with an accurate restraint that made all his statements seem carefully considered.

"He came to see me again the other evening," I said. "I

77

told him you were my headmaster. We went out for a drink."

Allenside smoked silently for a few moments, and then he said, "Did he ask you to lend him any money?"

For some reason I felt rather guilty.

"As a matter of fact he did."

"A lot?"

"Oh no. Only two pounds."

"Have you any brothers, David?"

"No. I'm an only child. I thought that was fairly obvious."

He paid little attention to my joke.

"Roger is my only brother: my elder brother. All through my boyhood I adored him. I thought he was wonderful. There is still a gap, an empty space where my admiration for him used to lie. I'd like to see him now. A few minutes in his company can make me feel reckless and ready to do something foolish. A nice feeling."

I began to speak, but Allenside shook his head.

"No David. Don't think of staging a reconciliation. We haven't quarrelled. There's been no estrangement. We have drifted apart by mutual consent. We have become so different, any communication between us would be quite meaningless. He has a contempt for my respectability, my seriousness, everything about me, which must include some sort of contempt for me. And I suppose I feel the same way about him and his works. To me, at best, he is just a seedy unprincipled journalist. I'm telling you this about my own brother . . ." he paused . . . "because I don't want him to take advantage of you."

Allenside spoke slowly as if every word was carefully considered. Then he added with a smile, "It might also be that I am suffering from a certain nervous jealousy. I know Roger is so much more entertaining and persuasive than I am."

It warmed me greatly to understand that Allenside valued my friendship. As a young man he must have had many friends. He had been a notable athlete and he had played rugger for U.C.L.: he had been president of the Student's Union. Many doors had been open to him, but he had chosen to train as a teacher. His first job was as Warden of a boy's club in Poplar. He had been offered a lectureship in Cairo, but he went to Poplar because of his socialist principles and

78

because he had become engaged to Janet, who was still an undergraduate. I fancied that had set the pattern: whenever a choice was involved Janet's need was the first to be met. Because Janet had secured a job in broadcasts to schools, their engagement lasted four or five years. Allenside remained in teaching jobs in the London area because Janet could not bear him to be far away. His two greatest friends of those years before his marriage were dead. John, an engineer, was killed in an air-raid in Spain; Hugh, a poet, had died of some obscure disease in India towards the end of the war. I imagined his marriage and becoming a headmaster may have cut him off from new associations. And yet he had a distinct gift for friendship; he was unselfish, reliable, modest, and helping others gave him pleasure and satisfaction. He suffered nothing from the torments of envy that so often put a limit to the capacity for fellowship in the man over thirty intent on getting on, who desires only to exchange mutual admiration with non-competitive cronies.

Perhaps with me he was able to renew something of the good-will and understanding he had shared with Hugh. He had made a collection of Hugh's letters and poems which he hoped to arrange for publication. I had mentioned them to my own publisher who had demonstrated the usual sympathetic unwillingness and advised us to wait until interest in the war years revived among the reading public. Meanwhile Allenside was tentatively engaged in writing a biography of his friend, but the fear of doing less than justice to his subject and, I suspect, a certain unspoken hostility on the part of his wife, made progress on the work very slow. It had reached the stage now when I felt it indelicate to mention the project although I was certain he had the ability to do full justice to his subject.

"Roger isn't easy to explain," Allenside said, staring across the garden. "I'll tell you about him. He might make a good subject for a novel."

Allenside smiled and I glanced at him, rather guiltily.

"You must have read my thoughts," I said, determined to be nothing less than completely honest. "As a matter of fact I had thought of him as a model for Sir Thomas Seymour."

"Really. Then I must read up Seymour's history. It might help me to understand Roger better."

I wondered whether he would see himself in my version of the Lord Protector. Perhaps not. He was infinitely more gentle. All they had in common was a concern for righteousness and resolute fairness and honesty. And also perhaps unhelpful wives.

"I'll begin at the beginning. Our father died when I was five. I barely remember him. Roger, who is two years older than I, claims to remember him very well. He was a gentleman of slender but independent means with vaguely literary aspirations. I have a novel of his in manuscript which I wouldn't dream of showing you. It's called *The White Tower*: imitation R. L. Stevenson. He was also a barrister but he never practised. He devoted a good deal of his time to lay preaching and the Liberal cause.

"Two years after his death my mother married Uncle James, her second cousin. He had been a friend of my father's and as far as I am concerned I find it difficult to distinguish between them, except that Uncle James was perhaps the more pious. I couldn't imagine him writing a novel. His literary efforts were very long and very dry sermons. He was Rector of Forley in Oxfordshire. For me Forley Rectory was the home of my childhood and youth and Uncle James, as we continued to call him, was my father. But Roger never accepted the new order. His dislike for Uncle James increased as he grew older; and he never liked the Rectory either. He could not forgive Uncle James for marrying my mother.

"It must have been difficult for poor Uncle James; he was a mild enough man. A weak heart gave him rather a high colour and the thick glass of his spectacles somehow made him more severe to look at. His manner was rather abrupt too. But he tried his best with Roger. It was no use. Roger practically forced him to treat him with severity. It was as if Roger wanted to make Uncle James to take him seriously as a rival for my mother's affection. When he was old enough to realise how much religion meant to Uncle James he did everything he could to upset the old boy in that direction. He associated with anyone whom he thought Uncle James would disapprove of. In the Rectory I was a neutral country in a small world at war. I can remember one incident rather vividly.

"Roger in short trousers in the drawing-room, his narrow

white knees, and a lock of hair hanging over his eyes, standing stubbornly in front of Uncle James who was saying '*Do you defy me, Roger?*' And the awful silence in which Roger refused to answer. '*Very well. Go up to your room.*' Uncle James helping himself to climb the stairs gripping the banister so tightly high-lights shone on his knuckles. I was as much afraid for him as I was for Roger. I stood at the bottom of the stairs, straining my ears. When I heard something I imagined to be a cry of pain I fled from the house, into the sunlight. It must have been high summer. I went into the wood beyond the churchyard and sat reading by a stream until my conscience forced me back to the house, with some vague intention perhaps of comforting my brother.

"The front door was open. I crept up the white stair-case. I paused for a moment outside Roger's door, then I opened it softly. Roger was sitting up and on the bed beside him my mother sat holding a pink plate with the soft yellow crumbs of a sponge cake on it still. They both looked at me without speaking. I have the impression I crept out as if my presence had not been observed. A little later from the gravel path alongside the house through the French windows of the study I caught a glimpse of Uncle James, seated at his desk, his hands together and his eyes closed."

Allenside paused. He spoke as if he could still see the scenes he described clearly before him. They must have occurred in the early nineteen twenties.

"I hope to goodness I'm not giving the impression that I suffered an unhappy childhood." He turned to smile at me. "I loved living in the Rectory. The Church and the Rectory were just outside the village. Uncle James was always kind to me. So was my mother in her rather absent-minded way. And I trotted round obediently enough after Roger whenever he would let me. The shadow in the house did not often stretch far enough to include me. And so I grew up to be my devastatingly normal and placid self."

We both laughed.

"But not Roger. My mother had some money by to send him to Cambridge, to our father's college. Uncle James paid for my education in London. When Roger was in Cambridge my mother was taken ill while staying with her sister near Brighton. She was moved to a nursing home. When Roger heard of this he borrowed a motor bicycle without permission and rode down to see her. He maintains that was the reason for his being sent down. I don't know. I rather suspect there may have been an accumulation of misdemeanours. My mother died that year in Forley. After the funeral Roger left the house for good.

"Poor Uncle James was left alone in the Rectory. I had begun to feel a tremendous affection for the old boy which was retrospective in a way. He had done his utmost for us. I spent as much time with him as I could, but by then of course I was in London. He had rather hoped I would become a candidate for ordination. I would have cheerfully gone on with the business if I could have believed it would have made the old chap any happier, even though I had become something of a socialist unbeliever. But he seemed to sense that I had no stomach for the job. When I said I fancied school-mastering he agreed quite readily. The same night, when I took him a glass of hot milk before going to bed myself he said almost à propos of nothing at all as I was leaving, 'You may not believe in the existence of a God, Edward, but I think you will always live as if there was one.'

"He was particularly anxious for a reconciliation with Roger. He wanted me to try to persuade Roger to come home. But Roger wasn't in the least inclined to relent. It was as if he blamed Uncle James and God jointly for his mother's death. About that time he was living with a girl of whom I had been fond, so communication between us had become rather difficult. Anyway, Uncle James died and Roger stayed away from the funeral.

"I suppose I sound unfair to Roger?" I shook my head but Allenside wasn't looking at me. "Maybe a difficult childhood is to blame for all his faults. Uncle James and my mother should have read the right books on psychology and treated him differently. But my ultimate impression is that even as a boy he made a deliberate choice of the course he followed. And all along with a quite alarming deliberation, he has always done just exactly what he wanted.

"As for myself it may be some hidden childhood jealousy still governs my attitude to Roger. My mother always gave him more affection that she gave me. But I fancy she gave me as much as I needed. Maybe I am still jealous because he walked off with Julia Shaw under my nose. But I honestly don't think so, because even now I would enjoy Roger's company. He has such a talent for liveliness. And the affections of childhood can never be entirely defaced: as time passes they remain like a sense of guilt. But it would be no good for us to come together again. He is set now in his ways and so am I in mine."

He got up suddenly from his chair.

"Come on, David. I'm depressing you and myself, and probably boring you as well. Would you like a game of tennis?"

IX

ALLENSIDE PLAYED TENNIS very well. To see him reach
out his powerful arm and ram the ball back at me filled me
with despair and a sense of bodily weakness that made my
racket hang leadenly in my hand. Such points as I managed
to win I obtained by an almost hysterically furious service.
I threw the ball up as high as I could and lashed down at it
with everything I had. After all I felt obliged to give Allenside
the best game I could. By tea-time I was unbelievably tired
and very hungry.

We lingered over our tea, drinking, smoking, and talking.
It was very pleasant. We pushed the trolley aside and stretched
our legs comfortably on the hearth rug. This was how Janet
found us. She entered excitedly, her eyes bright and happy as
if she had good news for her husband. She was rather put off
to see me in the other chair.

"Hello, David. Poof! What a stink of tobacco!"

We both rose to offer her a seat, but she motioned us
impatiently to be seated again.

"I'll take this thing out," she said and briskly wheeled away
the trolley in the direction of the kitchen.

I began to think of going. I didn't feel in the mood to be
nice to Janet. My evening could be more profitably spent in
the flat wrestling with the Seymour brothers. Allenside saw
me glancing at my watch.

"Now then David," he smiled. "Don't tell me you want to
go home. Or is it a more romantic appointment?"

I shook my head. That was one of the advantages of living
alone in London: you are able to present to your friends just
as much of yourself as you wish them to know. I had often
wanted to tell Allenside about Helen and myself. But on the
whole I preferred him to think of me as a solitary type of
young writer who had drifted away from his family and place
of origin. He believed the flat in Kensington was borrowed

from friends who were living abroad—which as far as it went was true.

"Janet will be disappointed if you go now. Stay a while then I'll run you home in the car."

No doubt he believed what he was saying; or rather he was expressing what he thought his wife ought to feel. My guess was Janet would be glad to have me gone. She tolerated me generally because I was something for which her husband had an inexplicable liking.

When we were seated together in the study, conversation did not come easily. Janet had something to say which she was holding back. She kept smiling at Allenside in an exclusive way that rather annoyed him. He wanted her to take due notice of me.

"You look very pleased with yourself my dear?" he said. "Has someone left you some money, or something?"

"Well," Janet said primly. "I have got good news." She placed her hands behind her head and leaned back so that the evening light glinted on the glass of her spectacles. Her hair was combed upwards in a way that gave her an aggressive air, as if she were arrayed for battle. She settled her large body more comfortably in her arm-chair. I could see that Allenside was inclined not to make the question she demanded before divulging what she had to say.

"Yes," he said interrogatively. That was as far as he was prepared to go.

"I'm not sure that I'll tell you. You don't seem sufficiently interested." Janet pouted in a way that might have been becoming to her twenty years ago. Marriage, I reflected, was an oppressive institution; especially other people's.

"Come on, tell us now, like a good girl."

This was Janet's Allenside speaking. The person I had once heard her call her *Teddy Bear*. I could not believe that Allenside would have chosen of his own free will to call his wife "a good girl." I leaned over to offer Janet a cigarette.

"You are generous, David," she said taking one. "Are you sure you can spare it?"

"I'm smoking my own today, Janet," I joked obligingly. It seemed to put her in good humour.

"Well, now, I'll tell you. It's a big secret mind." For Allenside's sake I hoped she wouldn't say what was coming.

85

But she did. "Don't you breathe a word, will you, David?"

Allenside sighed deeply. "Do tell us Janet."

"Now, Teddy, don't be impatient. Lady Mu whispered to me over the tea cups that the County are looking for a Director of the new Educational Research Centre at Forest Mount. And they're looking in your direction Teddy. Lord Whiteway is anxious that you should apply."

Allenside merely lifted his eyebrows. Janet turned to me for support.

"Isn't that wonderful, David?"

I nodded.

"Whiteway has not mentioned it to me. I saw him last week," Allenside said.

"He'll be calling in at school to see you on Monday afternoon," Janet stated triumphantly. She paused to gaze at her silent husband. "You don't sound very excited Teddy. Wouldn't you like the job?"

"Yes." Allenside knocked his pipe out in the empty fireplace. "I think I would."

"It's just what you've always wanted. The job's absolutely made for you Teddy and you know it. And you sit there as if you were waiting for someone else to take it."

Allenside laughed. "What do you expect me to do? Telephone Whiteway at once?"

"Don't be so annoying Teddy. Honestly, David, he does annoy me so sometimes. He doesn't have any ambition at all. In a man of his abilities it's a positive disgrace. Don't you agree, David?"

I nodded helpfully.

"There you are, Teddy. David thinks so too."

"All right, darling. I'm madly excited. You mustn't be taken in by my habitual restraint and calm."

Janet may have had more to say but Allenside was eager to change the subject.

"Janet, do you know who David met the other day?"

"Haven't the faintest. He moves in such exalted circles."

She was a little puzzled and angry that her good news had not had the desired effect, and she was inclined to blame me for the fiasco.

"Roger!"

"Your awful brother! He's certainly making his presence

felt." She frowned, exhaling smoke through her nostrils with undue fierceness. "Lady Mu was talking about him. 'My dear,' she said, 'why didn't you tell me about your brother-in-law?' I nearly sank under the table. I wondered what on earth he'd been up to. If only he'd stay abroad for good, I said to myself."

She threw her cigarette stump into the fireplace with an oddly masculine gesture.

"But the funny part was, Lady Mu was raving about him. He'd been such a good friend to her son Horace in South Africa, she said, and he was such a clever man. Her husband was most impressed with his political insight. They were even thinking of suggesting him to the Association as a candidate in the next election."

Allenside smiled. "And what did you say?"

"I just nodded and kept mum. It wasn't exactly the right time to give her a full account of dear Roger's history, including the fact that he still owes you four hundred pounds."

Janet spoke with mounting indignation, moving from irony to wrath like a train gathering up steam.

"I only hope and pray the Whiteway's don't see through him before your appointment is made. They're not likely to cherish the name of Allenside once they understand the kind of man he is. He'll probably borrow a few Whiteway thousands and fly to South America, or something of that sort. Honestly, your brother, Teddy!"

Obviously she was inclined to blame her husband for having such a disreputable brother.

"I only hope he keeps out of our way for the next few weeks. Once you've got the Directorate I wouldn't mind going after him and getting that money back."

Janet was attracted to money. The four hundred pounds was a very sore point. Rather inconsequentially I had a fleeting wish to see her married to Roger instead of Edward. They would have driven each other mad.

"What did you think of him David?" She looked at me. "You didn't see his wife of course?"

I said, "I gathered they had parted."

"Just as well. I must say I was sorry for Julia, odd creature though she was."

She stole a glance at her husband. No doubt she was still

jealous of her husband's first love. She was the kind of annoying woman who would be. I pitied Allenside as the husband of a possessive self-centred vulgar wife. Vulgarity was the most objectionable thing about her. But she was mean also, and a shamefully vigorous social climber. I think it was sympathy for Allenside that made me so strongly dislike her. She had done me no harm ever, but I could not forgive her the harm I imagined she did to a man for whom I felt a deep affection.

"I daresay you would have liked her, David. She wrote poems."

She glanced at her husband, who had sunk back gloomily in his chair.

"But I mustn't make fun of the poor creature. She's had rather an awful time really. She really wasn't Roger's type at all. Her parents were Plymouth Brethren and I suppose in marrying Roger she thought she was signing her declaration of independence. They lost their only boy, you know. It was rather awful. He was the only thing that kept them together. When he went they just hated the sight of each other. Julia wouldn't see anybody, and Roger went off to South Africa. Now you know all about the skeletons in the family cupboard, doesn't he, Teddy?"

Janet was proud of being an Allenside. As far as I could find out she was the daughter of an unsuccessful commercial traveller from Reading. No wonder 'getting on' was so important to her. She had a vast childhood of humiliation to exorcise: no pocket money at school, no car to fetch her home. '*Oh God make me as the other girls are, if not better. . . . I must work hard I will be top I must work hard.*' And here she was mistress of her own attractive house and of her own fine coming on so obviously a gentleman husband, with her one son in a progressive school and with the interesting career of her own: the very model of the successful smiling woman of the ladies' journals, the envy of all her tribe, written and produced by Janet Allenside.

"Mrs. Dell and Mrs. Downs—they do rather sound like a Music Hall pair don't they—I met them shopping in Croydon this morning. Mrs. Dell told me her husband was on the short list for a headship in Hull. I was rather tempted to ask her how many short lists he had been on by now. It must be quite a record. Don't worry darling; I didn't. Mrs. Dell said that she didn't want to move since their boy was at Epsom. She would prefer her husband to have the deputy headship of the Bilateral than a headship in Hull. You didn't tell me whom you were going to recommend, darling. Is it going to be Dell?"

My embarrassment was as acute as Allenside's. The idea of discussing his staff with anyone was abhorrent to him. It must have hurt him even more that I should witness his wife's ignorance of the principle he adhered to strictly himself. I imagined the good news she had heard from Lady Muriel had so elated her that she had forgotten the little restraint she exercised over her tongue in deference to what she probably considered Edward's eccentricities. No doubt she adored her husband, but she did not love him enough to understand him. She loved an image she had created out of Allenside; when the discrepancies between the image and the man became un-avoidably wide and glaring, she was puzzled and hurt and very annoyed.

Allenside got up to avoid the blank silence of not answering her question. I also got to my feet and murmured it was time I made my way home. My well-meant action was inopportune. It made it clear to Janet that I understood the rebuff she had received. It would have been better had I sat down calmly and begun to talk of something else. Allenside made no further attempt to dissuade me.

"I'll run David home in the car, Janet. Have you left the ignition key in?"

Janet nodded. No doubt she disapproved of Edward's wasting petrol on running me home. I suggested that I could quite easily go home by bus and tube, but Allenside would not hear of it and left the room.

To sketch away the silence I offered Janet a cigarette again. This time she took it without comment.

"If I were you," she said, "I wouldn't have too much to do with Roger. He isn't Edward's type at all. I never got on with him. The first time I met him, when Edward's back was turned, he began to make advances. I think it made him angry the way I told him off. He has disliked me intensely ever since. He'll probably run me down like hell if you mention me. I put a stop to the little game of tapping Edward. You know I discovered that in five years he had borrowed over four hundred pounds from Teddy. I put a stop to that. And then of course he turned quite nasty."

Allenside came back into the room, wearing an old trench coat.

"I was just telling David, darling, to beware of Roger." She wanted now very much to win back his approval.

"I don't think you need worry," Allenside said. "David is a novelist and they are supposed to be good judges of character."

In the car we talked politics in the dispassionate rather despairing manner used now by those who once expected so much, probably too much, from political action. It was a question we agreed on, how those men of good will who still had a concern for ethics could best exert pressure on those who angled for power. Allenside was more hopeful than myself of positive achievements in that direction. He was not convinced about my elaborate and obscurely phrased thesis on the necessity of martyrdom. History, I argued warmly and at length, demonstrated conclusively that every spiritual regeneration among human beings had grown like the mustard tree out of the seed of obscure martyrdoms. It was a pleasant and not altogether academic argument. It occurred to me that Allenside who was so reluctant to accept my embroidered intuitions, would make a far more resolute martyr than my soft self. In a small way he was a martyr already, living day after day with a woman who would shatter the nerves of any man not unselfishly steeled to bear the infliction. Whereas I myself had walked out of a home simply because I found it uncongenial, not to my taste.

If I were to explain to him that I still had irrational spasms of guilt about a course of action which was probably the best solution for all concerned, would he agree and understand? I would not have been a success as an ironmonger's son-in-law. Did Allenside believe I had no business to crawl out of the lower middle-class rut I was born in? He would not be so illiberal. The only distinction of any significance was between artists and intellectuals, and the rest.

How pleasant it would be to reveal all my hidden history to him, reveal it all, some evening in the flat, late at night perhaps with loaded pipes and punch to drink. There was no one I would more enjoy confessing to; and I would be willing to accept his judgement. I could think of nothing that would be of greater help to me, or give me more relief.

I knew I never would. It involved some risk that I was not prepared to take. Not that I feared he would consider me a poor sort of person to teach Scripture in his school, or anything crude like that. It might force me to clarify my mind to such an extent that I would be forced to face a line of action I was loth to consider taking. There was nothing I desired quite as much as letting sleeping dogs lie, in the hope they would eventually die in their sleep.

X

In my dream the blackboard was made of dark glass and I was teaching the most difficult form in school how to acquire a knowledge of God. These boys bulged like angry pimples in their desks which were too small to confine them properly. Among them like booby traps sat adults who had no real business to be there, disguised in mock humility. Visot sat in front, his hand under his chin, his eloquent eyebrows raised, his closed mouth creasing his cheeks, politely checking a smile. Briarman was behind him, half hidden, slyly glancing over Visot's shoulder ready to whisper a disparaging remark in Visot's ear when he thought I was not looking. In the classroom beyond the pitch-pine and glass partition, Allenside was teaching. I knew he could hear if my class got out of hand and I was most anxious that his help should not be required, desperately anxious not to admit defeat. In the back, a cigarette hidden behind his hand, Roger was seated leaning his back against the partition. His brother did not know he was there. The windows were open and outside the earth was tilted so that the window space was filled with roof tops that left no room for the sky. The slates were warm and colourless, too steep to lie upon.

I spoke with rapid nervous fluency.

"You have heard the wind howling about an empty house in which you crouch alone with your loneliness? You have heard the sea gnawing the crumbling shore? Within your small heads you have imagined the comfortless intercellular spaces, the ice that embraces planets, the fire of suns that consume. In your inch measured minds these galaxies of ice and fire revolve about a vacant centre. Visot, what were you whispering to Briarman in the desk behind you?"

"Neurotic." He answered firmly and promptly. "I said you were neurotic, sir."

I apologised.

"Let me return then to my original thesis. How do I know

92

that God exists? I have outlined to you already the Onto-
logical, Teleological and Cosmological arguments. It is a
remarkable thing I added that none of the Old Testament
writers made use of these arguments. They talked and trembled continually before their King of the Universe who was
too terrible to be visible; they lived in fear but never saw his
face. The hand of God that set the planets in their swift and
dangerous courses was a ring of endless light. The face that
they implored Him to turn towards them was more featureless
than a cloud and brighter than the Sun. The eternal arms
that nursed the universe might have been dark ropes of steel
that held the stars in place.''

"Conjecture," Visot said. "It can all be explained in terms
of sex and hunger.'

"Cash and crumpets," Roger grinned. The boys about him
chorused "Cash and crumpets."

"What I want to know," Briarman leaned forward earnestly, "what's it all good for? Where does it get you?"

"It's a supernatural insurance scheme," Visot explained.
"God collects the premiums. God is very wealthy. He made
a corner in planets."

"God is love," I protested wearily. "He created us so that
we could love each other."

Roger called out, "Now you're talking!"

"A corpse can't kiss."

"Who said that?" I demanded angrily.

"You said it yourself, sir. You said it yourself." The class
was getting out of hand. How could I keep it up much longer.
It would be wiser to sit down and let their noise flow over me
like water. Put my wrists on the table. Suicide in a warm bath.
I assembled my strength and spoke again.

"God keeps the universe together, he prevents it from
flying apart. God comes between two thousand million people,
he divides himself up two thousand million times into two
thousand million hesitations that preserve mankind from
holocausts of street by street slaughter, tube trains loaded
with vertical dead. The air we breathe that preserves us is
infused with His love and protects us from our brothers and
from ourselves. Each man acts through the envelope of his
conscience and God's love-driven air withers each evil act
but gives power and propagation to goodness, even among the

93

crumbling ruins of sin-infested Time, to multiply and prosper. Examine your mocking selves, let the light fall upon the secret clot of sin moving towards your heart. Learn, you machine minders, you kings of castles wrapped in evening papers, you potted Pharaohs, learn that the Lord God Reigneth!"

Exhausted with my own eloquence I flopped back into the chair and hammered the desk weakly with my fist shouting *The Lord Reigneth! The Lord Reigneth!* I hoped now Allenside would hear. My class was in an uproar. Visot and Briarman had begun an argument of their own. Roger had divided the boys into two sides for a convenient battle—Cash versus Crumpets—while he squatted on the desk to watch. But Allenside went on calmly teaching. He did not turn round. I was screaming now with desperation "*The Lord Reigneth! The Lord Reigneth!*"

Someone had switched on the bedroom light. I sat up rubbing my eyes. I shivered in the air and plunged back under the clothes. I was covered with sweat. It was Helen.

She wore a travelling coat and a plain hat of the type she favoured, the brim held up by a silver brooch. She seemed paler and thinner.

"Helen! I was having a nightmare. I am lathered with sweat. Isn't it ridiculous. Helen, you didn't say you were coming."

She sat on the side of my bed. She was wearing black gloves. I wondered whether to stretch out my hand and take her hand in mine. I wondered also how I would tell her about Phyllis's letter, refusing me a divorce. It was a little unreasonable, I felt, to arrive like this in the middle of the night.

She sat silently, until I noticed she had begun to cry. The tears rolled effortlessly down her cheeks. She was pale of course because she was dressed in black. At once I became full of solicitude.

"Helen my dear! What is the matter?"

Not without admiring my own selflessness I threw back the warm clothes and placed an arm about her shoulders.

"My dear! My dear!"

For a moment she let herself lean against me. She began sobbing. I wondered whether to reach for my dressing-gown. The cold was beginning to chill my spine.

At last Helen spoke. She moved out of my grasp and took out her handkerchief to dab her eyes.

"Nicola died last week."

The little invalid had gone. I was sorry, and a little relieved. It was better for the child; better not to linger in suffering. I took hold of my dressing-gown and put it on. Of course it would mean so much more to Helen. I should try to put myself in her place. This would be a difficult time for her. I would need to be acutely sensitive to her mood and very patient. It wasn't a cheering prospect but I was prepared to face it with persistent resourcefulness and fortitude.

"It was terrible. She was so brave and so cheerful, to the very end. She believed she would get better. One night I was sitting up with her and she asked me to draw the curtains. It was very dark outside. 'Where are the stars, Mummy?' she said, 'Where have they gone to?' "

Helen walked into the living-room. I hurried after her and put a match to the gas fire. I watched for my cue, waiting what to do next. Helen slumped down wearily on the settee. She rubbed her forehead with her hand.

"I can't cry any more," she said, a surprised note in her voice. "I feel empty. I can't cry any more."

She stared unblinkingly at the muttering glowing fire. I moved to her side to take her in my arms. She lifted a careless hand to push me away.

"It's too late now, David. It's too late for comfort."

She turned to look at me frowning. The frown seemed oddly to disturb the placid features of her plump round face.

"Why didn't you come out to Switzerland? You knew I needed you then. That was when I needed your comfort and sympathy."

I was too taken aback to think of an answer. I had never seen Helen lose control of herself to such an extent before. She was so habitually calm. I was the one to have little fits of temperament. It occurred to me that I had been living with Helen for the best part of two years without really having bothered to find out what she was really like. I had imagined it would be enough to anticipate the correct reaction from moment to moment, in return for what I gratefully acknowledged to be her loving concern for my welfare. But suppose that was not the basis of our relationship at all? The thought made me deeply uneasy.

"I am sorry for you David. I know what it is to be selfish. It is an imprisonment. I am no better than you: but at least I have become aware of my own condition."

How was I to defend myself? I was so used to complying with her wishes, on the few occasions when she verbally expressed them, there was no precedent to help me know how to act. Her postcards had given no indication of this. It is true they had not been arriving for several days, but they were so stereotyped anyway I had not minded.

"I've learnt so much these last few weeks. I began to love that child. Love came out of me for the first time; it was like a birth. It was something entirely new. I carried it about with me like a material thing; an unaccustomed burden strapped on my back, cutting into me, hurting me. Now it's gone, and I'm numb. I can't feel anything. I'm cold. Perhaps I've begun to die."

She was upset. She had had a rough time. I advanced to comfort her again.

"Don't touch me, David. It might make me dislike you. I don't want to do that. You can't help being selfish. You're a man. You can't help putting yourself first. Putting your self-importance first. Your particular self-importance is your writing. Your precious books."

She wasn't looking at me as she spoke, but she had sensed how I was mystified, and hurt.

"I'm not saying that I don't think your books are any good. I shouldn't have mentioned them. What I'm saying David is you are selfish and you don't know what love is, you haven't begun to know, you may never know. I wouldn't have known at all if Nicola hadn't passed it on to me, like a disease."

"Helen, why are you so eager to hurt me, when you know I love you?" I tried to prevent my voice from sounding plaintive.

"You don't love me David. You may deceive yourself into thinking you do. A man can make himself believe anything. If you loved me you would have come out to Switzerland; you would have come with me when I asked you. No. You put your independence first, your job and your work and your pride and your career, oh half a dozen things came before my need for you."

"You are misunderstanding everything now," I cried,

indignant at last. "I wanted us to get married on equal terms. It was the permanent basis of our love I was thinking of. It would have been wrong for me to have been dependent on your money."

"Our Marriage. Of Course. How strange. I had forgotten about it. Do you still want to marry me David?"

"Of course I do." And I added defiantly, "And you damn well know it."

This made Helen laugh.

"Still the same David. I had forgotten how much I liked you."

I smiled, perhaps it would all come out well after all.

"She was nothing to you, was she David? Just one of my little fads. One of my adopted children. Adopted to feed my child hunger. You were right perhaps in the beginning. But something big grew between Nicola and me, something far bigger than me, something I can never forget, something I shall hunger after for ever. Something before your eyes that you never saw. Something you couldn't replace."

I said I could. It couldn't have sounded very convincing. She smiled unbelievingly. Then she yawned and stretched herself on the settee.

"Leave the fire on. I'll sleep here tonight. I'm too tired to undress."

I went to fetch a blanket and placed it over her. She caught my hand as I leaned over her.

"Have I lost you forever David?" She gazed into my face with wide open eyes. It was curiosity more than fear that made her ask the question. I shook my head. She put her hands about my neck.

"Kiss me."

When my face was against hers she whispered:

"You must give me a child David. You must. You must. I must have a child."

She began to cry again. I stayed to comfort her until she fell asleep, then I turned down the fire and returned to my bed. It was a long time before I slept again.

97

XI

Dᴇʟʟ ᴀɴᴅ Eɢʟɪɴᴛᴏɴ sᴛᴏᴘᴘᴇᴅ talking as I entered the staff-room. Whatever they had been saying they didn't want me to hear it. I had Helen on my mind, and I was in no mood for their conversation. So I sat down at the table, going through the motions of a business-like bout of marking. A junior form had written me an account of the Siege of Samaria: thirty-two accounts neatly stacked before me. I murmured something about 'catching up with marking arrears.'

Dell was unusually restless. From time to time he walked across the room from his customary tattered easy-chair to stand on tip-toe and peer through the unfrosted panes of the window that overlooked the headmaster's corridor. Eventually, after they had glanced significantly at each other, Eglinton said:

"Have you heard the latest, Flint?"

It was something that gave both of them a certain pleasurable excitement. Teaching I reflected was a hum-drum occupation and teachers were easily roused by any variation in the day's routine. I put down my marking pencil and leaned back in my chair. A little gossip would be a relaxation.

Dell lit his massive pipe and watched me closely as Eglinton spoke.

The pair had become unusually close recently, as though they were running for the Presidency and Vice-Presidency on the same ticket. Briarman had been a little alarmed at the prospect of Allenside or anyone else getting the impression that a similar relationship existed between Brunt and himself. I imagined the other day he had staged an open disagreement with Brunt on some detail of administration in the presence of most of the staff in order to make known that no secret protocol or concordat existed between them.

"Poor old Vizzy's in the soup," Eglinton said.

I imagined some class-room calamity and I was vividly

98

reminded of my dream of the previous night. "What's up?"

"Bansdale's pa has complained to the Governors about Communist literature being distributed among the boys."

It did not take long to guess how Eglinton and Dell had found all this out. Miss Symonds. The apparently harmless and colourless could be dangerous. Eglinton had cultivated her for a long time. He had developed a technique of teasing her about Visot which increased her dislike for the man and at the same time deepened her dumb attachment to Eglinton. Among ourselves in the staff-room Eglinton talked sarcastically about 'Miss Symonds' impregnable chastity.' Dell also was a friend of hers. They shared a dislike for Briarman like a warm secret between them. Miss Symonds attached much importance to joining Dell and Eglinton and other members of the staff for coffee in the canteen during the mid-morning break. Perhaps she believed it enhanced her status. No doubt about the source of their information.

I said, "Surely no one's going to take serious notice. . . . Parents are notorious for writing crazy letters. . . ."

"Did you know about it?" Dell asked, rather too eagerly.

"No. Why should I?" I lied as best I could. It irked me to have to do so.

"Whiteway is in school this afternoon," Eglinton said. "He's in with the Head now."

"Do you think it's in connection with Bansdale's father's letter?"

"Yes. It looks as if the noble lord is taking a serious view of the matter."

"But it's too absurd," I protested.

"It isn't you know," Eglinton said placidly. "Our Commie friends are going to have to watch their step. I'm sorry it's Vizzy though. I respect him rather. He's the martyr-type. Not an opportunist like Brunt."

I said, "Have you mentioned this to Robinson yet?" Robinson was our Union representative. "He would soon put a stop to it."

"Nothing will come of it." Dell puffed away at his pipe. He sounded rather disappointed.

"Just a little harmless fun. Look!"

He sat bolt upright in his chair pointing at the corridor windows. Through the frosted glass we could see the large head and narrow shoulders of Visot. He was on his way to the Head's study.

"He's for it," Eglinton said excitedly. "What did I tell you!"

"You sound like a crowd at an execution," I said as drily as I could. Both Eglinton and Dell had risen to their feet. Dell sat down again with exaggerated calmness, but Eglinton moved to the door.

"I can get a view of the Head's study from the angle on the canteen stairs. I'm bursting with unhealthy curiosity."

Dell was quiet when he had gone out. I went on with my marking. "*They found the king's camp deserted. . . .*" By an odd coincidence it was Bansdale's book I was marking. "*The four leppers ate there fill from the loaded tables then one of them said we are a poor lot lets go back and tell the good news to the starving town. . . .*" Bansdale had a great interest in the Old Testament. *Narrative good*, I scribbled at the bottom, *Now include punctuation and correct each spelling mistake three times.*

Dell rustled his paper and cleared his throat.

"I shan't be here Thursday," he said. I was surprised to hear him accounting to me for his movements. In his eyes I always imagined I was an irresponsible youngster rather lacking in respect for his maturity and wisdom. I expressed polite concern.

"I'm going to Hull for an interview. A new Bilateral there: headship."

I wished him good luck. I expected now to be treated to a lengthy explanation, amply illustrated, of how such things were cooked. Instead he said:

"My wife is very much against our moving. As she says we live in our own house; and her mother lives in Cheam; and our boy Rex is doing quite well at Epsom."

I murmured sympathetically. To be taken into another's confidence imposes an obligation to be unreservedly sympathetic at least as long as the confidence lasts.

"I'm wondering," Dell said, studying the bowl of his pipe, "when Allenside is going to make his mind up about the Deputy Headship here. If I knew he had me in mind, I wouldn't bother to go to Hull."

Dell began to redden. It embarrassed him to be speaking to me of these 'personal matters'. It was then that I began to see that Briarman was Allenside's choice for the job, and not Dell. Briarman worked harder, he was more efficient, more enthusiastic, not so given to brooding over his wrongs and not difficult to work with. Disappointment was making Dell as temperamental as a woman in the menopause. I considered how careful I was being now, as I sat listening to him, disguising my thoughts with a mask of complete sympathy. He was so raw with the fear of failure.

"You are on friendly terms with Allenside, Flint." That he should so far abandon his pride to ask me such a question revealed the misery the man was suffering. "In strictest confidence, your honest opinion, do you think he has made up his mind? It's his own business of course—if I were head I would consider the matter with equal care before coming to a decision. In view of this interview pending in Hull I have been thinking of putting it to him outright. But I'd rather not do it outright. If you could help me I'd appreciate it, very much."

"I don't think he has," I said. "That's my opinion for what it's worth. And even if he had he wouldn't mention it to me or to anyone else that I know of. You know how punctilious he is about professional matters, as well as I do."

Dell looked distressingly disappointed. What on earth had the man been hoping for? Some miracle to overwhelm his growing inward conviction that Briarman was Allenside's choice.

I said: "Like most of the staff I hope you get it."

He nodded his thanks.

"Unfortunately it's what Allenside thinks that counts. I know he's never liked me."

"I wouldn't have thought that," I said protestingly. "I think he thinks very highly of his staff in general."

"Of those that creep and lick. Those are the ones he likes. Briarman and Brunt. You mark my word, they'll be the men for the job. Briarman deputy head; Brunt, special responsibility allowance. They've crept and sweated for the jobs these last two years. This damned unhealthy competition. I don't know what the profession is coming to, Flint. I've been teaching for twenty years in all sort of schools under all sorts of Heads, Flint; but Allenside's the most difficult I've ever had to work with. I just can't put my finger on what's wrong. I can't get to know him. He shoves up a barrier every time. There's something inhuman about him Flint. He doesn't think of his staff as men; he won't talk man to man. That's what I've got against him. It's as if he sets himself up as something perfect and challenges everyone else to reach his level. It's as if he's led a sheltered life and hasn't seen enough of the world or something."

He looked at me as if he had just recollected to whom it was he was speaking. I was hearing a modified version of Dell's complaint against Allenside which he was currently retailing to everyone he knew.

"Of course you are a pal of his. You won't agree with what I'm saying."

I said, with great show of fairness: "I grant you he's an idealist. He expects too much from everyone. But I admire him for it. I think he's an unusually upright and disinterested type."

"Is he?" Dell added with malicious force. "Is he though? I think that's the whole trouble with him: he's ambitious, terribly ambitious. That's the key to his behaviour all round. A crack Bilateral school, that's his aim. Big job ahead. A model school and an unqualified deputy head who won't share any of the credit. He's after big things is Allenside. He won't be here much longer. Up and Up and Up. His wife's the same. Why do you think she spends all that time on B.B.C. work? Increase their reputation of course. The brilliant Allensides. That's the kind of stuff that goes down big with Education Authorities. Stunts, that's what they like. Qualifications and hard work and years of service don't count."

Brunt hurried into the room and bustled across to his cupboard. He found what he wanted at once. His cupboard was the tidiest in the room. Then he studied the staff timetable for a moment, running his finger along it to trace the whereabouts of another member of staff.

"If you're looking for Visot," Dell said sourly. "He's in with Allenside."

"No, it was Mitchley I wanted: about table tennis tonight. It will have to be cancelled. We can't have the Hall. Eglinton's Dramatics bagged it before us."

"The tempo of extra-curricular activities has increased notably of late," Dell said. "I wonder why?"

I giggled appreciatively. It was the kind of innuendo that only Dell and Robinson could carry off successfully in the staff-room. Brunt glanced at me reproachfully, but did not answer.

"Your party colleague appears to be in a spot of trouble," Dell went on.

"Oh! Why? What's up?"

"He and the Lord Whiteway are closeted with the head-master at this moment. And I cannot believe that it's merely a matter of social intercourse, can you?"

Brunt gave me an elaborately puzzled frown. All his gestures were slightly exaggerated, as if he was always in front of a class or an audience that needed an immediate impression of his reactions.

"What's it about?"

"My guess is that it concerns a little matter of the boys being used to distribute *The Daily Worker*, or something of that sort."

Brunt controlled himself visibly. "What rot" was all he said, when Eglinton came in anxious to give the latest information on what was happening in the Head's study.

"Vizzy's standing in front of them like the boy in 'When did you last see your father?' Whiteway seems to be doing most of the talking. Vizzy's face is very red and very determined. He looks quite determined to make the worst of things. This is just what his martyr complex has yearned for. He'll be coming to school soon wearing a halo!"

His remarks were addressed to Dell and myself. Since the affair of the newspaper, he and Brunt had barely been on speaking terms.

Brunt said, "I think the way you are *gloating*, Eglinton, is about the most disgusting thing I have ever seen in this staff-room." Then he marched out, banging the door behind him.

Dell and Eglinton laughed, and I laughed too. Brunt was rather absurd at times. His virtuous indignation rose and fell like a temperature chart that never went lower than ninety-nine degrees. Dell and Eglinton were already discussing what would happen to Visot if it was proven that he had used the boys to distribute *The Daily Worker*. Dell enlarged on the unhappy position of a master accused by a boy of some offence, giving examples from his twenty years' experience which included the sacking of a headmaster in the Midlands for alleged homosexual offences which were never proven, and a case in which a headmaster was compelled to make a written apology to a boy and his parents for certain remarks made about the boy's appearance and parentage in the other boys' hearing. Dell's advice to all young teachers was that they could not be too careful. They should, he said, be above, outside, and beyond suspicion. That was why he maintained it was always wiser to keep the boys at their distance.

Eglinton nodded in the direction of the frosted glass.

"He's out again!"

We saw Visot pass on his way back to his class-room. Before Eglinton could say anything more, we saw Allenside's figure passing and then stopping outside the staff-room door. He just put his head in.

"Mr. Flint, could you spare a moment?"

When we were in the corridor, he said:

"It's about this Bansdale business, You are his form master. I thought it would be useful if you were with us when we question him. This is a wretched business." We entered his study. Lord Whiteway was seated alongside Allenside's swivel-chair, his conical bulk seemed to be balanced on an absurdly small chair. His chin rested on his chest and his blue eyes looked upward out of their baggy and bushy surrounds. He was glossily bald. He raised a large hand to greet me. His manner was archiepiscopal, as befitted a High Priest of Commerce.

"You remember Mr. Flint," Allenside said.

"The young man who writes novels." My hand was lost in his. "But I mustn't forget. He wants it kept quiet here, doesn't he?"

We all smiled. Whiteway was putting me at my ease. I glanced admiringly at the excellently tailored cloth that concealed his large shape. The jacket was double-breasted and there was enough material in it for a complete suit, waistcoat and all, for myself.

"I believe you know my niece, Helen Brown. Have you seen her lately? Or is she still in Switzerland?"

I wondered how much he knew about Helen and myself. It would be wisest to assume he knew nothing.

"A very independent young woman. Knows her own mind. A family characteristic, Mr. Headmaster."

He smiled at Allenside. An archiepiscopal joke. Certainly the remark fitted Helen better than his son Horace beach-combing in South Africa. I remembered Dell in one of his convivial moods describing to some of us in the staff-room how Horace Walker-Brown turned up at a school sports where his mother was to present the prizes. Half way through the second lap of the 440 he had staggered across the track waving a bottle and shouting incoherently. He became involved in the white figures of the running boys. He was a big fat chap Dell said, and the staff had difficulty in removing him. Downs claimed to have carried one of his legs. His mother had fainted and had to be taken home at once in their Daimler. She had thrust the high heel of her shoe through her straw hat which lay on the floor of the car. Her thin legs seemed rigid with a strange hysteria of its own. Lord Whiteway, Dell said, took the chair at the next Governor's meeting as if nothing untoward had happened.

Whiteway was still talking about Helen when Bansdale knocked at the door. The boy seemed cheerfully unaware of the disturbance he was causing.

"Bansdale," Allenside said, "this is a serious matter we have to ask you about. You have told your father that you were given two dozen copies of the *Daily Worker* to distribute from house to house. You did say that to your father, didn't you?"

"Yes, sir."

"Is it true? Think carefully before you answer."

"Yes, sir." Bansdale's eyes were wide with innocence. I doubted whether he realised that what he was saying might get Visot into serious trouble. Bansdale did not hate Visot. He was probably quite attached to the butt of his class-room antics. For Bansdale it was just a case of having to stick to his story: that was as much careful thinking as he did before saying 'yes'.

Allenside was distressed by Bansdale's unhesitating answer. He found it unpleasant to listen to a boy he liked telling a bare-faced lie that would land one of his staff in trouble. Allenside always had great expectations even of the most morally improvident: perhaps that was what Dell meant when he referred to him as 'inhuman'. I admit he was sometimes in danger of being blinded by his own virtue. He did not always appreciate that what was only mildly difficult for him verged on the impossible for others.

I said, diffidently, "May I ask Bansdale something, sir?" Lord Whiteway was drumming the top of the desk with his widely padded fingers. Oh guardian of civic welfare, I apostrophised him silently, behind your expanse of chrome and glass shop window, what fish are you quietly frying by the latest unobtrusive methods? Why should you trouble us so much over this railway clerk's letter?

"Bansdale," I said, fixing him with the most piercing stare I could muster, in the old-fashioned schoolmaster manner.

"Yes, sir." He gazed at me with respectful apprehension. (I carry more weight among the unfranchised section of the population.)

"You took those papers out of Mr. Visot's attaché case, didn't you? You meant to play him a trick didn't you? You didn't mean any harm did you?"

"No, sir." This time the boy was more hesitant.

"You didn't take them out of Mr. Visot's case?"

"No, sir."

"Mr. Visot has told me he didn't give you them. Where did you get them then?"

Bansdale looked down as if he would refuse to answer.

"Tell me where you got them." I sounded quietly inexorable.

"Penge took them, sir, from Tibbot's locker. Tibbot had kept us in, sir, twice last week and when Penge showed me them I thought I'd give them away to get my own back."

I felt rather pleased with the success of my cross-examination. Allenside said: "You may go back to your class, Bansdale. I shall want to see you again at four o'clock."

Lord Whiteway knitted his bushy eyebrows. A wave of frowns broke against the bald beach of his lowered head. When he raised his eyebrows they were swept away.

"Who is this boy Tibbot?"

"A sixth former," Allenside said. "A good lad. An excellent prefect. I've not heard before about his political opinions."

I was glad Allenside knew less than I did. It would leave his conscience undisturbed.

"Could we see him, do you think?"

Allenside hesitated before answering. He got up from his seat to study the time-table on the wall. I sensed how much he resented Lord Whiteway's ponderous and interfering presence. He usually referred to Whiteway as "a very good friend" of the school; which, publicly speaking, was true enough. Our Bilateral was looked upon by the authorities as an experimental model of great interest, efficiency and promise. The Education Office was tenderly sympathetic toward our needs. Whiteway was responsible for this. Whiteway was chairman of the Governors; honorary president of the O.B.A. There were Whiteway Cups and Whiteway Prizes. He was a "good friend of the school." That was why Allenside had always cultivated his society: for the sake of the school, not personal pleasure. And now also there was this directorship of the Educational Research Institute in view. Janet was right. It was a job after Allenside's own heart. He wanted it very much. It made him hesitate now to tell Whiteway that he knew how to run his own school. He was looking at the time-table for an excuse.

"I wouldn't like to disturb him now." Allenside turned round. "It's rather an important lesson for him."

"Hmm." Whiteway began to drum the top of the desk again a little impatiently. "Perhaps we can see him again."

Allenside said nothing.

"Frankly, headmaster, this is an unsatisfactory business. It seems to me rather worse than I had first imagined."

Allenside said carefully, "As I said before I have every confidence in both Mr. Visot and Mr. Brunt. They are admirably conscientious and hard-working teachers."

Whiteway got up from his chair. He was a formidable figure. If I had been in Allenside's shoes, so dependent on his good-will and co-operation, I would have been afraid of him.

"These people," Whiteway said, "put their party allegiance before everything else. I don't believe that they can ever be completely reliable. I am opposed on principle to giving them any posts of special responsibility. However good this Brunt is, it still seems to me sheer madness. I feel very strongly about the matter."

"Special responsibility in a school," Allenside said wearily, "is just a euphemism for extra work, donkey work usually."

107

"It's a matter of principle," Whiteway said. "This school is a model for the future. We need to be especially careful. Don't you ever read your brother's articles, Mr. Allenside? They're about as sound as anything being written on present day politics."

Allenside smiled but did not answer. His silence seemed to increase Lord Whiteway's displeasure. Whiteway displayed approval or disapproval by calculated manipulations of his bushy eyebrows and extensive mouth, as if they were parts of some temperament barometer announcing the weather of the Whiteway world. It was easy to see he had long experience in terrorising regiments of under-paid clerks. He glanced angrily at the clock.

"I must be going. Perhaps you could call at the Hill one evening. We ought to talk the matter over more thoroughly. I won't take up any more of your time now."

He turned to me.

"Good day to you, Flint. If you see my niece do tell her we would appreciate a visit. Tell her our address hasn't changed."

He bared his teeth at me unmirthfully.

Allenside escorted him to the school entrance. His Daimler was parked in the road outside. I waited in the headmaster's room.

"I'm a blasted fool!" Allenside slammed the door when he came back. "If not worse. I should have told Whiteway to go to hell right at the start, and take the bloody letter with him so they could burn together."

I wanted to smile. Allenside didn't usually swear and it sounded funny.

"You can see what I've done, David. I've been trying to humour Whiteway so as not to lose my chance of the Director-ate. I thought I was smooth and clever enough to handle him so that Visot would be cleared, Brunt would get the S.R., the school would continue to prosper and I would get my pro-motion. Something to call out all my powers of tact and diplomacy. I've under-rated Whiteway and compromised myself. I've made a mess."

There was nothing I could do except listen sympathetically.

"And now I've got to salvage what I can. I'll pick up my self-respect first, so it's good-bye to the new job."

I made sounds of protest but he shook his head. He stood

by the window, staring at the brickwork of the wall across the square area occupied by the bicycle sheds.

"Janet will be disappointed. I feel disappointed myself already. But to think I've been living in a sort of fool's paradise these three years. I imagined I had learnt to handle old Whiteway. I thought of him as a 'harmless old buffer' whose oddities I tolerated and even pandered to, for the good of the school."

Allenside rubbed his forehead with the back of his hand.

"For three years I have been able to deceive myself. It's frightening to know we find bigger ways of making fools of ourselves as we get older. We shake off the wilder illusions in order to adopt the subtler kind that aren't so obviously ridiculous. I feel this morning as if I had just woke up. I don't like the man, David. I never have. He's made use of me and of the school. And all the time I kidded myself that I was handling him beautifully for the good of the school; this glorious combination of state and independent school virtues. He gives us new dressing-rooms on the playing-fields; I see that he's eulogised in the local press. He gives us cups and shields and prizes and I build him up as the school's fairy godfather. I've given him quite a bright jewel in the crown of his civic reputation. I must have known all the time I was doing it. Like some bad habit, I pretended it wasn't there. Do you think I'm a hypocrite, David?"

I shook my head vigorously. I was touched by the honesty and the loneliness of the man. That wife of his would be no help to him now. She would nag him incessantly for not getting the Directorate. She would never understand. For Allenside this trivial incident over Bansdale's letter had become a moment of truth. It had not only become cruelly clear to him that in order to become director of the new Research Institute he would have to withhold the special responsibility post from Brunt, and allow Visot to be 'investigated' at Whiteway's pleasure; it had given him a sudden glance at his own behaviour for the past three years that made him loathe himself with the clear fervour of religious conversion.

With a gesture of tired resignation he sat down at his desk. He glanced about the room as if he were seeing it for the first time: the neat notices and cyclostyled regulations that decorated the walls, the efficient filing cabinet.

"Do you think I am pompous, David?"

"Of course not."

"I do. This room is a restrained advertisement. I can't tell you how much I dislike the person whom it advertises. The super-efficient, scrupulously fair, quietly enthusiastic headmaster with all the right kinds of advanced ideas. Determinedly on his way up. Prepared already to speak with nostalgic affection about the school he was reluctantly obliged in the interest of the eternal verities to leave. Write a book about a Tartuffe of a headmaster, David. I'll give you all the material you need. I could almost do it myself."

If only I could have framed the right words without sounding unctuous or sentimental, I would have told him that he was a man whose integrity I admired and envied. But how can you say that to a man who is examining himself so candidly? Nothing you say could endure the scorching heat of his own strictures. I would be better employed exposing my own secret pride to the same blistering light.

To my relief the bell rang before Allenside could say any more. He waved sardonically as I went through the door. I had never seen him make so inconsequential a gesture in school before. It was all too disturbing. It was as if the minister had winked in the middle of a sermon. I would not have him appear anything but what I was convinced he was: an intelligent, self-controlled, strong character; a man who was no passion's slave; an arbiter of righteousness and justice, a man of good will, good sense, and sensitive conscience. It would have been unbearable to discover he was no better than myself.

XII

I FOUND IT DIFFICULT to get used to Helen in the flat again. Having been in solitary possession for so long I had acquired an affection for the place as something of my own. It required self-discipline to persuade myself that I was not master of the house. A dinner party I had arranged with two writers I admired had to be cancelled with almost indecent haste. Marriage, I concluded, would be the only happy issue of my little afflictions. Marriage would stabilise my unsettled position and my hectic conscience. It was the simple solution we all reach for out of the complexity of our conflicting desires like the one fit word that eludes the tip of the tongue.

When what I deemed to be the auspicious moment arrived I showed Helen Phyllis's letter. She read it with such calm that I was at a loss to explain the perturbations that had made me hesitate showing it to her.

"From what you have told me about her, David," she said handing the sheet of notepaper back to me, "this is exactly the kind of letter I would have expected her to write."

I wondered what kind of picture of Phyllis I had drawn for Helen's benefit. Probably an unfavourable sketch designed more to exonerate my own behaviour than to give a true picture of the girl I married. Phyllis was not a bad example of the provincial housewife; the presiding deity of a cosy well-ordered house: a devoted mother, dutiful daughter, and deserted wife, moving in her restricted circle like a well-trained mare. Her chief fault, her inability to rise above her surroundings, had probably obscured all her virtues from my view. Incompatibility of temperament usually entails an inability to understand. It had been more than enough at the time that Phyllis completely failed to understand me.

Helen said, "I wouldn't consider it an insuperable obstacle."

"What do you suggest?" After all Helen had a great deal more practical ability than I.

"How long is it since you last saw her?"

"Nearly three years."

"Desertion?" Helen said thoughtfully.

"But I am doing the deserting." Aloud it all sounded rather harmless and absurd. Why should the word so unpleasantly disturb me when I thought of it in the solitude of my mind?

Helen did not answer. She was thinking. Thinking for Helen usually meant deciding a course of action. Economic independence had given her the habit. She spent less time than most in day-dreaming. Naturally enough since she so often had the means of translating fancy into fact.

"I suggest," she said at last, "that you leave it all to my lawyers. I have found that given sufficient money lawyers can settle practically anything. For a few hundred pounds they could take a simple divorce case like this in their stride."

I should have smiled, because Helen was practising her own brand of realistic humour. But I was disturbed by what I felt to be a lack of sensitivity on her part; and I was uncertain whether I ought to allow her to undertake such an expensive operation on my behalf.

"It will be for my own benefit, David," Helen said softly. "I very much want you to marry me."

It would have been graceless not to give in; it appeared to be the only thing to do.

"Did you ever ask her to join you in London?" Helen sat curled in the corner of her large chair, sleek and smooth and self-contained and quietly calculating as a favourite cat. I wished she would not be quite so objective. It made me feel rather a fool.

"No." A note of protest in my voice as if I had been accused of some unworthy action.

"Pity. But I am sure there is a line of progress there if properly worked up. Your job was in London; you had to be in London. It was your wife's place to join you."

I nodded uneasily. All I could vouch for was my intention to put as many miles as I could between Warrington Avenue and myself. With more nerve and greater linguistic ability I would have spent the last three years wandering about Europe instead of teaching. But I hadn't the money and I wanted to be in London to nurse my reputation as a novelist.

Helen was disappointed to find what little progress I had

made with the project on the Seymour Brothers. She spent an evening reading through what I had done. I came back late from a party in Maida Vale to listen to her judgement. My heart thumped with absurd perturbation. The importance I attached to her opinion was a superstition which had no rational foundation. I knew Helen's mind was essentially a business one. Her criterion of success was too material. We had once discussed publishing together in a small way; my literary judgement combined with her gift for business. The enthusiasm was brief and petered out. Helen would not have remained interested for long in publishing elegant experiments that made no money. I did not blame her for that because strong instincts in myself shared her commercial point of view.

"It isn't any good, David." Cigarette smoke eddied about her. The ash tray on the floor was crammed with stumps. When concentrating on some business to which she attached special importance she liked to smoke continuously until the task was done. At other times she smoked very little. "It won't do."

I sat down, guilty and miserable. She was quite right, probably for the wrong reasons.

"You know what I think is the matter?" She spoke with firm conviction. She thought well of herself in the role of patron and critic. I felt weakly ready to be overwhelmed. Whether she was right or wrong the force of her conviction would flatten my sensitive hesitations. "These Allenside brothers. I admit there are similarities—but therein lies the trap and you seem to have tumbled into it. There are inconsistencies in the behaviour of Edward Seymour; in some scenes he seems all Allenside; mild and conscientious, pre-occupied with the scruples that worry men of smaller stature than the Lord Protector. Edward Allenside has robbed the Lord Protector of all the marks of greatness. Seymour was ready to dare his soul to achieve his purpose. He had an inspired ruthlessness that your little Allenside would never understand. It's muddled you see. I wish I could express myself more clearly. But you see what I mean?"

"You are probably right," I said glumly. "I shall burn the whole damn thing. I wish the notion had never crossed my mind. In any case I know it would be a far more suitable story for a play than for a novel. Oh dear why didn't I face all this long ago. I've been pecking away at the thing half-heartedly for weeks, and it's got me absolutely nowhere. Damn, damn, damn."

"David darling, don't be downhearted my dear. You know you usually have to make one or two false starts before you hit on the right theme. You told me that yourself, several times. I know exactly what you ought to do."

I looked at her eagerly. I was greedy for any suggestion.

"Come down to Boscombe with me. The garden there will be delightful now. We'll fix up a studio for you over the stables. There are the chauffeur's rooms: they could easily be done up. Then you could reconsider the thing at your leisure. Decide whether it's to be the Seymours, or the Allensides, or something new and exciting and quite different. Let's do that David, shall we? It would be wonderful. You'd have all day to work instead of these sneaked hours between dinner and bedtime. Peace and Quiet and Freedom to think. That's what you need."

"But school, Helen. . . ." I can imagine how plaintive I sounded.

"Blow that awful school. Resign. Give in your notice, or whatever it is they do. You should have done so long ago. It's perfectly absurd the way you've tried to carry on two full time jobs. I don't know how your health can stand it. Really I don't."

"If I resigned," I said, "I'd need to give Allenside two months' notice."

"Surely not. That's enormously long. I'm sure a week or two would be quite enough. Two months is absurd. It might as well be two years."

"It might be three," I added cautiously. "In lots of counties it's three." I did not want to do as Helen wished and I was fighting for time in which to fathom my objections. The situation was all the more desperate since it had arisen so suddenly and found me completely unprepared. I had not lived with Helen long enough to develop the matrimonial gift of gliding over the springs that set off the clockwork of a woman's cherished purposes. The money was hers; the flat was hers; the ability to come and go was hers: I was at a considerable disadvantage.

"Really, David, for an artist you seem exceptionally over-laden with bourgeois taboos."

It would have been out of place to tell her I was trying to be a Christian as well. It would have sounded absurdly pretentious coming from me.

"Allenside and I are friends, Helen. It would cause him great inconvenience if I just walked out on him. It would seem as if I attached no importance at all to the good-will between us." I added a final touch to the portrait of my virtuous hesitation. "He's having a lot of trouble in school just now. He needs all the good-will he can get."

"Now you are just making excuses." Helen straightened her legs which had been drawn up comfortably. She sat on the edge of the sofa, and weighing on her hands, lifted her legs as if she wanted to view her feet without looking downwards. It was an oddly schoolgirlish gesture somehow meant to accompany an outspokenness that was not altogether pleasant for herself or the friend who was present to hear it. "You have enough faith in your talent, have you? Or haven't you enough faith in me?"

I became quite eloquent. It was abundantly clear, it seemed to me, that there could be no satisfactory basis for living for either of us other than marriage. Everything depended on that, our happiness, our peace of mind, my work, and Helen's work. I tried to express as much of what I felt as I believed Helen could understand. I did not dwell on my distractingly uneasy conscience, or my determination to live by my own labour, or my obligations to Allenside and the school.

"We've got to be together more, Helen." I became franker and bolder, impelled by the spate of my utterance. If there was to be any prophecy it would only come when freedom of speaking bordered on the ecstatic. "If we are to create a way of living, to live creatively and not merely to exist, both you and I must forego a lot of the freedom we enjoy as free lances. I must give up my school, my dabbling in educational theory, my compensating urges towards good works, my cultivation of minor and inefficacious austerities and all the unattractive aspects of my porridgey character that annoy you only less than they distress me; and you, my dear, must circumscribe to some extent your passion for travelling, your taste for taking up and dropping expensive projects. What you and I need is a taste of the simple life together, something resembling what we captured in the Cotswolds, Helen, on a permanent basis. London doesn't really suit us, you know, does it? Either you or me."

My eloquence spent itself. Helen was making no enthusiastic response.

"I never realised before," she said smiling coldly, "you considered me vacillating and unsteady. Is that why you distrust me? Or have I other characteristics that distress you more?"

My prophetic insight had been no use. She made no effort to understand what I was striving to express. She persisted in considering the whole business on the lowest possible level. Now it was my turn to sulk. We had never had a scene of this kind between us before but it seemed too familiar to be the first and too inconclusive to be the last. The element of mystery in our relationship which had depended so much on restraint and silence—the poor poet aided and beloved by the silent princess who bestowed upon him her favours as rich gifts in return for his secret ecstasies, who came and went disguised in the wide cloak of her unrevealed purposes and designs—had gone for ever. We had reached the stage of knowing too much about each other to be able to maintain even the quietest and most tastefully tailored illusions. It seemed clear to me, at least, we had no course but to proceed forward to the frank daylight of marriage.

Helen recovered sooner than I did. Perhaps she realised that as long as we lived together in unofficial cohabitation, we would need to make the best of each other's company. She suggested that we should go out somewhere for dinner and perhaps dance. After a little persuasion, I unsulked, and by the time we were in the taxi it had become the occasion of some unspecified celebration.

The next day while I was in school, Helen spent the morning with her lawyers. It was arranged that I should go and see them and place the divorce business in their safe hands. Mr. Buss the lawyer struck me as being oddly like Helen. He was smooth and sound, restrained and efficient, polite and rather ruthless in the unmistakeably Brown fashion. Their power rested not so much in themselves as in what they could do; the key positions they occupied in the great machine. I thought of asking whethere there was any blood relationship; or could it be entirely a class-mark, like the lean, scrubbed, hungry look of the English proletariat?

Before the negotiations had begun, I came home from school one day to find a telegram on the table. Helen was out shopping. I picked it up. It was from Phyllis. Telegrams were obviously her perfect medium of expression. *Father passed away peacefully last night funeral Friday 11 a.m. Phyllis.*

I did not discuss the telegram with Helen. But I spent surprisingly long sessions debating in my own mind whether or not to attend the funeral. Was it or was it not my duty to go? It was the kind of nice problem that my conscience could gnaw at with scholastic persistence for a whole day and still be fresh for the renewal of holy warfare when my head lay on my pillow.

The old man was in my view—and all views of character are limited and relative—a complete horror. I can see him now standing at the entrance of his large and gloomy ironmonger's shop in top coat and bowler hat; proprietor, commissionaire and shop-walker; discreetly placed to keep a close watch over his overalled shop assistants, and the affairs of the town as reflected in the traffic of its High Street. Mr. Rayment, ironmonger, town councillor (twice Mayor), Methodist deacon, my father-in-law. To think of him was enough to make me feel sorry for myself. And to think that I had once gone out of my way to ingratiate myself with him, to make myself acceptable, amenable, and inoffensive; to think that I had flattered the man, listened respectfully to his advice, which he distributed with lavish freedom; it was an exercise in humiliation.

And now the house-fly could settle on his cold nose as he lay in the open coffin and his hand could not be lifted to brush it away. The loose false teeth had been removed and those moist clacking lips were shrunken shut with the vice-like firmness of a vein in stone. The Polonius of Warrington Avenue. But I myself would never have dared to kill him. Death made me sorry for him. He had become poor old Rayment. It was all I could do to stop myself going to the funeral. He got a lot more out of me than the passing tribute of a sigh. I may also have been curious to see Phyllis and my son Stanley, but any desire to see them entailed an even more powerful desire that they should not see me. I would willingly have lain under the laurel bush at the top of the back garden, in the rain, to watch them through the window before the curtains were drawn at night. But I could not bear the thought of shaking hands with either of them and attempting to make conversation. In any case Phyllis probably had no desire that I should attend the funeral in person. The Rayments were a large tribe and it could have been very embarrassing. No doubt all she required was that I should send a wreath; which I did.

XIII

We had been reading the story of Jacob and Esau.
I had attempted to modernise it in my own way. I was always
more at ease dealing with the Old Testament than with the
New. It made fewer demands on the teacher. Talking frequently about Christ makes a man become either mealy
mouthed or agonisingly uncomfortable. I seem to have hoped
that I would make some spiritual progress as I continued with
my teaching—or as I grew older and set my moral house in
better order—that would eventually allow me to pass the
parables over my mouth without defiling them and to describe
the progress towards the Cross without being overcome with
embarrassed shame. The two most difficult names to say in
the language, Jesus and Christ. A graveyard of heresies nestle
in an intonation and the germs of martyrdoms and massacres
are broadcast in spitting syllables, from Jack Jesus to King
Christ. A name to conjure with. I could not go around saying
this son of God I'm telling you about ought really to be King
of the World with his G.H.Q. in every heart especially mine
which you all see clearly, you boys in the back stand up if you
wish to see clearly, dangling on my sleeve. Vulgarity is
thoughtless sincerity.

Munday, a conscientious hardworking boy with neat hand-
writing who came from a respectable socialist home had (as
I had intended someone would do) drawn the line at Jacob.
Munday had received careful instruction in ethics from his
serious-minded father. I had taken care to emphasise that
Jacob was a swindler and a cheat in the hope that an objection
would be raised that would allow me to proceed smoothly to
the next stage of the argument. He was this and he was that
I was going to say but he was still better than Esau. However,
Munday had taken the thing too much to heart. He had
flushed deeply and his protest, coming from so well-behaved
a boy, was a declaration of irreconcilable and unshakeable
disapproval of Jacob. Without warning I was put to the test.

Munday's valuation of me as a man and a teacher would rest on my handling of the question.

"There's evil in all of us, Munday," I was saying. The boy watched me closely. His cheeks were flushed but his eyes did not waver, and he did not blink. "Jacob perhaps had more than his fair share." A weak bid for a smile. I did not get one. "But he had in him the raw material of greatness. When passed through the furnace of living this ungainly ore became the finest tempered steel." Although the metaphor was borrowed, usually it had some effect. But Munday just frowned. His stupid honesty was the front line defence for the preservation of his sinewed citadel of prejudice.

"Take Paul . . ." I addressed the class in general, a note of appealing exasperation in my voice, but I got no farther. A breathless prefect had knocked the class-room door and entered hastily. Breathing heavily after chasing up two flights of stairs he gave me his message.

"You're wanted on the phone, sir. In the staff-room."

"Stay with the class, will you, till I come back." I turned to the class. "Take out your text-books and read the chapter on the Patriarchs until I come back."

I sped down the stairs three steps at a time, the palm of my hand polishing the wooden banister rail. The phone lay on the window sill alongside the receiver, the round mouth and ear turned upwards, waiting curiously alive. Bill Hawkes was in the room, and Mitchley, who sat at the table marking. "Come on, Flinty," Bill said grinning. "Don't keep the lady waiting." I wondered who the lady could be.

It was Helen. She made no apology for ringing me up in the middle of a lesson.

"David?"

"Yes." She was telephoning from the flat. I wished Hawkes and Mitchley were not in the room. One was marking, the other was reading *Punch*, and I was supposed to assume that neither was listening.

"Roger Allenside has been here this morning."

"Oh!" I said uneasily. "What did he want?"

"You didn't tell me he was friendly with Peter."

There was no time to pause for an answer. I had to think of something to say that would give nothing away to the two men in the room, and yet give Helen satisfaction.

"I didn't imagine it would interest you."

"You didn't tell me he had taken you and Peter out drinking."

"No." I made my voice sound as agreeable as I could.

"This is what I want you to understand David: the man's not to be trusted. He's a criminal. He came here this morning wanting money."

"Good God. He's never seen you before." I was so surprised I forgot the two listeners in the room for a moment. "He wouldn't have the nerve."

"He wanted me to invest in a company he has formed for buying and selling second-hand cars. He thought I would be interested because Peter was in it. Had you heard about it before?"

"Heavens no. Did he say I had?"

"Not in so many words. But he has a way of hinting things which I find extremely distasteful. What I wanted to ask you, David, was whether you could come home to lunch. And perhaps take the afternoon off too because I'm rather anxious to settle Mister Roger Allenside before he goes any further. I want to consult Buss and I'd like you to come with me. Allenside's game is polite blackmail: and I rather suspect he is involved in other rackets too. He made a great show of being very friendly with Uncle Harold and Aunty Muriel." (I was a little slow in catching on that she was referring to Lord and Lady Whiteway.) "He knew Horace awfully well in South Africa. It shocks me to think of Aunty Muriel being taken in by him. Approaching age is softening her head I think. I can't tell you how much I distrust and dislike him."

"I'm rather glad to hear that," I said. "He fancies himself as being a great success with every woman."

"Well, how soon can you get home?"

"I can't easily get away for lunch. But I have a free period at the end of the afternoon. I could be at the flat by three thirty. Would that do?"

"I suppose it will have to. You might tell your Mr. Allenside about his crooked brother. But I mustn't keep you."

"Three thirty," I said, "if not sooner."

"Goodbye." She had put the receiver down smartly.

"Bye," I said although I knew the line was dead. "My class is waiting." I smiled fatuously at Hawkes and Mitchley and

121

rushed out, wondering how much they had made out of what I had been saying.

I was uncomfortably aware of not having risen to the occasion. As I climbed the stairs, I wished I had made up my mind to go to Helen at once. She would not have rung up unless she needed me. I never remembered her ringing up the school before. I could have rigged up an excuse to Allenside. He knew me well enough to know I would not ask to leave work unless the matter was urgent. I need not have mentioned it was about Roger. Was that why I had been unwilling to go? Not wanting to bring so unpleasant a story about Roger before his brother: not wanting to assist in damaging the name of Allenside. No, that was not my excuse. There was no excuse. I had deliberately shirked an unpleasant duty and my hypocritical devotion to my time-table was a clear case of moral cowardice. Nothing upsets a man more than being forced to contemplate and condemn his own weakness. I did not feel up to coping with Roger or even learning from Helen the real depth of his iniquity. I had no difficulty in believing the worst of Roger, but I could not bring myself to adopt a positive attitude towards him. My instinct was to avoid not only his presence but even the thought of him. Helen would have me preoccupied with both. She wanted to declare war on Roger and attack at once. My instinct was to keep out of his way and act as if he had ceased to exist. I had lost all professional interest in him now: Sir Thomas Seymour or no. He was too dangerous to play with. Not my type of character at all. I was more of a bird watcher than a big game hunter. If Roger charged me I knew I would be rooted to the ground and trampled upon never to rise again; a provincial Hamlet accidentally killed in the first Act.

By three o'clock in the afternoon, however, my exaggerated fears had lifted like smoke scattered by the morning breeze. At lunch I obtained Allenside's permission to leave at three, and hastening down the steps of the main entrance while the school was still caught in the time-table's tight net I felt something of the elation of a boy enjoying an unexpected half-holiday. Like a film actress devoted to her complexion, I was always at pains to preserve a youthful impulse in my reactions. The bus was delightfully empty. I occupied the front seat on the top deck and surveyed the common as we rumbled gently on our way with the friendly condescension of visiting royalty. The wooden windmill was neatly posed against silvery clouds and vast expanses of blue sky. The trees and shrubbery displayed their assorted green, but the herbage of the peaty soil was still dominated by the blend of winterburnt grass and the sombre green of young rushes.

In Putney High Street only the housewives were about in any number, darting in and out of the flourishing shops with quick birdlike movements. The newspaper sellers had time for talk of horses and football with longing acquaintances; or to think of sensational headlines for their posters before the rush hour began. The traffic swam along its different routes with the graceful leisure of gold fish in a pond. Elderly men leaned over the bridge and studied the manœuvres of a white river bus about to moor at the pier. Innumerable prams were being pushed to and fro along the Fulham Embankment and in and out of Bishop's Park where a troup of gardeners were gently busy, with the calm persistence of their craft, over something large but still indistinguishable in the ornamental gardens. It was very pleasant to be on one's way home in mid-afternoon.

Helen was not in the flat when I arrived. I was breathless from running up the stairs (the lift was out of order). There was a brief note scribbled for me on the mantelpiece on the back of an invitation to a private view of the recent paintings of a friend of mine. *Gone to see Buss. I'll be back for tea.* I was beginning to realise what a prominent part her solicitors played in Helen's life. They adopted children for her, managed her estate, protected her interests, engineered her divorce no doubt as they were about to fix mine, bought and sold her houses; they fought her battles on every front. Whenever personal relationships became too much for her she would retire behind her solicitors' barbed-wire entanglements. I felt a little envious. It seemed rather like something I myself needed.

In the kitchen I drank half a pint of milk and armed with a plate of biscuits I retired to my room. For this room alone— I felt a sudden emotion taking hold of me as I opened the ivory painted door—I owed Helen undying thanks. It was my sanctuary, and she had meant it to be such. Whatever her shortcomings she had all the instincts of a patron of the arts.

The Seymour brothers were now definitely set aside. They would make a play perhaps when my reputation as a novelist was sufficiently established to make a venture into the theatre a practical proposition. My notebook now occupied the most prominent position on my desk. It consisted of ideas and impressions. The ideas were numbered. I would continue to jot them down until the 'real thing' occurred and then the notes would all be centred on that. My life would begin to revolve about it for twenty-four hours a day, until either I was thrown out of the saddle or until the new machine collapsed under me, or until the new book like a new house rose firmly against the landscape and I could shut the front door, hand the keys over to the publisher and walk away myself in search of a new site for my ant-like urges.

This afternoon I had no ideas and I did not mind in the least. I browsed among my books and among Helen's father's. When Helen called my name I was pleasantly immersed in William James's *The Varieties of Religious Experience*.

I found Helen in a combative mood. I stood about helpfully while she prepared the trolley for tea. I studied her shape critically as she bent over the kitchen table making cucumber and tomato sandwiches. Her small hands moved with surprising speed and dexterity. She had comparatively narrow hips but heavy thighs and thick but still shapely legs; for so plump a young woman her breasts were surprisingly small. Not Rubens; perhaps Paolo Veronese—but too small for that too. Her white necklace suspended above the table seemed as militant as war-paint and gave an unusually aggressive air to her rotundly passive figure.

"Do you think I have no sense of humour, David?" she asked me seriously.

"Dear me, no." I answered at once—and then began to consider the question seriously.

"That's what your friend Allenside said. He really was the limit."

"Tell me about it." I was not over eager to hear, but it had to be gone through.

"Push the trolley in there. I think that's everything." Her eyes surveyed the trays with critical satisfaction. If Helen had less money she would have made an excellent housewife.

We made ourselves comfortable in the living-room.

"When I opened the door," Helen said, "I thought it was somebody selling things."

I laughed: "You weren't far wrong."

"A man who uses his appearance as a calculated advertisement, for something better than what he really is." Helen was very pleased with her appraisal of Roger. She had, of course, less power and less money by far than her uncle, Lord Whiteway, but she had the advantage of a more thorough and leisured education.

"The kind of man who sets my teeth on edge. 'I'm Roger Allenside,' he said. 'A friend of David's.' 'David isn't here,' I said. I didn't ask him in. 'Well as a matter of fact, Mrs. Bayly, it's you I want to see.' It's been a long time since anyone called me Mrs. Bayly. It must have put me off my stride because quite against my intention, I asked him in. He began to talk about Uncle Harold, and my cousin Horace, and how friendly he was with Uncle Harold, and my cousin Horace, and how friendly he was with Uncle Harold. They were planning a trip together to the States. 'For business and political reasons,' he said," Helen gave a satirical flour'sh with her hand.

"Big shots," I said laughing. "The reality of power."

Helen frowned. "He asked me in a horribly playful tone if Uncle Harold knew about you and me. He spoke as if everything was a joke. I can quite see his manner would be an enormous success in a saloon bar and with certain types of women. Most people would find his witty high spirits rather infectious. I must be the exception. I took a violent dislike to him right away. I knew he was edging round for my point of view so that he could stand beside me as it were and see the world from my angle, making sarcastic and satirical remarks about people he guessed I disliked, hoping to win my approval!

"Then he tried his private life; how he had lost his only son and how the loss had preyed upon his wife's mind. He came nearest there to winning my sympathy. I almost told him about Nicola. But the thought that he was after something, trying to get something out of me, put me on my guard. I have a sixth sense about people who are after money. I can shut up then like a clam."

We smiled at each other.

"I think my silence was beginning to wear him down. It wasn't all quite what he expected. He must have got quite the wrong impression of what kind of a person I was. Perhaps he thought because I lived with you I was some sort of a sentimental poet's mistress—all dressing gown and glossy magazines. I don't know what Peter had been telling him either. He went on to Peter when all else had failed. He referred to him as 'Poor Ol' Pete', and tried to give me the impression that he was Peter's father confessor. By this he had begun to regret having called. Some plan or other of his, based on a completely false idea of my personality, had fallen through. But he refused to accept that the whole carefully planned visit had been wasted.

"It was then that he began to talk about this second-hand car business in Shepherd's Bush. Having outlined its wonderful possibilities he went on to say how nice it would be to have Peter in a decent steady job to keep him out of mischief. 'What kind of mischief,' I asked. 'He drinks rather heavily you know,' Allenside said, 'and in his cups he's inclined to talk too much. It would be an advantage from every point of view, Mrs. Bayly, if you could see your way to supporting this venture.' I wish now I had given him a piece of my mind there and then. Ever since I've been thinking of all sorts of cutting and crushing things to say. But instead I merely said coldly that I would have to ask him to excuse me as I had to go out to attend to some business. He offered me a lift. I opened the door for him and thanked him, saying I wouldn't dream of keeping him. I saw him getting into his car from the kitchen window. Very spivish looking, a new green floating bloater."

We laugh again. 'Floating bloater' was an expression of my own invention that had amused Helen. I was always pleased and flattered when she demonstrated traces of my influence in her speaking. At such moments vague fears about the unreality of our friendship were utterly dispelled.

"What action have you taken with Buss?"

"Well, I told him the whole story. He said there were no grounds for any legal action in what took place between us. He had used no threats or made statements that could be interpreted as blackmail. All he has done is to make an unsuccessful appeal for support of a business venture. There's no law against his doing that."

"What does Buss suggest?"

"Nothing at all. Unless your friend Roger tries again we have nothing at all to work on."

I nodded as gravely as I could. "That is what I would have said." To myself I added, without charging you the earth for the advice.

"But I think, David," Helen spoke emphatically, "you and I ought to deal with him."

"How, my dear? What can I do?"

"He could make himself very unpleasant. I've no objection to Uncle Harold knowing about you and me, but I would rather tell him myself than have him hear from such a polluted source. And I don't like the influence he claims to have over Peter. He's got to be stopped David. And it can be done quite easily. We've got to expose him."

I stirred uneasily in my chair. Helen was eager for battle. I felt like a smaller Power bound by alliance, with no stomach for a fight.

"I'm convinced he's a crook, David." Her enthusiasm was roused. What could I do to restrain her. "He made a great mistake intruding himself upon me. I don't like that sort of thing. It makes me quietly but wildly angry. He's put his nose in a hornet's nest. We've got to plan our attack carefully, David. There's a great deal I've thought that you could do, to begin with."

My heart sank. What could I do against Roger? The faintly indignant thought that it was none of my business crossed my mind with a *'but what's it all got to do with me.'* Shocked at my own disloyal thoughts, I nodded my head slowly, as if I was in complete agreement with her aim, and already engaged in considering ways and means of putting Roger Allenside in his place.

XIV

SCHOOL HAD BEEN DISMISSED at the end of the second lesson in the afternoon. The black blazered boys who a few moments ago had seemed chained forever to their wooden desks had deserted the three-storied building. Only a prefect or two lingered in the cloakroom or by the bicycle shed, shouldering a bag or inflating a too soft tyre.

In the staff-room chairs had been arranged about three walls of the room. The headmaster's chair had been placed ready for him at the head of the rectangular table, and Robinson who kept the Minutes, was already seated on the right. Each member of staff had a copy of the Agenda and also his own stiff-backed mark book. The main items on the Agenda were the formation of a School Council; the regulation of extracurricular activities; the question of Penge being sent to an institution; and a revision of the rota for Saturday duties.

But no one was thinking of the Agenda at the moment. All the staff were assembled in the room except Briarman and the headmaster. Groups were busy drawing their own conclusions. "After all," Glide said to me, swallowing so that his Adam's apple genuflected and his long teeth slipped into view as soon as he opened his slack mouth to speak, "he can't put it off much longer. The Governors will be meeting on Thursday." Glide knew the date of every important event all the year round. He was also an established and respected staff-room authority on the ways and customs of the Education Authority.

I glanced at Dell who sat in his customary chair, listening to Eglinton who talked with a low rapidity which Dell did not seem to follow very closely. Dell kept washing his face with his dry hands as if to wipe away any tell-tale traces of embarrassment. I gathered that Eglinton was urging Dell to support his impending attack against the School Council, a project which was mainly Brunt's idea.

"We'd better find a seat." Glide gazed about the room unenthusiastically.

"Come on!" Robinson made a characteristically autocratic gesture. He was a small man in a profession where inches often helped. (The boys called him 'Half-Pint.') "Get yourselves seated. The sooner we start the sooner this thing will be over. Anyone would think some of you hadn't got wives to go home to."

"Now then," Hawkes protested, grinning, "don't you get personal."

I sat down next to Eglinton. When we were all seated the two empty chairs became more conspicuous than ever.

"Do you want to be answerable to a bunch of kids inspired by Comrade Bert?" Eglinton said to me, tapping item two on his agenda sheet.

"I don't really know," I said hesitatingly. Dell seemed relieved at not having to listen to Eglinton for a moment. He gazed longingly at the open door.

"It's wrong on principle." Eglinton smiled faintly. He always made it a point of not appearing too serious. "And it will be a perfect damn nuisance. I'm absolutely against it, aren't you, Dell?"

"What I always object to," Dell said, still staring at the door, "is unprofessional behaviour. As far as I am concerned the man's opinions—which I disagree with of course—are neither here nor there. He lacks professional standards."

"That's what I mean." Eglinton seemed satisfied. He slipped his hand under his jacket to bring out his cigarette case. Uncertain whether to smoke or not, he left it there. Dell's gaze was filled with undisguised longing. In spite of the bald head and the moustache he looked pathetically boyish. He believed some last minute miracle might still bring the job to him. It was not impossible that Briarman in a moment of inspired honesty might refuse it in order to give way to the better man.

"Do you think we can smoke?" Eglinton asked.

Dell said, "We usually wait, don't we at these meetings until the Head tells us to carry on."

"Dell, I believe you are a ritualist at heart."

Dell gave a vague smile. He had heard the tone only, not the joke and had estimated a faint smile would be enough.

"You can't be too careful," Dell said, "with Allenside. He looks straightforward enough, but you never know where you really are with him, that's the snag."

Nothing on earth would ever reconcile Dell to Allenside again. That was the answer to failure, Allenside was to blame.

"He'd take the school to bed with him if he could," Eglinton said grinning. "No home life, that's his trouble." He turned to look at me. "Formidable woman his wife, isn't she?"

My smile was a sign of collaboration. For Allenside's sake I would have prevented it, but as far as Janet was concerned Eglinton was quite right.

"Ambitious woman," Dell said, "just like him. That's all they want; to get on. That boy of their's packed off to a so-called Progressive School, out of the way. No home life at all, as you say. . . ."

Downs had crossed the room and placed his hands on the wooden arms of Eglinton's chair, so that his watch chain dangled between them.

"Got to stop this Boy's Council business," he whispered conspiratorially, glancing from Dell to Eglinton. "The old man's bound to want Brunt as chairman. Shall I propose you Dell?"

"No damn fear," Dell said.

"My dear Downey bird," Eglinton tipped the watch chain so that it began to swing to and fro, "your tactics are too short-sighted. Propose someone 'neutral'. Somebody like Robinson. Or why not Flint here? Or why not Visot if it came to that? That would be a master-stroke—Vizzy for Chairman."

Downs grinned, displaying two rows of decaying teeth, gums and all with exceptional fulness. Nothing could persuade him to go to the dentist.

"What about Hawkes?" I suggested helpfully.

"Bill won't take it," Downs said. "He's like me: too bloody lazy."

I wondered how Hawkes would have liked the comparison.

"I think you ought to take it on, Flint. Don't you, Dell? Holy Moses for Chairman. Vote for Holy Moses."

Dell wasn't listening. He heard only the footsteps of the headmaster and Briarman approaching down the corridor; loud, arrogant, aggressive, successful footsteps. That was where his feet should have been treading. Could it be that his deepest disappointment was that Allenside had spurned the intimate friendship and loyal deputy headship of P. B. S. Dell? To prefer Briarman's company in the seclusion of the headmaster's office, to attach more value to Briarman's advice and judgement; inexplicable and unforgivable. And yet he listened now to the approaching footsteps with such intensity, it might have been good news he was expecting.

Briarman walked in behind the headmaster. With conspicuous humility, having carefully closed the door, he chose a hard chair by the cold radiator. As if to discourage anyone from whispering to him, he stared downwards, studying the conditions of his nails. He appeared a democrat who had reluctantly allowed his name to go forward not from personal ambition, but out of a stern sense of public duty. He would never have admitted even to himself that he had just obtained something very near his heart's desire.

I understood Allenside's choice: but I wished he had chosen Dell. Not only because Dell was a more amiable fellow: in the long run I am certain he would have made the better job as deputy head. In striving to be fair, Allenside had probably given undue weight to Briarman's ostentatious bustle and enthusiastic overtime. Allenside, I concluded, was an excellent man himself, but he lacked the insight that would allow him to penetrate the façade of men who were over-anxious to please. Had I been in his position that would at least have been one mistake I would not have made. These reflections, however, only combined to make me fonder of the man than ever; it was his devotion to justice that had led him to make the misjudgement. And I was not so overwhelmingly positive about Dell as to exclude the possibility that, after all, Allenside was right and I was wrong.

Allenside wore a neat blue suit and a white shirt with buttoned cuffs. He had left his gown hanging on a peg behind the door of his office. Between his fingers he held a silver propelling pencil on which his name was engraved. As he spoke, he turned it about as if the small activity with his hands helped him to speak.

"You may know that the Governors will be meeting next week to appoint a deputy headmaster for the school, and also to confirm an appointment to a post of special responsibility. I think it is right that you should know now that I shall recommend Mr. Briarman for the deputy headship. I do not feel it is necessary to go outside these walls to fill a post which is essen⁺ially that of senior master."

Briarman looked up for a moment straight at the headmaster, as if to indicate he was listening respectfully, and then quickly looked down again.

"I am not yet in a position to say anything about the second post."

Mitchley had gone red in the face. With an effort he drew his lips tightly over his protruding teeth. Eglinton had taken out his flat cigarette case and was tapping it lightly with his finger nails. Brunt was pushing his close clipped moustache up and down with his lower lip.

Allenside picked up his copy of the Agenda. He invited members of staff to smoke if they wished and then he asked Robinson to read a summary of the Minutes of the last meeting. There was a rustle of noise as the smokers lit up. The tension was relieved. Mitchley whispered with fierce intensity into Glide's ear and it was like steam issuing from a safety valve. Eglinton muttered something to Dell as he offered him a cigarette, but Dell out of his daze of disappointment barely seemed to hear. He even left his charged pipe unlit, poking the bowl with the ball of his thumb until it became quite unsmokable.

Allenside found it painful to look at Dell. It made him acutely uncomfortable to consider the pain his decision had imposed upon the man. Dell would be on his way to Hull the day after tomorrow. Allenside no doubt had given him the most glowing testimonials he could invent. But it was unlikely he would get the job. He wore an injured look that made successful city councillors shy away from him; they shunned the hurt look of failure as if it were leprosy.

Allenside signed the Minutes. Then he read the report on the project of a school council. It was mainly the work of Brunt and Ship, an enthusiastic young physicist who had left at the end of the Christmas term. Allenside said that he assumed most of the staff were still in general agreement with the aims of a school council: to give the boys practical experience of self-government and a sense of sharing in the administration of the school. I could never tell him that most of the staff found the idea distasteful; and none of them dared admit it. In a way it was up to Allenside to find out such things for himself. Could he not see now that Mitchley would have loved to oppose the whole notion? The way the thin form was bunched up and held in by elbows dug into the back of his chair.

Eglinton's opposition was more subtle. Having expressed his admiration of the report, he suggested amendments which would mean watering the council down to an ineffectual debating society closely guarded by four or even five members of the staff. In addition to a staff chairman he suggested house-masters should be ex-officio members of the Council. Downs said he would like to second Mr. Eglinton's proposals, and then like a rabbit that has rashly ventured to the centre of a busy road he scuttled back to his obscure burrow of silence.

Visot opposed the amendment. So did Mr. Thorpe, a young man who always blushed at the sound of his own voice, and so did Robinson, for some reason beyond my understanding, unless of course he actually approved of Brunt's scheme, which I found difficult to believe. Another difference between Allenside and me: he took everyone's disinterested behaviour for granted. He systematically thought the best of everyone. I do not mean that he lived in a fool's paradise. He was probably more acutely aware of human depravity than I was. 'Thinking the best of everyone' was a standard rule for his own behaviour. Like all good men he was more possessed with the correction of his own faults and weaknesses than the desire to linger (as I so often did) with leisurely assurance over those follies and shortcomings of his fellows from which he himself did not suffer.

We talked for some time to no particular purpose. It was clear enough to me that the majority of the staff were waiting for Allenside to disclose his views before bringing their own into the open, while Allenside, considering himself a thorough chairman, waited to express what he felt would be the feeling of the majority of the meeting. It was like a Cabinet meeting in which ministers under-rate the Premier's disinterestedness and open mind concerning the subject under discussion, and keeping in mind how much their own fortunes depend on the Prime Minister's goodwill, wait too long for some indication of his viewpoint in their anxiety to please and to avoid making a false step.

Eventually the headmaster proposed that there should be a staff chairman and that there should not be more than two members of staff present at Council meetings at any given time, in the capacity of silent observers. This suggestion was at once adopted. Only Mitchley, a look of martyrdom screwing up his thin face, and Dell, whose thoughts seemed elsewhere, did not raise their hands. Downs lifted a listless right hand which he let drop as soon as he felt the Head was not looking.

We proceeded to elect a member of staff to act as Chairman. Our interest in the meeting revived. Eglinton and Mitchley, to name only two, would do all they could to keep the job from Brunt. Visot and Thorpe would be equally keen to keep out Eglinton. Hawkes, Dell, who was beginning to show a flicker of renewed interest, and myself would abhor the notion of Briarman getting the job. Visot, seconded by Robinson, proposed Brunt. Mr. Glide, who seemed to swallow as he pronounced the name, proposed Briarman. After a slight pause, he was seconded by Leggitt, the P.T. Instructor who usually slept in the corner on Allenside's left and almost out of his view. Leggitt's snooze was traditionally overlooked, and we all smiled to hear his voice. Leggitt grinned and recrossing his legs settled himself comfortably in his chair. He usually came into his own swopping blue stories with Bill Hawkes, in what amounted to a competitive exhibition.

Then Eglinton proposed me and was seconded at once by Mr. Dell, now fully revived and speaking at his weightiest. Allenside suggested that to avoid embarrassment we should vote by ballot.

While he and Robinson were counting the paper slips the telephone rang. Eglinton, who sat nearest, lifted the receiver. Everyone watched him as if each were expecting a personal message they were anxious to hear and yet reluctant in such a place and at such a time, to take. I hoped it wasn't Helen.

"For you, sir." Eglinton held the receiver out in Allenside's direction.

"Allenside speaking." He made his voice sound brisk and discouraging. I thought I detected a woman's voice. He turned away from us all and bent as if to listen more closely. Politely we all began quiet conversations with our neighbours. When he put down the receiver and turned around I was struck by the pallor of his face. He returned to his chair. Robinson pushed along a slip of paper showing the result of the count. I thought Allenside studied it, head downwards, for longer than was necessary.

Raising his head he said: "Mr. Flint has been elected Staff Chairman of the School Council." He smiled at me. "I suppose we should congratulate you Mr. Flint, and hope that you won't find the burden of office too·unbearably heavy."

There was general laughter. Everyone seemed reasonably satisfied with the result. No one seemed as surprised as I was, although after my first blush of self-satisfaction I realised it was the intense desire to keep the other two out that had put me in.

"Yes, Mr. Brunt?"

Mr. Brunt wanted to speak.

"I merely wanted to say Mr. Chairman," (in staff meetings Brunt always addressed the headmaster as Mr. Chairman) "that Mr. Flint can count on me for any support or assistance he feels he may need."

Allenside nodded with hurried approval and went on to the next item on the Agenda: what to do with Penge? Was he to be removed, or allowed to stay, or was there some other alternative? How should he advise the Authority who would ultimately decide? As his form master I gave my views first. Then Mitchley, Eglinton and Brunt entered into an open competition for displaying the greatest educational wisdom. Beginning with 'I've done everything I could for that boy, no one could do more' Mitchley spoke at length of the disappointment the lad had been to him. Brunt said what Penge needed was love. 'It's obvious,' Brunt said impatiently, 'the boy's absolutely craving for it.' Eglinton, staking all on a burst of honesty, said, 'Quite frankly I could never find it in me to love the little horror. And I doubt if any of us could. For the sake of the rest of the school, he ought to go.'

I was impressed by the intensity with which Allenside followed the discussion. He always gave polite attention to everything we said, but now he listened intently to every word, as if he were Penge's father, or even Penge himself, looking hungrily around the faces of his judges for one cooling drop of mercy. In the end I proposed we should give him another chance at the Bilateral; also recommending that he should be

135

taken from his uneasy foster parents and placed in some convenient institution as near at hand as possible.

Allenside plodded on conscientiously through the remainder of the Agenda. Whatever it was that weighed upon his mind, he was determined not to let it interfere with his duties. But the result was to make his progress painfully slow. Most of the staff had become bored and impatient long before we had finished. I imagined the groans and curses of universal disapproval that would rend the air in the room, in the corridor, in the lavatories, once he was out of earshot. I longed for him to reach the end quickly for his own sake. I was tempted to go and whisper in his ear *"For God's sake, old man, step on it."* If I had done, he probably would not have minded, but I was not prepared to take the risk. At last it ended. Most of the staff ostentatiously hastened about collecting their things. Eglinton and Hawkes galloped off noisily to catch their trams. Allenside collected his papers slowly and neatly.

"Mr. Flint."

"Yes?"

Brunt and Dell from their different positions in the room were listening.

"Could you call in my room before you leave?"

I guessed it was something to do with the phone call. Could it be something about Roger? When the staff-room had emptied, I hurried along to Allenside's office. I found him standing by the window. It was half-past four. The sky was blue but no sunlight lightened his office. His room had only the morning sun.

He turned around. "Is that you, David? The most extraordinary thing has happened. My son Howard has run away from school."

XV

IN MY RECOLLECTION, Howard Allenside was not a very impressive looking boy. I had seen him last during the Easter holidays. He had emerged at his father's bidding from beneath their car, clad in greasy overalls, his adolescent face and recalcitrant hair smeared with sump oil. He regarded the world with an unnecessarily suspicious and defensive look.

He appeared again at tea time, washed and brushed up, but any confidence his overalls and spanners had given him had also been removed. His mother spoke to him as if he was one of her admirers who did not always come up to expectations; and at the same time she spoke to me about him with critical frankness, as if the boy himself had not been there.

"I'm afraid Howard doesn't take great delight in academic studies, David," she said. And a little later: "It's rather a worry sometimes, what will become of him. He shows no interest at all in books. I can't understand it. It isn't as if his father and I were a pair of morons. . . ."

"I don't know, Janet," Allenside interrupted. "We're not all that intelligent. It's soon enough to judge Howard. By the way he's shaping now, he seems certain to become a Nuffield the Second, or at least an Emperor of Austin Sevens."

I was not sure how much the boy appreciated his father's defence. But it was obvious that his mother's strictures were a familiar agony. She could not reconcile herself to the fact that her darling boy was not a happy combination of her own brilliance with the more solid virtues of her husband. It was impossible that she had given birth to anything less than a genius. She recoiled from any sign of backwardness on the boy's part as though from a physical disfigurement.

Allenside asked me if I would like to accompany him to Bearings. He thought I would find it an interesting place. Characteristically he controlled his worry by considering me. I telephoned the flat, but Helen was not in. We drove out to

Bearings after a hasty unpalatable tea in the school canteen.

It was delightful to get out into the country. The new leaves perched on their branches like small green birds assembled together after an arduous migration. The grass in the ditches having outgrown its first strength leaned over to catch the dust that rose from the road. When we arrived at the Lodge, the gravel of the drive crunched in a friendly familiar way beneath the car's tyres. Ayrshire cattle grazing the rich green of the Park, remarked our progress with patrician indifference, content within their own glossy brown and white beauty.

One would have thought it was a good place for a boy to be in. There were no houses anywhere in sight and even the school, red brick and Virginia creeper, was partially hidden by successive planes of trees and tall hedges.

The evening light emphasised the space between objects: the clear air embraced each green form, passed between blades of grass and curled about the surface of stones and tree trunks, separating each individual object more efficiently than any index system; and the same air fixed the meaningful entity beneath the hard sky; a sky softened to some extent at each horizon by piled up clouds, which were castellated, yet smoother than mountains and permeated with light.

It was difficult to believe that Allenside had been mistaken in placing his son in such stimulating surroundings. Away from a house-infested suburb and a nagging mother, the boy would have time and breathing space to feel for and find the frontiers of his own personality; to find a basis for self-reliance and independence. I would have liked to offer him some comfort now by re-affirming this. But the thoughtful silence we shared on the way out was difficult to break. The boy had to acquire independence. The view, which we shared, that there was no justification for the freedom of the individual unless he was able to make right decisions, demanded this. For this occasion, I was all Allenside; the elastic virtue of sympathy allowed me to put myself in his place. It was strange to think I had a son of my own. I found it much easier to think clearly about Allenside's fatherhood than my own, which was so vague as almost to be non-existent.

As a reasonable opening, I asked Allenside about the school. He was glad enough to speak.

"Bearings was started by this chap Templeton in Hampstead. When he saw the war coming he was smart enough to get hold of this place. They've been here ever since. He sold the house in Hampstead for four thousand odd to the Ministry of something or other and he bagged this place for three thousand."

"Smart lad," I said. "An educationalist with his eyes open."

Allenside smiled. "He has a pose of woolly other-worldliness, but he's as shrewd as if he'd been nursed on the Stock Exchange. He's quite a character. I hope you get a glimpse of him."

"Perhaps he'd do for *Best,*" I said. Allenside raised his eyebrows. "An American magazine which runs a feature called *The Most Curious Man I Ever Met.*"

Allenside smiled, "My Uncle James had a story about a cook who consecrated himself Archbishop of the Azores. Do you think that would do?" He wasn't without the family humour.

"I think that must be the kind of thing they are after."

We drew up in front of the house, at the edge of the lawn facing the way we had come. Someone was practising the piano in a room on the first floor above the door. The music stopped while the player ran to the window and then started up again. On the lawn, a few yards away from the car, a long haired young man with a tweed coat over his shoulders sat on a low stool, a drawing board resting on his knees. He regarded us with an impersonal stare as we emerged from the car. Allenside lifted an arm in greeting. The young man frowned. His features were made even more hawk-like when he opened his long thin mouth to speak.

"If you are looking for Templeton, Allenside"—his voice was high, cold and precise—"he's not here. He's bloody well gone."

Allenside introduced us. "I'd like you to meet David Flint. David writes novels. David, this is Rupert Martingale. Rupert is the resident poet and painter."

"Delighted," Rupert said with stony indifference. "Of course you know the novel is no longer taken seriously as an art form?"

Allenside was looking expectantly at the house. I didn't quite know what answer to make.

Rupert rose to his feet. He was so thin he gave the impression of being unusually tall, but in fact Allenside was quite two inches taller.

"I've been working for some time now," Rupert said, "on a sonnet sequence about birth and death. Would you like to hear it?" He smiled at me suddenly: a surprisingly attractive smile. "You look intelligent I think. This is the first sonnet, the form is a modification of my own. '*Out of the fissured tomb the gutted unction's lingering odours come. No dolmen or maenhir dare now deny. . . .*'"

Allenside said: "Did you say Templeton was away?"

Rupert frowned. "I really think you ought to listen. I really do. It is the least one can expect."

He bent to pick up his board, and marched towards the house. His shoes were too big for him and as he walked they revealed great holes in his black silk socks.

Allenside smiled. "He's rather Lewis Carroll, Rupert, isn't he? I shouldn't have interrupted him really. If Templeton isn't here we'd better find Taylor. He's the Bursar. He rang Janet up to say Howard was missing. Janet wanted to phone the police at once. But I felt it would be wiser if we made some inquiries first."

Most of the rooms in the house were barely furnished, with polished wooden floors. In the library which seemed very well stocked with books, a young girl sat at a desk, possibly acting as librarian. She was writing letters.

"Where is everyone?" Allenside asked her.

"There's a General Meeting," the girl explained. "In the gym. It's about Food. The food's been ghastly this last week. Templeton has taken the cook with him to Italy and we've had a woman in from the village who doesn't know the difference between a cabbage and a potato."

As we walked on a boy came rushing at us at top speed. I caught him in my arms.

"Somebody after you?" I asked.

"Excuse me." The boy's voice squeaked breathlessly. "I'm late you see. Rupert will be waiting. It's time to open the kiln."

The boy raced on. We walked on until we came to the doors of the gymnasium. They would not open. There seemed to be a press of bodies on the other side. Allenside knocked softly at first; and then much harder. The door opened and for a moment we had a glimpse of tables arranged in a circle at which boys and girls of varied ages were sitting. The rest of the school seemed to be crowded around them like spectators at a great roulette table. A tall boy was on his feet, outlining the best way to boil potatoes for one hundred and forty people. A plump youthful-looking man wearing corduroy slacks and sandals and a coloured shirt, with rolled up sleeves that displayed plumb freckled arms, slipped out and closed the door softly behind him. He smiled at us in a brisk business-like way.

"Mr. Allenside, isn't it? You know I telephoned Mrs. Allenside." His accent was faintly north-country. "I am sorry about this business. Shall we go to my office?"

We went through a door on which was printed in small black letters *T. Taylor. Bursar's Office.* Taylor showed us where to sit and gave us cigarettes, while he himself sat on his desk, with his feet on his chair, and began to fill his pipe. He was studiously informal, as if in such a home of Freedom and Culture he were rather ashamed of his own efficiency.

"I really haven't much to add to what I've already said to Mrs. Allenside. As you know everyone here has so much freedom we can't easily account for their movements although we watch their development closely enough. Howard just left. He just packed his bags and walked out. There's nothing to stop any of them doing that. I can't guess how he managed to transport all his luggage without attracting our attention to what he was doing. It is possible that someone met him with a car. Or, of course, he could have taken the stuff to the station piece by piece in the Chev. As you know he is our school mechanic. Everybody acknowledged his wizardy with cars."

It rather suggested that Howard wasn't any good at anything else.

"He wouldn't be old enough to have a driving licence, would he?" I said.

"Nobody round here would notice that," Taylor laughed easily, "especially if he was in his overalls. And Howard spent as much time as he could in them. We didn't object of course. We saw they gave him ease and confidence."

I nodded as if I had understood his point. Taylor had a way

of laughing after each statement he made that deftly suggested the truth of his statement was self-evident and you were very dull indeed if you did not see it.

"Young Terence Wavertree who has the next bed to Howard said he'd been talking a lot about his uncle lately. I wonder whether you've contacted him?"

"Which uncle?" Allenside sounded astonished. "My brother you mean?"

"Yes." Taylor laughed.

"Has he been here then?"

"Yes. Quite often these last few weeks. We were always glad to see him. He seemed to do Howard tremendous good. Brought him out of himself. They were great friends."

Allenside was so lost in thought, he merely nodded his head at Taylor's last remarks. He rose to his feet.

"There's nothing more we can do here now, is there?"

Taylor walked with us through the corridors to the front door.

"I'm sorry this has happened just now, especially since I am in charge."

Allenside said absently, "What does Templeton want in Italy?"

"Chickens."

"I beg your pardon?"

"Chickens." Taylor laughed, this time I thought a little bitterly. "He wants to breed chickens on the shores of Lago di Maggiore."

"Not a bad idea," I said.

"In itself no." Taylor's laugh grew still shorter and less hearty. "But he's losing interest in the school."

"In what way?" I asked.

"He forgets things. Forgets to give a lesson, forgets to take out a walking party, forgets to give me my cheque, forgets to pay the staff."

"Dear me." Allenside was puzzled and worried.

"And what is more awkward still," Taylor was laughing freely again now he had seen how perturbed Allenside had become, "he wants to sell the house."

"Has he had an offer?" I asked.

"A firm of Custard Manufacturers have offered nine thousand."

"What on earth do they want it for?"

"As an egg-farm. And they'll use most of the house for storing sugar. I've made a memorandum, Mr. Allenside, about all this. I intend to circularise the parents and directors. I hope to call a general meeting soon."

Allenside nodded approvingly. We got into the car. I noticed Rupert looking down operatically from an upstairs window. He still wore his coat over his shoulders. I wanted to ask Allenside what would be emerging now out of the fissured tombs, but he looked too worried for such persiflage.

Allenside said casually to Taylor when we were about to leave, "When was my brother here last? You don't happen to remember?"

"Sometime last week I should say. He came fairly often and of course I may not have seen him every time."

"I see," Allenside nodded gravely. "Howard may have gone to stay with him. We'll soon find out. Goodbye now."

We drove off.

XVI

I WAS ABLE TO GIVE Allenside his brother's address. I was tempted, too, to tell him about Roger's behaviour with Helen perhaps hoping he would kill two birds with one stone and save me the trouble of quarrelling with Roger. I never did like quarrelling with anyone. It's the chief reason why I always take so much pains to be amiable with everyone I know. If I find myself unable to be amiable with anyone, I take pains to avoid him.

A Quarrel: that was what I imagined it would be like. Allenside would take firm hold of Howard, and then tell Roger what he thought of him; and I would stand behind Allenside, nearer the door, and perhaps have my word about Helen as a Parthian shot, just before we left. Roger would say nothing and smile in a provoking way behind clouds of cigarette smoke.

But I did not tell him of Roger's encounter with Helen. I felt the poor chap had enough to worry about at the moment. Perhaps an opportunity would come later, when we had found Howard.

"It's rather revealing," Allenside said on the way back (he drove faster than I found comfortable; but my faith in him was sufficient re-assurance) "to have a problem child on your own hearth." And a little later he said: "I have always regarded problem children as a reflection on their parents."

He was taking too much blame upon himself. His wife was to blame. Allenside was to be pitied for having so unfortunate a wife. During the war, when Allenside had been away, the stupid woman had assiduously laid the foundation of their misfortune: with hourly persistence she had built up this ant-heap of misery. What could Allenside do more than he was already doing; suffering her folly, allowing her to prick at his nerves with the needle of her thwarted ambitions, meeting unflinchingly the daily impact of her scalding vulgarity. My own cowardice was a measure of the submerged depths of his courage. I had fled before the menace of an uncongenial home; but compared with Janet, Phyllis was pale and inoffensive. Of course, I had no real knowledge of her; only the vague memories of dissatisfaction. Had our marriage continued to develop, it might well have grown into some quiet hell like this; a damnation transfusion, dripping drop by daily drop. Considering the misfortunes of our close friends, we sometimes become ashamed of our own petty and undeserved comforts, and forget the crushing afflictions under which we groaned the moment before. Thinking of Allenside, as the car swept down the Edgware Road, I counted myself lucky until shame of my own exemption from suffering overtook me and I became restless to make amends to Fortune by taking upon myself voluntarily some misery equal to his.

It was dark when we reached the Embankment. The light from the street lamps writhed in gleaming brassy ropes across the heaving surface of the incoming tide.

We took the lift to the third floor and I felt I was making some contribution to Allenside's support when I rang the bell.

Howard opened the door. He was wearing a yellow polo jersey that obviously belonged to his uncle. His ears glowed red from vigorous washing, like a mechanic's. He did not seem surprised to see his father. The boy was taller than I had expected him to be. He stood confidently still and looked straight at his father. Allenside frowned. Confidence was what the boy needed of course, but this seemed rather an absurd exaggeration. No doubt Howard was thinking himself enormously clever. He'd given everybody a shock; made a real impression. He had something to crow about. From one extreme to the other, from debasement to exaltation: a common phenomenon. Schoolmasterly thinking.

Roger appeared at the end of the corridor, actually smoking. "Aren't you going to ask them in, Howard?"

No doubt Roger was enjoying the situation. This was his flat and he knew more than his brother did about Howard's movements. For Allenside, and for me, his sympathetic shadow, an embarrassing position. The large flat wasn't very clean.

It was mostly in use after dark, when shaded lights smoothed over dust and stains. Something about the place suggested orgies, the combination of luxurious fittings and disorder and dust. My curiosity, like that of the reader of a Sunday scandal sheet, was roused; saliva in a dog's mouth before a heaped plate. Here, there had been the kind of parties part of me would have enjoyed watching. It is a rare comfort to sin second-hand. I doubt if the flat had been cleaned since I was last in it. The dust had been undisturbed or trampled on so long it had begun to turn into dirt. The bathroom door was ajar and I caught a glimpse of an array of empty bottles under the bath. It was an incongruous setting for a family conference.

"I came here myself," Howard explained coolly. "I wanted Roger to help me find a job."

"Suppose you tell me first," Allenside spoke as lightly as he could, "why you just walked out of Bearings."

The boy had reached some decision that gave him an assurance Allenside had not seen him use before. He spoke with careful adult formality as if he were anxious to explain things as simply as he knew how to.

"I don't think that school is any good for me, Father. It's all right for arty sort of intellectuals and bookish types I suppose, but not for me. I'm not that sort and nothing will ever make me be. I'm interested in engines, but I'm not good enough at Maths to make a scientist, but I am a good mechanic. Everyone says so."

"We won't discuss that for the moment." Allenside would never have used so unsympathetic a tone to a boy at school. With his own son, he was too involved to be able to maintain objective control over his own reactions. "What exactly did you think you were doing, just walking out without any warning or explanation? Didn't you realise you would cause everyone a lot of trouble?"

"I thought of writing you a letter," Howard said, still surprisingly calm, "but you know how poor I am putting things down on paper. I thought this would be the best way of showing you and Mother what I wanted."

I had a glimpse of Janet over the teacups saying 'If only he had some idea of what he wanted.' This interview should have been for Janet. It was unfair that she should escape. It was totally unfair that Allenside should have to bear it.

"But why bother your Uncle? It was hardly fair on him, dragging him into it, was it?"

"I thought Uncle Roger could help me get the kind of job I wanted. I know I'll never be any good at academic stuff.

I thought Roger could introduce me to something in the motor trade."

"It didn't occur to you that your mother and I would have liked to be consulted."

"Mummy treats me like a backward child. I know I'm a disappointment to you both."

The fragile skin of newly acquired composure was beginning to crack. Howard sat up straight in the centre of the deep, stained settee—which I imagined had lulled so many women into a sense of false security—his palms pressed into the soft cushions and his chin buried in the absurd neck of the yellow polo jersey.

"You know that's rot." Allenside got to his feet. He needed time to think. This wasn't a boy any more. The slow process of growing up had been fast enough after all to catch him unprepared. The progressive school had become too narrow a space in which to shelve this problem. "It's time we went home. It's getting late."

"I'm not going back to Bearings, am I?" Howard expected a decision not a postponement. He had keyed himself up for a show down, not for carrying on as if nothing extraordinary had happened. "Honestly, I don't want to go back. I hate the place."

"We'll see."

"Roger can find me a good job, can't you Roger? You say I'm not cut out for the academic stuff don't you. You know I've got a flair for machines. It's my gift that Mummy is always worrying about."

"You've sprung this rather suddenly. We haven't really had time to think, have we?"

"If you're going to send me back," Howard glared determinedly at the empty grate, "I'd rather not come home."

"Don't be so melodramatic."

"Roger could easily get me a job if you were willing. He said so, didn't you, Roger?"

"Better get your things. And take that polo jersey off. Your mother wouldn't like to see you in it."

When he used a conciliatory tone, it came too late.

"Come on old boy. Try and be reasonable . . ." Before Allenside could finish the boy had already rushed blindly out of the room.

Allenside began to move after him.

"Best to leave him alone," Roger said. "Have a cigarette." He held out his case. Allenside shook his head.

"I rang up Janet, some time ago. She was relieved to know the boy was safe. She told me you had gone out to the school. I was wondering whether I'd run him home myself or wait until you came here. He seems to have had a lift into town with a fruit lorry. He walked here from Knightsbridge. The boy's got guts."

Roger seemed to take the view that Howard's adventure was a very creditable affair.

"I understand you have been visiting Howard quite a lot recently. Is it you who put this notion of running away into his head?" Allenside stared angrily at his brother.

"That's most unfair." Roger looked genuinely injured. "I admit I think that place is a crack-pot institution and I think the lad would be better employed in a gas-works, but I've never made any suggestions at all to him about his future."

"Why did you go there to see him in the first place? How did you find out he was at Bearings?"

"Lady Mu told me."

"Lady Mu?"

"Lady Muriel Whiteway. I always call her Lady Mu; she likes it. She said Janet was worried about him; he didn't seem to have the family brains." Roger grinned.

"But why did you go to see him?" Allenside seemed to compel Roger to make straightforward answers. As if they were boys again who knew each other so well, subterfuge and disguise were quite useless. Anyone would have thought Edward was the elder brother. "Why couldn't you leave him alone?"

"Curiosity, at first." Roger seemed unusually truthful. "He was Peter's age. I wanted to see. Just curiosity. But I took a liking to the lad. A real liking. It's true about his flair you know, Edward. Quite seriously I'd be very glad to help him. I have an interest in a new garage in Shepherd's Bush and I have good connections in the car trade. Some of these big firms run excellent courses, and award diplomas and things. It would be much better for the lad you know. It's what he wants definitely."

Roger glanced at me as if he were about to ask my support. Hastily I looked at a coffee stain on the carpet.

Allenside was unrelenting.

"You don't expect me to take all that on face-value, do you Roger. If Howard was entering any firm with which you had connections, there would be certain preparatory investigations I would want to make first."

Roger flushed angrily. "You don't believe I am genuinely interested in the boy do you. I like him a lot. He's got fine stuff in him."

"If you were so interested in his welfare," Allenside said, "you might have thought fit to contact his parents some time ago. You seem to have gone out of your way to keep your friendship with Howard a close secret."

"I was trying to be tactful," Roger said. "I had begun to tell Lady Mu of my interest in the boy so that she could pass it on to Janet and to you. I thought it was the better kind of approach. By the way, I hear rumours that you are due for a new promotion. Whiteway speaks highly of you. But he isn't entirely happy about your politics."

Allenside was in no mood for conciliation, especially on Roger's terms. Everything Roger said seemed to goad him to more intense anger.

"I'd like you to understand Roger, quite clearly, that you are to leave Howard completely alone. I consider your influence on him now would be the most undesirable thing that could happen to him. I hope I am making myself perfectly clear."

I never heard Allenside sound so deliberately nasty.

Roger said, "You sound just like Uncle James."

"It's a pity you never listened more to Uncle James. It's because you could never tolerate any form of criticism that you've made such a success of deceiving yourself." A conciliatory note entered Allenside's voice. "When will you bring yourself to face things as they are and not as you wish them to be?"

"Let's not have a lecture." Roger glanced at me. "Is he like this with the boys? You've no idea Eddie how sanctimonious you sound."

Allenside called his son. When the boy entered the room, he was carrying a small suitcase. Allenside relieved him of it.

We left Roger after the briefest of 'good nights.' When we were going through the door Roger called my name. I paused and looked back. If he beckoned me I determined to shake my head and slam the door.

"I rang your flat this afternoon, about tea-time. You weren't in."

"No," I said, feebly. "Well, it's getting late, isn't it. Good night."

I hurried after Allenside and his son. I wanted to get into the back of the car so that the boy should sit next to his father. I watched them as we drove away. The wall of silence was difficult to break. The boy stared straight ahead. The first thing Allenside would need to do would be to establish contact on some new more cordial basis, and do so before they got home: some understanding with which to face Janet. Allenside spoke once or twice; the lad answered with a monosyllable. Allenside could not touch the boy across the wide abyss of misunderstanding. Sitting alone in the dark back of the saloon I was witnessing the dumb agony of a parent whose child refused to have applied to him the resources of his love. If Allenside placed his hand now on the boy's narrow shoulders it would not be a father's friendly touch Howard would feel but the heavy policing interfering hand arresting his free flight. From now on Allenside would be compelled to exercise the patience and the cunning of a hunter to regain the boy's affection. I did not doubt that he would succeed, although in this brief encounter, his over-wrought nerves had sent the elusive game flying out of his reach, like a gun going off too soon. I wondered much what Allenside would do.

Janet would be no help to him. She was too intent on her social climbing. If he asked my advice what would I say? I would have loved nothing more than to help him. I would spend day after day devising endless schemes to capture Howard's erring spirit.

But when he drew up alongside the entrance to the flat in Kensington, he seemed self-absorbed and distant in a way that I had never seen him use with me before. I realised then he would never ask my advice. He had withdrawn in some indefinable way from the intimacy we shared, as if what I had witnessed that night had erected some new limit to our friendship, I would not be allowed to cross. He was deliberately isolating himself. In order to do better battle for the soul of his son with sharp unblinking vigilance, he was denying himself his former consolations and comforts. I was too saddened by Allenside's predicament to resent the personal loss such a withdrawal would mean to me. Because a man, preoccupied with literary ambitions cannot afford many friends, the few he has are all the more valuable to him. But when his car had gone, and I found myself standing alone on the deserted pavement a sudden flood of self-pity welled up inside me bringing me to the verge of tears. I raised my arm as if to call back Allenside and his burdens to populate the desolation in which I dwelt, to mitigate my limitless isolation. This was God's country and He had left it. Then suddenly a couplet presented itself in my mind

> *Knock, Son of God, I am alone*
> *And unentangled as a single stone.*

My spirits rose as I repeated the words to myself, as if they were some trinket upon which I had stumbled in the desert of self-pity. Going up the stairs I resolved to begin work on something new at the first opportunity. There was some kind of salvation to be found in words.

XVII

THE FLAT WAS EMPTY. The note Helen left to account for
her impulses as if they were thoughtful and considerate
actions, was rather longer than usual.

*I'm sorry David, I can't tolerate London a moment longer. I hoped
you would have been home in time to take me to the station. I'm
catching the six-thirty down to Boscombe. Roger Allenside telephoned
this afternoon. He wanted to know whether I was prepared to reconsider his 'offer'! I warned him you would deal with him. I telephoned Buss and he advised a complaint to the police. I don't know.
What do you think? Give up this teaching business David and come
down to Boscombe as soon as you can. Buss says the divorce may take
another two or three months. Your wife isn't being very co-operative.
There are lots of things in B. I must attend to. I want to see how
Sigrid and Maureen are settling down at their new school. Come as
soon as you can. I don't know when I shall be able to face London
again. Love, Helen.*

It seemed as if a postcard régime was to be reinstituted:
I did not dwell on the possibility that Helen was trying to
force my hand, it was so delightful to have the place to myself
again; I walked around the flat light-heartedly as if I had been
restored possession. I left all the doors open and marched
solemnly around like a parson beating the bounds of his parish.
I poured myself a glass of sherry, but set it on the table untouched while I executed an absurd gig on the carpet, lifting
my knees and kicking the air, collapsing on the floor in
attempting a clumsy somersault—delighted to have hurt my
shoulder so that I could rub it energetically and feel newly
awakened. I wanted to measure the flat from outer wall to
wall in feet, my own feet. Before finishing I had become bored
and ashamed of my little orgy. It was disgusting to be so
delighted merely because every problem was shelved, to be
so ready to drift on in smug irresponsibility and empty independence, without the inclination even to sin more than was
necessary to wrap me in a cocoon of convenient oblivion. It

was as if I hoped my passivity would exempt me from the agony of attempting to act whatever my conscience nagged at me to do.

I slept late next morning and I had to rush off to school without any breakfast. I took the underground because I hoped it would be faster, and I clattered down the steps at Gloucester Road just as the doors of a District Line train were closing. Four minutes were wasted fuming up and down the platform and gazing stupidly at large adverts for beer and bleach.

I arrived at school sweating uncomfortably just in time to teach. The boys were already trouping out of Assembly. I apologised to Allenside who smiled and nodded—efficiency I thought is the most marvellous of all masks, nothing is shown except the well-controlled smile of the man beneath, and rushed off to Room 20 where the waiting form was already growing noisy. I pushed in the doorway, spectacularly grim, allowing my eye to travel sternly from face to face until the room was completely silent. It was a kind of game really: I was the fierce master who would unhesitatingly devour the first boy who dared to speak, and they were spectators who enjoyed the pantomime devil's frightening actions. I enjoyed class teaching: it was a parlour game in which you were boss at your own party and at which everyone had to play the way you liked. It was a way of earning a living; and teaching scripture could be even something more. I was planting the Law and the Prophets like the seeds of revolution in row after row of suburban gardens. It was more effective than if I stole out at night and pasted on three hundred front door windows posters in capitals which read *THE LORD REIGNETH*.

During the break when I bustled into the staff-room in search of my morning coffee, I found Brunt, Briarman, Glide, Robinson and Hawkes assembled about Visot, all registering the disturbed sympathy colleagues bestow upon an injured brother. Visot, who held his coffee cup in both hands, sipped with the heroic fortitude of a sufferer who has steeled himself to suffer more.

"It's damnable," Brunt was saying, his face red with indignation.

"What's up?" I said, joining the group.

"A witch hunt," Hawkes said grimly. "That's what it is."

"It's degrading to think of it happening here." Glide swallowed authoritatively. "I mean to say what's the use of talking about free institutions. . . ."

"Victimisation," Hawkes said. "I've seen it happen often enough in industry."

"What's up?" I said again.

Visot explained patiently. "I've been asked to attend the Governors' meeting. It's about a letter Bansdale's father has written to Lord Whiteway apparently about Communist influence in the school."

"Oh!" I looked as surprised as I could.

"Allenside could have squashed the whole thing right in the beginning," Brunt said darkly. "If he were a strong head-master he would tell Whiteway to go to hell."

"How were you notified?" I asked Visot.

"A letter from the clerk to the Governors"—Visot tapped his breast pocket—"was waiting for me in the rack this morning."

"But he didn't tell Whiteway to go to hell." Brunt pursued his theory. "Why? Because he's interested in the Directorship of the New Institute. I heard his name mentioned several times at County Hall last Saturday morning. Naturally he won't want to damage his good-will with Lord Whited-Sepulchre."

"That's completely unfair," I burst out, suddenly enraged at the thought that Allenside would forfeit his chances for the job he wanted in order that this Brunt should get his special responsibility allowance. They all seemed to be looking at me and I became suddenly tongue-tied and embarrassed. Mitchley had joined us and was swivelling his long neck around enquiringly.

Brunt regarded me coldly. "It's a fair deduction from the known facts. Or do you know more than we do?"

I longed to shout, "*Why don't you say this to his face? You creeping licker.*" But it wouldn't have been any use. It wouldn't have done Allenside any good. I lacked the nerve to create a row. I remained silent.

"It should be put in the hands of the Union right away," Glide said, "on the highest possible level."

Robinson had been thinking sternly for some time, frowning into space, working out the problem. Now he spoke.

"My advice to you Visot, is not to go."

Hawkes said excitedly as if he saw what Robinson was after, "That's it, exactly. Don't go."

"You are in no way obliged to attend," Robinson went on as if he had not been interrupted. "You could either send them a short note declining the invitation, or just not go. I think I would advise the former course."

Brunt was nodding approvingly. Now most of the staff were listening, even Downs and Dell who had been talking confidentially in a far corner of the room. Eglinton was out on corridor duty and Thorpe had not yet come in. His coffee looked cold beneath the skin that had formed on its surface.

"You see," Robinson said, "once you step inside a meeting like that you have committed yourself. You can't very well sit there with your lips firmly shut. And if you once say something, make an answer—even assuming your eloquent tongue doesn't run away with you"—(we all smiled)—"They've got you, just like that."

Robinson clapped his hands together expressively.

We were all united in our concern for Visot, even Eglinton would have shown some sympathy had he been present. The atmosphere of the room was warm, cordial, fraternal, for the first time for many weeks. Had an appeal been made, each man would have dug deeply into his pocket or pledged himself on solemn oaths to fight in Visot's defence. I heard Dell quote to Downs, 'I don't agree with what you say, but I'll fight to the death to preserve your right to say it.' Downs' mouth was open. He nodded but I doubt if he understood what the phrase meant. He had that atrophied dullness which is peculiar to a certain type of middle-aged teacher who has one eye on the clock and the other on his pension.

The new unity and universal brotherhood was snuffed out by Visot himself. He shook his head slowly.

"No," he said. "I shall go to the meeting."

Advice, protest, criticism, came popping from all quarters. Robinson walked away from Visot's side to put down his empty cup on the tray. Visot stood firm, his heels together. My feeling was in favour of Robinson's suggestions because I thought it would be better for Allenside that way, would avoid an unpleasant clash and perhaps give him a chance to salvage something out of the whole unhappy business. But I could not resist admiring Visot. This was his hour, and nothing was going to deprive him of it; this sweet chance to defy, in the name of the people in the name of justice, the naked force of capitalist power.

"Do you think that would be wise, Jack?" Brunt spoke to Visot but most of us were listening. "There's a great deal in what Robby says, you know. I would be inclined to agree with him."

Visot shook his head firmly. Brunt did not press the point. Brunt may have had his special responsibility post in mind. I would have liked to see them discuss the problem in private. Brunt had a far more impressive public façade than Visot, but in the long run Visot was by far the stronger man. His was the view that would prevail in the making of policy and decisions because it was born by dedicated perception out of steely strength of character. Visot, butt as he was of every schoolboy's pimpled wit, had something of the authentic stamp of greatness. Sooner or later the fiery Brunt would compromise. His patience would give out, his personal ambition would demand fulfilment, the opportunity he could not bear to let pass would come his way. '*A headship will give you so much greater scope in working for the cause,*' temptation would successfully whisper. He would degenerate from a trusted member to fellow traveller and ultimately drop out into a suburban semi-detached house paying his mortgage, reading *The Daily Herald*, often bewildered and miserable and constantly grumbling about the weather.

Visot, I fancied was of sterner stuff. Nothing would change him. He would either go forward to power with the party or be a ready, acceptable sacrifice that the cause might still live. He was a man made to help change the world, or to be crushed by the world's unyielding unwillingness to be changed.

"You've a perfect right to refuse to go," Briarman said indignantly. "In my opinion they had no business to ask you. The Union should take this up at once. It's a test case." Briarman had a gift for using righteous indignation when it was not needed. He liked to be thought of as a straightforward chap and a man who had the interests of the staff at heart. I often wondered what mental adjustment he would have to make if he overheard Hawkes calling him a 'sneak in the grass' or Robinson calling him 'the creeping first mate with a phoney certificate'. He always spoke to Robinson and Hawkes as if they were among his best friends.

"I've done nothing inconsistent with my duty as a teacher. I've committed no crime. It's a deliberate attempt to discredit a teacher because he happens to belong to the Communist Party, and says so openly. I intend to tell them as much. I shall accept their invitation—not without a certain amount of pleasure." Visot banged his empty cup down on the empty tray, looked at his watch with unnecessary calmness and then walked out.

"Good old Vizzy!" Hawkes laughed. He addressed me as the most likely person present to share his point of view. "He's got guts; you must admit that."

I smiled and nodded, but Robinson shook his head soberly and Brunt frowned as if he was still thinking out his attitude to his problem.

"Vizzy versus Vhiteway!" Briarman was ready to join in the fun: but as so often his eagerness to be included blurred his perception of the sentiments we were sharing. He assumed because we were laughing, we took the matter lightly.

I was anxious to discuss the matter with Allenside. I studied him carefully at lunch. He ate quietly, apparently nodding from time to time at what Eglinton and Briarman were saying, but it was obvious to me that his mind was far away. I wondered what had happened to young Howard. What was that fool of a mother saying to him when they were alone in the house all day?

She might even forgive Roger the four hundred pounds and other past misdemeanours if she came to believe that he exercised influence on Lord Whiteway. Allenside had a wife and a son and a brother to contend with. He had to cut his way out of the net their actions threw about him.

I felt that in this school matter I could help him, or at least help to release some of the tension in his mind. But I found it more difficult than I would ever previously have imagined to persuade myself to speak frankly to him. The notion of the previous evening was still strong in my mind, that Allenside had drawn up the bridge and had retired within himself to dedicate himself entirely to coping with his family troubles alone.

We spoke for a short while as we drank our coffee in the staff-room after lunch. It was about the School Council. I was to convene a meeting of a steering committee consisting of Briarman, myself, and three boys to draw up an agenda based on the resolutions sent in by the different forms and groups. Our conversation was formal, and polite, in our usual public manner, but on this occasion I had the uneasy feeling that from now on our conversations on any subject even when in private, would be little different. With an effort, just as he was about to lift himself out of his chair, I said, "Could you spare me a moment or so at four?"

"Yes." He nodded with polite readiness. "Excuse me." He moved across the room for a word with Robinson.

When four o'clock came Miss Symonds told me, not without a certain pleasure, that Mr. Allenside was engaged and would I mind waiting a few minutes. I asked her to tell him I would be waiting in the staff-room.

I never liked hanging about in the staff-room when the rest had gone. Without human beings it seemed an untidy dingy cloakroom with book cupboards instead of wash-basins around the walls. It had something of the deadness of a railway station waiting-room, a room in which to while away a time-tabled day in order to hasten on to a more pleasant tomorrow that will be spent elsewhere. An empty room in the factory into which the hand is led when her headache becomes unbearable. In our society we go out of our way to make the surroundings in which we work as distasteful as possible; no doubt in order to increase the pleasure of escape. Vast sums of money are expended on moving large sections of the population from one place to another on the assumption that to stay in one place would have the ultimate effect of either killing a person or driving him mad.

While I turned over the pages of an illustrated paper and looked with angry boredom at photographs I had seen before, and debated in my mind whether I should bother to read the captions and print inserted around them, Dell came in to collect his hat. Dell sported a green pork-pie with a band of twined piping and a gay feather. In his tweeds, at a reasonable distance, Dell looked like a country gentleman especially when his pipe was in his mouth. It was only at close quarters you could detect the chalk dust in his pores.

"I didn't think you would be in today," I said chattily. "Are you taking the night train to Hull?"

"I'm not going." Dell clapped his hat firmly on his head. "It would be a waste of time. These things are cooked. Wirepulling. There'll be a local man you know. Skerries from the Tech was telling me last night about a fellow he knew in South Wales who had spent four hundred pounds in getting a headship. Oh I'm not saying it's so bad up here. But it's pretty bad everywhere. I'm sick of the whole thing, I can tell you. Good night Flint."

Poor old Dell. He couldn't take another failure. His cure would be to go on trying but to give up wanting, then maybe he'd get it. But was I such a raving success myself? I'd done nothing lately. The Seymour brothers story was a fiasco, an empty flagon. I had no ideas worth working on. I had not even bothered of late to cultivate my literary connections. It was ages since I had entertained. Redvers Cloudspeake of the Third had mentioned asking me to do a programme on Ahab and Elijah but I had heard nothing from him since. No books had been sent on to me for review. I had had no poems printed. I might have been on an icy mountain in Greenland I shivered so much at the revelation of white open spaces of literary isolation. I wanted to rush to a telephone there and then. Why should I worry about Allenside when my own career was at stake? Then I remembered the flat was at my disposal and I decided to have a party again as soon as possible, and my calm was to some extent restored.

Allenside looked in.

"Sorry to keep you David. What shall we do, stay here or go into my office?"

"Better go into your office," I said. "Is Miss Symonds there?"

"No. She's gone."

Allenside closed the door.

"You will probably disapprove of what I've got to say," I said before he could turn to face me again.

"Let me hear it and then I'll let you know."

"It's carrying tales out of school."

"Oh." He became more serious. "Then perhaps you had better not tell me."

"You know Visot has been summoned to appear before the Governors' Meeting."

"Yes. He told me so himself this morning. I told him not to consider himself in any way bound to go."

"That was our advice. But he's made up his mind to go. I think he's ready to make quite a thing about it all."

"I see." Allenside frowned. "Is that what you wanted to tell me?"

"No." I cleared my throat nervously. It was even more difficult than I had imagined. "You told me you intend to see that Brunt got the special responsibility post, even though Whiteway is against it."

"Yes," Allenside nodded. He was probably regretting having told me, but he refrained from showing it.

"Brunt has been saying that you have allowed Whiteway to call Visot to the Governors' Meeting because you want to keep in Whiteway's good books."

Allenside pressed his lips together firmly. I knew he was annoyed with me, and that he was considering now what to say. He was inclined to attach significance to his considered statements and usually took time to make them.

"You were right David," he said at last, "in thinking I would disapprove. I do. Very much."

I spoke now to defend myself.

"I see no point in you throwing away your career for the sake of securing an S.R. for an ungrateful disgruntled malcontent like Brunt."

Allenside looked down at his desk and did not answer.

"I know it must be distasteful to you to have to humour a pompous potentate like Whiteway. But that's the way things are done in this imperfect world." I plunged on desperately. To stop would be to sink. "Even the most upright man must compromise sometimes in order to salvage some decency. It is far more important that you should become director of that institute than that Brunt should collect ninety extra pounds a year."

Allenside smiled suddenly. "I agree with that last statement."

I was all ready to cheer, and to congratulate myself on my sensible intervention. With difficulty I restrained myself from hopping about in front of his desk.

"I've tried to persuade myself along much the same lines. I haven't succeeded. Mr. Brunt isn't as far wrong as you seem to think. He's right enough to make me feel more guilty. It must be Uncle James's fault, making me hunger and thirst after righteousness as earnestly as an evangelical curate."

"It must be a long time since you met a curate," I said. "They talk about the necessity of Dogma now with a capital D and aesthetic ritual and artistic plays and tableaux to be performed before the altar in keeping with the Church's calendar."

"Uncle James was an evangelical low churchman." Allenside smiled happily. This was like the usual tone of our conversations. "In his youth he had wrestled with Darwin like Jacob with the Angel. He claimed to have won but he had a certain vagueness which I fancy was a legacy from the struggle."

At any other time I would have snatched at the opportunity of talking about morals and religion with Allenside. There were so few to whom I could speak of these things with honest and unaffected simplicity. With my literary friends I could become as heated and as excited as I liked in academic apologetics but had I become personal and expressed my own doubts and fears and longings they would have become acutely embarrassed. It was something I would never risk doing with anyone I knew (I might have been able to once with Helen but the kind of familiarity we had achieved did not allow it. All such delicate matters were tacitly postponed until we had reached the haven of marriage) except perhaps Allenside, and not often with him. He had all the Englishman's reticence about discussing the state of his soul. The steely restraint that was the backbone of his high standard of behaviour was equally effective in stiffening his resistance to talk that threatened the privacy of his conscience. His conscience may have been a book in which God inscribed his Will more clearly and distinctly than in mine, but Allenside treated it as a very private diary. I wondered, too, how far his reticence was due to the misfortune of having a foolish wife. There were so many things it would have been disastrous to tell her, he had been compelled to cultivate the habit of keeping his own counsel. Allenside was the decent kind of married man who would tell no one anything he would not tell his wife.

I needed someone to talk to as frankly as possible about right and wrong, and the existence of God, and the nature of Christ, and the salvation of my little soul; but this was not the time or the place. My business now, my mission, was to prevent Allenside from sacrificing his career for the welfare of Mr. Brunt.

"You're wrong about Brunt," I insisted, a nagging note creeping into my voice in spite of myself. "You think he's efficient, keen, disinterested, devoted to the school and the welfare of the school and all that. He isn't really. All he wants, the same as everyone else, is to get on, as fast as possible. He just puts on a noisier and more persistent show that's all."

"You may be right," Allenside said calmly. "I'm not going to discuss this with you David. I can't deal with people's motives. I'm a headmaster, not a novelist. My criterion is the good of the school and my judgement is on results. Brunt deserves the S.R. on results. I'm going to see he gets it. That's all there is to it really. I've got to see to it, or I could never respect myself again. I'm cross with you now, because you are making me say the things that my generation don't approve of saying in so many words. Good intentions put into words are tarnished immediately by the act of expression. Are you coming home?"

We walked together as far as the underground station. We bought evening papers and glanced at the cricket scores.

We had a mutual interest in cricket and we had spent several pleasant Saturday afternoons together at Lord's. Before we parted, Allenside squeezed my arm. Left alone, I walked on to the bus stop considering whether after all I had the right idea about our friendship. In Allenside's view I was a well-meaning little boy. He may have known far more about me than I had ever guessed and given me his tolerant friendship because he felt I was a weak creature that needed it. Men do not look to little boys for advice or comfort. My effort at advice he would regard as the ingenuous outburst of a good-hearted boy more partisan than perceptive. A talent for story telling and word spinning did not necessarily bestow upon me maturity or wisdom. Could it be I was immature or unwise?

Allenside's standpoint was no accident, no outburst of stubborn pride. It was considered, a chosen act to which as to a standard, he was nailing his manhood. My attempt to interfere had bounced off like a tennis ball off a stone wall. I was dismayed and dispirited by my own ineffectiveness. There was a peculiar humiliation in having lived for thirty-three years without exerting more influence on the lives of those around me than an unusually docile boy of six.

XVIII

Eglinton interrupted my lesson with Form IV in Room 30. I was day-dreaming about the sherry party I had in mind, going over a mental list of guests and deciding how to invite them, when he knocked the door lightly. I rose to my feet with guilty speed and moved among the nearest desks to glance at the maps my well-behaved pupils were making.

He came up to me and whispered in my ear, "Someone in the staff-room to see you." He grinned delightedly. "A lady."

To conceal my resentment at his implied familiarity, I gave a puzzled frown.

"I'll keep guard here, until you get back."

If it was Helen I was prepared to be annoyed. She knew well enough I did not like to be interrupted at school. Perhaps some new crisis had developed, or she was trying to force my hand, compelling me to put some need she had of me before the school. I went towards the staff-room with unwilling speed.

The door was open. I caught a glimpse of a woman seated before the empty fireplace. She was dressed in black. It was Phyllis. My wife. I wanted to turn back before she saw me. In the space of a few seconds I examined and rejected two or three possible plans of escape: turn back, leave the school, go down to Boscombe, and send my resignation from there with some excuse for my inexplicable behaviour; or walk out on everybody and find a job or go abroad. I suppose it was my Christian-trained conscience that restrained me and then pushed me in through the open door.

Outside her own home Phyllis had no confidence in herself. When we faced each other her face was already red with embarrassment. To me it seemed as if she had stepped across a chasm in time from ten years ago to the present moment. She had grown thinner and for some reason the Phyllis that stood before me was closer to the girl I married than the woman I came home to, three years ago. Becoming thinner had restored some of the delicacy to her features which had once sent me into ecstasy. Something of the old physical attractions, which during the week in her father's house we had never begun to recapture, reasserted itself magically in the first moment of our encounter to such an extent that I almost forgot my own freedom and said at once how pleased I was to see her. Phyllis abroad, small, slimmer, neat, well dressed in her mourning clothes, was more agreeable than the housewife managing her home hearth and household like a waspish A.T.S. sergeant.

But her accent wouldn't do at all.

"I'm sorry to disturb you Davie." Here, immediately upon the voice of Eglinton, it sounded on the verge of 'eeh bah gum'. Was that why Eglinton was grinning so? "There was no other way of finding you quickly. I want to speak to you Davie. Can we arrange something?"

"I'll be free soon after four."

"Shall I meet you outside?"

"No." I smiled apologetically. "The boys. . . . Better not. I'll meet you outside the Southern Railway station at four fifteen. Will that do?"

She nodded. "I'll go now then," she said. I walked with her towards the main entrance. She seemed tame enough, but women are unpredictable creatures and she might be tempted to shame me by making a scene in the corridor.

"Is there anything serious?" I asked with cautious anxiety.

"It's the divorce, Davie. I've heard from your solicitors. I thought you and I ought to talk about it first."

I nodded hastily.

"Stanley all right?"

Her face brightened. Without that question she could have gone out reciting to herself 'he didn't even ask how Stan was' over and over again with increasing despair and perhaps bitterness as well. If the divorce could be secured amicably so much the better.

"I'll tell you all about him afterwards." I watched her run lightly down the steps. She still had something of her old light-footedness. In the old days before the war she could contrive to play a strenuous game of hockey or tennis and still look attractive at the end of it. There was still nothing wrong with Phyllis physically. She was slim, firm, contained. Helen seemed gross in comparison. It was just that she was dull, and narrow-minded and house-bound. She was so different from me it might have been an Asiatic I had married.

I took no account of her slowness in the days when I was infatuated with her. It didn't seem to matter then that she didn't like poetry when I tried to read it to her. In those days it was for her to judge and for me to struggle to reach her expectations. I would accompany her to the open-air swimming pool and sit watching her in the water with the great Stanley, a mass of sunburnt muscle, and a girl friend of hers called Doris. I had never learnt to swim and so I decided to make the best of sitting fully clothed watching. I remember how she floated in the bottle-green transparent water and how I noted eagerly the water lift her swimming costume to expose for a brief moment her small breast to my view showing at the centre of such whiteness the dark circle of skin about her nipple.

When I returned to my class such memories from my first youth continued to assail me as if I had suddenly become aware of advancing middle age and wanted to fix my recollections of youth in face of the danger of losing them for ever. My last lesson was with Form Six. It was meant to be something of a free discussion about religion and kindred problems, but this particular Sixth was a collection of uninspiring scientists and technicians and our discussions tended to grind on mechanically on a basis of artificial question and unsatisfactory answer. They seemed difficult to awaken, these large solemn, spectacled boys, overburdened already with the weight of specialist swotting and the prospect of earning a living. Today, remembering my own youth, I saw them in a more sympathetic light. Perhaps the bright world hit them as forcibly as it had done me and they too had secretly washed their faces in the morning dew, or had lain with some silent watching girl on the edge of a field of ripe corn, or sat alone in the shade of a tree by a meandering summer river.

Phyllis had been part of the inarticulate poetry of my youth. The blurted sincerities that the more suave early twenties had hurried to burn. Dark haired angel, neat and decorative as a summer dress, my religion lay then in the smooth movements of her limbs. Phyllis was the magic being that, all unconsciously, converted words into flesh and clothed them with sunlight.

Being with or near Phyllis had smothered my earlier desires to escape from that small town. It was the war that forced me away, gave me the release I had been unwilling to give myself. To go away was an unthinkable heresy. In the country around the town I built up a small world of unique virtues and singular beauties: the ruined mill buried in the heart of Braddock's Wood, alongside the gurgling stream that kicked brightly at the moss-drapped stones; Trentwell Hall and the great Park; the deserted lodge where roses choked the blind unbroken windows and overwhelmed the fallen shutters; Shaw's Farm, the tenants of which were distant relatives of my mother's, who always gave me a welcome and were delighted when I brought Phyllis with me. They took a deep delight in my marriage which I found difficult to explain then. They made jokes, Bert and Ella, a middle-aged childless couple, which made me blush. Their delight in the wedding, which they attended—without them it would have been a dull, undistinguished, hurried affair—was nothing however to their pleasure when I bicycled over on a Saturday evening and told them that Phyllis was pregnant. Phyllis didn't much care for them. She was all for bourgeois refinement and she found Bert and Ella crude, vulgar, earthy, and lacking in restraint. . . .

I found her standing in the shade of the hall before the booking offices. Her black dress and coat made her conspicuous on such a warm heavy afternoon. Her face was cool and neat, but troubled and uncertain. I had been thinking so much about her in the course of the afternoon, I could compare her with the younger Phyllis, as if she and her former self stood side by side. The lips were narrower now, even pinched at the corners, and her whole face seemed midway through a transformation from tender and soft to hard and solid. The texture of her skin had coarsened, as if it had been stretched, slackened, and filled up again. I felt a compelling desire to see myself in a mirror and pass myself under the same test.

At my suggestion we had tea in the café on the top floor of a large multiple store. By the way Phyllis looked about, I guessed how much she could have enjoyed herself if only she could forget the occasion of her visit. It would have been quite fun to show her around London, but that would hardly help the divorce.

Over the plate of rich cakes wrapped in cellophane paper she handed me Buss's letter. His line of attack followed closely what Helen had suggested. I wondered why Helen bothered to use a lawyer, she had such an acute mind herself.

"If it's a case Davie," Phyllis said earnestly, bending forward towards me, a sliced cake resting untouched on her plate, "of my deserting you by not coming to London to live, well I can do that now poor father's gone. That's what I want to tell you. I would sell the house. Houses are not difficult to buy over a certain price, are they. If we lived in London that would suit you all right wouldn't it Davie? You could live the way you want, teaching and writing. That would suit you, wouldn't it?"

Good God. I suppose she believed for the last three or four years I'd been living in lodgings, with celibate virtue, sauce bottles and indigestion. When we say so little to each other what vast illusions we allow to grow unchecked in each other's minds.

"Don't you want a divorce, Phyllis?"

She shook her head and blushed.

"I know I'm to blame Davie. But I couldn't leave father. No one else could have looked after him and I think he would have died without seeing little Stan every day."

No doubt this was the explanation she gave to the neighbours and taught to herself. She had kept it up and worked everything in to fit it. "*My husband has a good job in London, but I can't leave my poor old father.*" I wondered if any of her more inquisitive neighbours asked her when she expected to see me home again. And I wondered what answer Phyllis gave. She was so stupid deceiving herself was easy and any lies she told would have the enormous advantage of ingenuous simplicity. No doubt a divorce would upset the whole illusion, compel her to embark on a venture of fabrication she knew she had not the intelligence to keep up. Her social position was threatened. The solicitor's letter with its swanky address was an ultimatum that she could not ignore. It had brought her to London.

It was up to me now to tell her about Helen. I no longer relished discussing our affairs in the housewives' haven. We went out and took a bus to the Common. We must have appeared an odd pair walking gravely among the untidy overgrown gorse bushes, Phyllis in her formal mourning black, and I myself soberly dressed carrying an ample brief-case that Helen had presented me with on my last birthday.

We sat down on a bench before a stagnant pond.

"I want you to release me," I said solemnly—I was too nervous and uncertain of myself to do it in any other way—"because I want to marry again."

And then I told her something about Helen, but not that we had been living together. Some scruple restrained me; either fear of hurting Phyllis unnecessarily, or some shame or inhibition I had not rid myself of. Talking with Phyllis I could never forget my origins: that was her last remaining claim on me. When I heard Phyllis's voice I was not far from the smell of varnished pews and the wheezing of the Sunday School harmonium.

It was some time before I noticed she was crying, because as I spoke I avoided looking at her face. Two large tears were rolling effortlessly down her cheeks. But she did not move or sob. I was acutely uncomfortable. I wished now I had not suggested leaving the café. It would have been better to endure the curious glances of strangers than feel compelled now in this quiet place to give her some comfort.

There was nothing I could do. But unescapably a weight of obligation descended on my shoulders. In spite of her athletic powers in youth Phyllis wasn't a modern woman. There was nothing self-sufficient about her. It was up to me at least to see her back to her boarding-house.

I asked her where she was staying. She gave me an address in Gower Street. We made the journey there in an atmosphere of unrelieved gloom. It might have been a funeral we had attended on the Common. Once or twice in Knightsbridge and Piccadilly I attempted to draw her attention to the sights of the town and she made a gallant effort to show a lively interest, but the bright look of awareness on her face vanished behind the dull cloud of unhappiness even before the great buildings were out of sight. She could not follow my directions. I indicated one place and she gave a brief admiring smile at another. I wanted to tell her she was the most uncompromisingly womanly woman I had ever known and that she should get married again to a manly man, a steady type, and have several babies, and that she would make a perfect wife for

169

nine men out of ten. I wanted to tell her that I wasn't her type and that she was far too good for me, an over-statement I was prepared to defend with mutually flattering arguments bent with great art and cunning to reflect two ways at once.

Outside her boarding-house, it suddenly occurred to me to say, "Phyllis, did you see my last novel?"

She nodded.

"I'm sorry Davie. I forgot to congratulate you on it."

I smiled.

"Did you read it?"

She nodded again, but rather hesitatingly.

"All of it?"

"I haven't finished it Davie. I read a bit every night, but I am so tired usually I fall asleep after a couple of sentences."

I wanted to laugh uproariously, but I restrained myself. She might not have understood. I just looked at her standing on the step above me, a pretty woman still. Suddenly I felt her arms around my neck and she kissed me quickly on the lips.

"But don't think because I don't read your books I don't love you, because I do."

Before I could speak, she had gone into the house.

XIX

I FOUND PHYLLIS'S unexpected declaration confusing and
annoying, as if a sudden breeze had scattered a neatly arranged
pile of papers on my desk, compelling me to pick them up and
sort them out again. All the way back to Kensington I found
myself thinking about her; I was a prancing impressionistic
photographer taking innumerable shots from endless angles,
determined to capture the soul of his subject. She was my legal
wife. She was twenty when I married her. She still had a well
balanced attractive figure. Her shoes were size three and a
half. Her eyes were blue but her hair dark. It was possible
she stained white streaks in her hair with hair-dye. She was
intellectually slow. She never passed her matric. She cooked
well but in her own home she had a tendency to nag and
domineer. She spoilt her son and pampered her father. She
had the devotion to duty of a well trained animal. And it
seemed that throughout the vicissitudes of almost ten years,
she continued to love me.

I was not flattered. I did not, or not for long anyway, think
that some endearing quality in myself fastened her love to me
as the scent of a flower draws the bee to its heart. Love
illuminates and transfigures the lover more than the loved
one. My religion taught me that the capacity to love without
reservation was the crowning glory of human personality.
It was disconcerting to find something of this virtue at the root
of all Phyllis's faults. I suppose I considered her love for her
father and her son and for me as faults. It was because of
these, this overpowering blanket of attachments, that I had
left her. It was upsetting to find a rare metal in such ordinary
clay. (It would be improper to style Phyllis 'common'.) If
only it could be painlessly transferred to someone else: grafted
on someone who could return the love and give it increase,
and never hear the grating note in her kitchen voice, or feel
her prejudices and ignorance or see her spoil her Stanley the

second, or feel the incessant nudging of the hard elbows of her lack of taste, discrimination, and intelligence.

My attempts to educate her. In a field on a summer's day I read her an Auden lyric . . . *And all the summer through the water saunter.* I looked up, pleased with the sound of my own voice; pleased with having read something she could reasonably be expected to enjoy. She sat leaning on an arm, decoratively enough, gazing, as far as I could make out, at cows grazing in a meadow across the river. Indulgently, I allowed that as legitimate precedence of the eye over the ear; but I insisted on her telling me what she was thinking of while I was reading. "Next door's wireless," she said, innocently enough.

In their front parlour there were two volumes of verse among the commentaries, children's books and pious memoirs. The poems of Ella Wheeler Wilcox, and a small fancy copy of Omar Khayyam with Beardsley decorations. Phyllis knew a few verses from both volumes by heart; some early adolescent passion and despair must have driven her to them. She understood that Ella Wheeler Wilcox gave me no pleasure; but since I had expressed admiration of it she quoted *"Ah love could thou and I with fate conspire . . ."* rather frequently in the difficult months preceding our marriage. At the time I imagined Mr. Rayment and Warrington Avenue were the sorry scheme of things entire; but a longer view reveals that Phyllis too was among the objects due to be remoulded nearer to the heart's desire.

By the time I reached the flat I was prepared to admit that Phyllis was a woman whom I had never understood. Between the idolised image of my infatuation and the shadow of her father's house, the true Phyllis had passed unnoticed. All the time she had been there to look at, but I had not seen her. And now, thank goodness, I was to be relieved of the responsibility and obligations of ever getting to know her. If I had lost something rarer than radium, let it be my punishment not to know what I had lost. Sentimental memories of the pre-war past were of no practical assistance to either of us; between two people whose relationship had been committed to lawyers, they verged on the unseemly. From my most austere standpoint as a moralist, much of it came shockingly near infidelity to Helen. A man who leaves one woman for another is like an emigrant who has crossed over the ocean that separates one continent from another. He must take upon himself the whole paraphernalia of a nationality; a language, a loyalty, and the passport of a way of living which stretches over him from head to foot as close-fitting as a new skin. Any communication with the past could easily topple into sudden treason.

I picked up the day's mail that lay on the door mat. The letters were mostly for Helen. At once I took out my fountain pen and re-addressed them. It was the kind of thing I did immediately for fear of forgetting to do it at all. Helen took her mail very seriously. She spent a good deal of her time dealing with her correspondence. There were also two or three postcards for me in an envelope. Views of Dorset. I set them up on the mantelpiece. Maureen and Sigrid were nicely settled in their new school but Sigrid was suspected of chicken pox. There was also a smart envelope containing a printed invitation to Lady Whiteway's At Home, Thursday evening, eight p.m. Could this be Roger's doing? At Home at the Hill. Or did Lady Muriel want to see what kind of a man her niece wanted to marry? That was more like it. I did not feel inclined to go. They were not my kind of people. There was nothing to gain from such a visit.

Although I had the flat to myself, I was unable to write. In my notebook were Ideas which refused to come to life. I played about with the notion of a short vivid novel on the Conquest of Mexico, seen through the eye of a boy caught up among Cortez's followers. Then there was an idea of a dictator's right-hand man who escapes from his defeated country and settles down incognito in a mid-western town, where he gets involved in local politics very much against his will. And a third about a trade unionist who becomes a Minister of the Crown and is captured by Communist bandits in the Malayan jungle. An unhappy missionary acts as interpreter between them. The Big Issues pushed about like giant stage scenery by willing little shifters: Communism, Capital, Culture, Colour and Christianity. A novel 'informed with intellectual passion' and stiff with 'contemporary significance'! Visot would be my model for the bandit's political commissar. I myself would be the missionary, worn with home-sickness and secret drink. And perhaps Allenside would be the Minister of the Crown. It seemed an excellent idea—if only someone else would come along and write it.

I decided I would be more usefully employed arranging a sherry party. A reputation never needs more nursing than during inspiration's closed season. These were preliminaries that could best be gone through on the telephone. First catch your hare.

"Redvers? This is David. David Flint. Hello! How are you? I want you to come to dinner on the twenty-second. Can you make it? Well how about the twenty-fourth then? I want to pick your brains! Seriously, I badly need your advice. Good. That will be lovely. See you on the twenty-fourth then. Seven thirty to eight? Fine. Love to Imelda. Splendid. Well goodbye then. Goodbye."

Replace receiver. First objective gained. Flush of victory. Next move? Griselda Fox of *Vanity Fair* or Theodora Pearlman of *Grant Groves*? Griselda was prettier and more entertaining, but Theodora more influential. Nice point. Try both.

Someone rang the front door bell. We were not accustomed to unexpected visitors. I resented the intrusion. For some reason I imagined it might be Roger. I did not want to see him. Blast him, he had no business to intrude. Sink of corruption, moral cesspool; let the police deal with him, inspect him and condemn him; have him put away or destroyed. He annoyed me like a bad smell. Damn him absolutely. But I had no stomach for damning. I wanted very much to be left alone as soon as any such intrusion threatened. The bell rang again. On the other hand it might not be Roger. I answered the door.

"Evening, Flint." It was Peter Bayly. His moustache drooped mournfully, and his straight hair was a little out of place, otherwise he was very neatly dressed in a city suit and a hard collar. In his hand he carried a bowler hat. He was a good-looking fellow in a horsey sort of way. But hardly Helen's type I would have thought. He looked the type of post-war young Englishman who considered it part of his breeding to be stupid about everything outside the strict code by which he lived. It might be a cruel necessity for him to earn a living by selling cars, but the great thing was, in private life, to maintain the standards of the mess. A kind of neo-nineteenth-century Stoicism, based on patriotic resolve. Good form was all. Among most of these men, whose discernment was only for the detailed observation of established ritual, Roger would be accepted as one of them. "Is Helen here?"

I invited him in. He carefully refrained from looking about him. He stood by the window and fixed his gaze on the yellow flowers in the window box. The sun's light was filtering gently through the trees of the park and an occasional taxi flitted down the wide brown-tinted street.

"I have nothing at all against Helen," Bayly said, eyeing me carefully. "She was too good for me, that's all."

I seemed to remember him saying all this before—in the lavatories of *The Green Huntsman*—in the same tone of voice.

"Too clever," he added. "I'm not clever. Never was. Maths and History were my worst subjects at school. Did you like school Flint?"

I shook my head.

"You're a schoolmaster too aren't you? That's rather funny." He did not smile. "Schoolmasters don't like school either. If nobody likes them why do we bother to keep the damn things open? '*The silly fool the silly fool was even sillier at school but he beat the bully as a rule.*' Helen taught me that one. She said it was poetry. I expect you write poetry, Flint. Helen would like that. She was keen on poetry. Never could see anything in the stuff myself."

It was obvious he had drunk enough to enable himself to ramble on like this indefinitely. Rather loudly as if I was addressing a rather dull pupil, I invited him to sit down and offered him a drink. He shook his head.

"I've resigned," he said. The word was not easy for him to pronounce but with a little extra effort he succeeded. "That bloody man Allenside has gone too far. Wish I'd never set eyes on the swine. It's a scandal the people they let into good schools. To think that I fagged for that awful swine."

"Shepherd's Bush?" I suggested helpfully.

"I'm not going to get mixed up in any shady business," Bayly wagged his finger at me accusingly. "And that's exactly what it is. Very bloody shady. Allenside's a crook, Flint; nothing better. Now what I want to know is, is he a friend of yours?"

I shook my head.

"I hope not. The police called at the garage this morning. What do you think of that? A lorry they said, loaded with sugar, ditched near Chelmsford. Traced here. To this garage. My name on the registration book. My name!"

Peter looked outraged.

"I said to the bloody policeman I said, 'look here. I don't own this obscene garage or any of the obscene trucks and cars that are found in it. I am merely an employee old boy,' I said. Just a poor bloody worker. The place belongs to a cad called Allenside. Used to be my senior at school. After him, John Peel, I said. As for me I'm resigning this very day this very moment. And then I just walked away."

I nodded approvingly.

"It was a good gesture," said Peter. "A noble deed in fact. But not very practical. They owe me a fortnight's pay."

He shook his head sadly.

"Look here, old chap," I said, ready to adopt an idiom and a tone he would understand. "You really must have a drink."

I prepared him a gin and tonic. He watched me thought-fully.

"I've been doing a lot of thinking today," he said. "A ruddy great heap of thinking. Tick, tick, tick, tick, tick." He rapped his forehead with his knuckles. "Types like Allenside will ruin this country. There'll be no decency left."

"Come on, sit here," I said. He flopped tiredly into the settee.

"Very decent of you Flint. Very decent indeed." He clasped his glass firmly with both hands. They were narrow white long fingered hands. Beneath the shell of his assumed personality there was no knowing what sensitive creature lay peering out at a hostile world. I began to like him very much. He called out parental-protective instincts in me. He appeared to be even weaker and more helpless than myself. And yet he had been decorated for bravery, for defying death. Perhaps he found life more difficult to defy. We were not exactly in the same boat, but the sea and the storm that tossed us about were the same.

"I'm glad you've seen through Roger," I said. My tone was congratulatory. "He's been making trouble here. He had the face to come here and ask Helen to put money into that Shepherd's Bush place. I thought that was the absolute limit. You see he's rather pally with Helen's uncle, Lord White-way . . ."

I stopped suddenly. Bayly had put down his glass and he was holding his head in his hands.

"What's the matter?" I said anxiously.

"Think I'm going to be. . . . Mind if I go to the . . ."

He staggered out of the room. I thought it was kindest to leave him alone. Should I go to the kitchen and get some tomato juice, or make some coffee? I heard the W.C. being flushed. He reappeared in the doorway, the colour of death, a bright red spot under his left eye. He was frowning as if a dizzy headache made it difficult for him to see. I was impressed by his fortitude. Under similar conditions, I would have been groaning away like a heifer in labour.

"Look here, Flint." He held the doorpost for support. "I'm going to bank on you being a good chap. I'm going to tell you something about Helen. Nothing to her discredit mind. But something that's made a mark on her. Her father died in prison."

I did not immediately realise the information had any personal implication. I showed polite surprise.

"Rather a bad show. It happened just a few weeks after we were married, in April, nineteen forty-four. I had been under the impression the old boy had died before the war. Actually he was due out in less than a month. Helen hadn't told me anything about him. She never really forgave me you know for looking up the case in the Law Reports. Her feelings about the business were very complicated. Sensitive girl. Too much for me to cope with. Naturally she didn't want people to know about him. The old boy had been sane enough to save her endowments from the crash. But she didn't forgive him for getting himself into trouble. She never wrote to him or visited him. The thing worked on her mind. As I say she's a sensitive girl."

So this was the secret behind her chilly reserve, behind the careful way in which she told me only what she wanted me to know; behind her restlessness and her reserve; her moving from place to place; her constantly changing plans. What kind of love could relieve her of her burden? Not mine. She made no use of mine.

"Like a bloody fool," Bayly said gloomily, "some time ago I told that swine Roger, the story. I thought I was clever telling him something he didn't know. He talks so damned well

177

himself it makes you feel you've got to say something pretty sensational to deserve his attention."

"That's how he's been getting Helen," I murmured.

"You didn't know about her father?" He looked at me inquiringly.

"No." I shook my head.

"Of course not. I always think it's a mistake that husband and wife should tell each other everything. There are many secrets that are best kept."

He walked across the room very steadily and picked up his bowler hat.

"Don't go," I said. "Stay and have something to eat."

"Must be off I'm afraid." He hesitated, and then added, "If I were you I wouldn't tell Helen what I've told you."

I nodded obediently.

"Doesn't always pay to be too frank, does it?" He smiled weakly.

"Don't think Allenside will be bothering you much longer. My guess is he'll soon be clearing out of the country again, and Rufus Wod will be clamped away in jail."

"The Whipping-boy?"

"That's it. Bloody Wod thinks Allenside is God." He spoke seriously, but it sounded like a joke.

"What will you do now? Without a job I mean?" I tried to sound helpful.

"I've put in for a police job in Malaya. I wouldn't mind joining the Army again. It's a hard life perhaps, but at least you know where you are."

As the lift went down I caught a glimpse of him clapping his bowler firmly on his head.

XX

That night, for the first time, I felt uncomfortable being alone in the flat. My imagination began to get out of hand, and I wished Helen was back. As far as I knew, Roger's activities did not include violence. But although I feared violence more, I knew Fraud and Corruption were deeper sins. My mind made an alarming catalogue of Roger's criminal activities. Once you started that kind of career there was nowhere you could draw the line. Black market and blackmail; black magic and black mass. Roger was unclean. Behind the tall distinguished exterior, the predatory teeth and glittering darting red eyes of a rat. No doubt I imbibed too many gins and tonics before going to bed. I had violent dreams of a slaughter-house kind. Blood everywhere, and silence. There was an episode in which Roger and Rufus Wod forced me to join them in the back of a lorry, half loaded up with frozen meat. The lorry went screaming silently through empty streets, pursued by motor bikes and police cars. Roger gave me a gun and compelled me to shoot at our pursuers over ramparts of meat roughly covered in thin sacking. Hoping to deceive him, I fired low. They decided to throw me out. I clung to a side of beef my nails sinking into the cold flesh, but Roger kicked at my fingers compelling me to let go. The alarm bell mercifully woke me up. Shafts of morning sunshine streamed cheerfully into the room, illuminating the abstract painting that hung on the far wall. It was a fine day and I was able to smile at my nightmare.

Nevertheless I found the routine of going to school as refreshing as a new experience. I was suitably pleased with the comparatively empty compartment which bore me southwards against the stream of traffic, the body-packed trains making for the city. If there was duality in the Universe I wanted to be on the side of space and light. At prayers I regarded my colleagues with tolerant benevolence, until I remembered that the headmaster, who sat listening intently to the lesson, rather inaudibly read by Mr. Downs, was Roger's younger brother. It was time, I decided then, I took control of my hysterical alarm and began to regard Roger more dispassionately. Was he a crook by inclination or by necessity? I had always imagined that criminals were mostly motivated by the desire for gain. I remembered Visot eloquently explaining over the lunch table how criminals in the just society would disappear and how corruption was an inevitable corollary to capitalism. No doubt Roger needed money. He liked to impress and live on a lavish scale. No doubt he had women whose luxurious needs had to be catered for and he may never have been free from pressing debts. But what impressed me most was the jaunty unconcern and humorous lightness with which he pursued his various businesses. He was not without social ambitions, he was anxious to impress the world with his own importance, he could give utterance on political matters with a fair imitation of the gravity of a *Times* leader, but beneath all that I fancied I could discern a startlingly consistent anti-social motive. He was able to achieve his criminal success, his brazen frauds, because in the last resort he didn't give a damn for people. He didn't even bother to hate them; he just didn't give a damn for anybody except himself. He was a man whose conscience had been neatly removed, as if by a surgical operation. With a little more coarsening he would have made a successful operator of a gas chamber; with a little more refinement and restraint and persistence the czar of a business empire. I was so pleased with my analysis I was eager for a chance to put it to Visot, '*Now Vizzy, in a Socialist State how would you cope with a man like this?*' But a little further reflection showed me that Visot's prompt answer would be 'Put him behind bars'; and I was back where I started. With deflated pessimism I concluded that the world was getting too much for me. If only I could rid myself temporarily of my body and observe all that happened as a wise invisible spirit I would not be unduly put out at whatever lengths Roger went to. But there was no way of depositing in safety the body for which I had so tender a regard without removing my entire self from the scene of the action.

In the staff-room during the mid-morning break Briarman announced, not without self-important solemnity, that Mr. Robinson and Mr. Hawkes had certain proposals which they wished to place before the whole staff. He asked Mr. Visot to be kind enough to replace Mr. Thorpe on corridor duty since the proposals concerned what action the staff should take as a united body in support of Mr. Visot tomorrow afternoon.

Robinson outlined his proposals in the calm and matter of fact manner which always lent such weight to whatever he had to say. He was an experienced committee man and his judgements and opinions were always received with attention and respect.

"In my view," he said, "this is a matter which affects the integrity of our profession. We all know that Mr. Visot is a Communist. He makes no secret of the fact. We also know he is as conscientious and as honest a teacher as anyone else on this staff. The allegations made by Bansdale's father are complete nonsense. We all know that. And it is up to us to say so, unanimously. If we can show proper solidarity as a staff I am pretty certain the Governors would not dare take business any further. They would be only too pleased to let the whole matter drop. Hawkes and I would like to suggest that we can deliver them a letter either through the head or better still by means of a deputation. We've got to stop this kind of thing here and now and Hawkes and myself suggest this might be the most effective way of doing it."

Brunt moved restlessly in his chair as though he were anxious to speak. He said with unusual quietness, "I'd like to speak but perhaps it would be wiser if I didn't."

Hawkes raised a large hand and grinned. "You keep out of this Bert. The less you say for the next forty-eight hours the better."

For once I fancied Brunt was glad to retreat into the background.

"Well," Briarman said in chairmanly fashion, "would you make that a formal proposal?"

Robinson nodded.

"And you second it?" Briarman said to Hawkes.

"Yes," said Hawkes. He was enjoying the business. Hawkes pursued women with the intensity and devotion of a sportsman, but nothing warmed and uplifted his genial soul more than a demonstration of masculine solidarity, especially when directed against Authority which Hawkes disliked on principle. He was the engaging type of man found among the crusading wing of the Labour Party, enjoying nothing more than a Protest March or a mass meeting in Trafalgar Square and suspicious of his Party for not providing him with enough of them.

"Has anyone else got something to say?"

Briarman glanced at the clock. There were five minutes left before the bell was due to go.

"I think we might have had more notice," Dell said. He rubbed his face with his hands as if to remove any signs of embarrassment. "It isn't right you know to rush the matter through like this. If the letter is to represent the views of the whole staff there ought to be a thorough discussion beforehand."

"Do you mean," Robinson said coldly, "that you are not in agreement with what I have said?"

"Of course not." Dell fumbled testily for his pipe and pouch. "But the wording of the letter. What exactly is it going to state? Some of us are not prepared to go as far as others. A working agreement ought to be reached."

"Exactly." Eglinton crossed his legs carefully. In the beginning he had appeared apprehensive and uncomfortable, but now Dell had spoken, he was more at ease. "No one will dispute the general principle. But the strength of the wording of the letter, the way in which the case is put in this particular instance, should be carefully considered. God knows I don't wish Old Vizzy any harm, but there's no doubt about it but that he has been unwise. And there is no doubt either that Communist influence in schools has to be watched."

"Hear, 'ear," said Downs, dropping the second 'h' as a result of too much effort to include the first.

"I was afraid of this," Robinson said. "You're going right off the point! The question at issue is, is a teacher to be penalised by the Governors and perhaps by the County as well, on the strength of a boy's evidence which can easily be proved false and inaccurate in every detail. If there was no *prima facie* evidence, the case should never have gone forward. I thought that would have been plain enough to you all. Hawkes and I are not so much concerned with getting Visot out of trouble. Obviously that's exactly what he himself is longing for. We are concerned with preserving the rights, and privileges if you like, of our profession; in which I would have imagined every man jack of you would have been automatically unanimous."

Robinson sounded very angry, and Dell and Eglinton had no answer to make.

"Right," said Briarman striving to conceal his pleasure at Dell's confusion. "Right. What is it to be then, a letter with or without a deputation? There's just a minute left before the bell goes."

"Let's have a ruddy deputation," Hawkes said jovially.

"I second that."

Briarman said, "Mr. Flint has seconded it. Any other proposal?"

Dell and Eglinton were silent.

"Just send the letter," said Downs, glancing at Dell and Eglinton for approval. But they realised they would be outvoted and did not bother to speak.

"How many men do you want?" Brairman asked.

"Two would be enough," said Robinson. It was his show now. Everyone accepted his figure.

"I propose Mr. Robinson and Mr. Flint." Thorpe spoke up suddenly from his corner.

"Hawkes," I said hurriedly, "not me."

"No," Hawkes said generously. It was obvious he would have loved to go. "You speak better English. You go, old boy."

The bell rang. Its impatient clamour echoed throughout the school. Dell, Eglinton, Downs and Mitchley rose from their places, eager to be gone. For a moment as they stood up they looked like the nucleus of a party. But their unity was purely negative. It had no positive force and it could never prevail. There was a political lesson there if one had the time to examine it with care. For myself, I was preoccupied with wondering why the new burden had fallen on me. *The lot fell upon Matthias.* . . . Although I was uneasy and unwilling there must have been some power or instinct in me that, almost in spite of myself, reached out to accept the chance even as it fell. Could it be that if the conscience was exercised at all sooner or later with autonomous force it would precipitate actions that were repugnant enough to the unregenerate nature in which, like a jewel in the head of a toad, the bright thing lay?

"Is that all right then?" Briarman raised his voice to make himself heard.

"Yes, yes," Hawkes nodded. "And let them compose the letter between them and read it to us in the dinner time."

"All agreed?"

There were noises of general approval as each man hastened off to his class-room.

XXI

"DAVID?"

I knew it was Roger's voice, but I said 'speaking' as if I had no idea who was there. My heart thumped nervously.

"This is Roger. I missed you at Lady Mu's last night David. Anything the matter?"

I remembered the invitation card. I had made no answer, one way or the other. I left myself open to the charge of having been rude. My confusion was increased. As often happens when I am put out, I began to stutter.

"Speak up old boy! I can barely hear you. Something wrong with this blasted phone I think. Can you hear me?"

"Yes," I said weakly.

"Good. Why didn't you turn up?"

I said, "I forgot."

"That's a good one! You must be a genius after all. Complete disregard for the social verities: 'I call, I creep, I conquer!'"

It wasn't true—I had licked boots in my time—but I was warmed as if by a compliment.

"It was a very nice party. Lady Mu asked me where you were. She was very anxious to meet you. Seriously, David, you must make amends. The Whiteways have far-reaching interests you know. Did you know they were part-owners of The Bell Theatre and The Mummers?"

I didn't. It was devilish how my interest in them was at once quickened and how I began at once to realise it was possible to see them in a different light. If they showed a benevolent interest in my work they would at once be elevated to the Patronage of the Living Arts.

I spoke into the telephone: "I didn't mean to be rude. I honestly forgot."

"Is Helen there?" Roger inquired. I did not at once fully appreciate his impudence. Did he assume that Helen would not tell me about his blackmail threats? But of course he himself did not regard them as such. That was how he sustained his breathless cheek. Having no regard for Truth, he was able to regard anything he said at any given moment to be true. Never for one moment did he think of himself as a criminal. He was a clever man who deserved all the rewards of cleverness and enjoyed the process of being clever. It was expected of his friends that they should share this enjoyment and be vastly amused by what he said and did. His intimate friends were those whose view of Roger most closely coincided with his own; as a man who could, if he would, filch the sacred fruit off the altar of greatness. An uncrowned king among men, with an attractive dash of Robin Hood and Jolly Roger about him. A leader of men who at any moment might be called upon to step into the limelight of History, and in the meantime kept his wits and abilities in practice by various ways of making money in a world where money was not easy to make. Men who did not share this valuation of himself were uncouth boors, men of ill-will; potential enemies.

"Are you listening?" His voice impinged itself upon my thoughts.

"Yes." I had no idea what he had been saying.

"I'll be over in about half an hour then."

"No." I protested weakly. "I mean . . ."

"This phone is absolutely no good tonight. I simply can't hear you. I must have a chat with you about old Edward. We must do something to help him. I'll hoot for you three times. We'll go out for a little spin. 'Bye now."

My indignation against him did not take long to evaporate. Why did Edward need help and what help could Roger possibly give him? The more one thought about Roger, the more difficult it became to be afraid of him. He deceived no one more than he deceived himself. I felt renewed confidence in the superiority of my mind over his; my courage increased as if I had been endowed with a weapon of unanswerable power. I had no need at all to be afraid of him. He was not violent. He was just a cheap crook; someone to be sorry for. No doubt had he committed any offence against me I would have been alight with indignation. Had he cheated me of a few hundreds or injured me in any way, I would be howling for the police. It was true that he had blackmailed Helen, the woman I was going to marry, but the attempt had failed and in any case Helen had plenty of money. If he was able to pull wool over Lord and Lady Whiteway's eyes, it just served them right.

His journalism was contemptible. The grandiose effusions of a man who over-rated his own knowledge and acuteness, composed in a floridly knowing style, calculated to impress in what he considered 'the right quarters' and to flatter the prejudices of those from whom he hoped to gain most. To my mind, the stuff seemed more disgusting than his black market activities; somehow a more premeditated and hypocritical fraud, and a deeper prostitution. Those guilty of Fraud, Treachery and Flattery inhabited the lowest circle. I imagined Roger in a frozen hole, gnawing frenziedly at Rufus Wod's skull. . . .

He was hooting down in the street. I went to the window. Another new car: a bold red thing glistening assertively alongside the pavement. The hood was down and neatly packed beneath a waterproof cover. Roger wore a duffle jacket and a cap. He had long leather gloves on his hands. He waved at me cheerily. The world had an unlimited supply of friends who would be bought by a favour and a smile. Free market for friends. Right reactions bought and sold. Stooges to order. Pick-ups at fancy prices.

"Where would you like to go?" He smiled at me.

It was a fine evening. It would be exciting to go anywhere out of town. But I did not wish to place myself under too deep an obligation to Roger. There was no knowing when he would make use of it.

"Anywhere you like," I said. I saw his highly polished shoes gleaming in the small twilight where his feet rested on the controls. It was delightful to speed through London on such an evening. Crossing Battersea Bridge the whole river westwards seemed alive with light. The mind was lulled into a stupor of satisfaction as the fresh wind tingled a smiling face.

"I wanted to talk to you," Roger said, gazing calmly at the road ahead, "about old Edward." His hands gripped the wheel firmly. His self-possession was unassailable. He had all the three dimensional solidity and self-satisfaction of a man about to do a good turn. Did he know the police had been nosing about his garage at Shepherd's Bush? Did he know Helen and her lawyers were after him? Sitting next to him, he seemed tougher, more successful, more formidable than my private estimate had taken into account. It was an effort not to become afraid again. Cleverness had a better chance of prevailing over toughness when a safe distance lay between them.

"We've got to help him," Roger said. "This Directorate. He's keen on getting it. It all sounds like my-eye and Fanny Adams to me, just academic balderdash. But if Eddie wants it, he ought to get it. The trouble is Whiteway has decided he isn't reliable. Politically reliable I suppose he means. As if old Eddie could ever make any difference one way or the other. He'd be too busy turning over his conscience at any crucial moment."

He expected me to laugh. I managed to induce a smile. He did not seem to have any idea of the underlying strength of his brother's character. Having known him a life-time, he preferred to cherish a distorted view of his brother's nature, because it was in harmony with his own view of himself. If he acknowledged where Edward's real strength lay it might involve a mirrored glimpse of his own weakness that he was under no circumstances prepared to examine.

Roger said: "Old Whiteway thinks he's shielding Commies on the staff. Is that true do you think?" He looked at me as if he had asked my advice, with trust, and eager to have my answer.

"Not really. It's a question of professional standards really. Loyalty to the profession."

"That certainly sounds more like Edward." He nodded wisely. "Janet was at the party last night. I expect you know that she and I . . . well, we didn't get on. She used to look at me as if she wished I were dead. Between you and me, Eddie and I would never have drifted apart but for her. But there's no point in picking old sores, as the Kaffirs say. Janet sucks up to Lady Mu for all she's worth. It's rather comic really. And since she's discovered that Lady Mu and Whiteway are well disposed to yours truly, her attitude towards me has distinctly sweetened. I had a little talk with her last night about Edward's prospects. The poor girl is so dead keen actually, it's likely she might do more harm than good. I warned her not to mention the subject all evening to anyone. It must have been hard for her. I guessed old Whiteway had the matter on his mind and would bring it up with me at the first opportunity. My waiting paid. We had a drink together, behind closed doors as it were, in his study. What it all amounts to is this. Whiteway will see that Eddie gets the job provided Eddie gives some measly ninety pounds or so to anyone on his staff except the two Commies. I don't remember their names. He might even give it to you? Why not?"

He grinned happily. I hadn't realised before how much affection he had for his brother. It was almost as deeply-rooted as his belief in himself. He was enjoying himself tremendously trying to engineer something to his brother's advantage. There was something pathetic about it. In the space of an hour I had held Roger in contempt, I had been afraid of him, and now I was sorry for him to the point of liking him.

"What's your view of the situation?"

I looked gloomy. "I'm afraid his mind is absolutely made up. He won't give way."

"Stubborn old devil, isn't he? Real old mule." His voice was full of real admiration. In a moment if I was not careful we would be singing Edward's praises in unison. I repeated the words 'black market, blackmail,' in my mind; a charm to prevent me falling under his spell. As soon as Roger saw you were liking him, he would start thinking how to make use of you.

As we passed through Streatham I thought of Visot. Would he be standing in the front parlour boldly rehearsing his speech of defence: Bertie and the old man watching Gerald with awed approval? I doubted whether the Governors' Meeting would be quite the occasion he was preparing for. With the exception of Whiteway, the Governors would all be inclined to pour oil on troubled waters, and even Whiteway's real objective now was to force Allenside into withholding the Special Responsibility post from Brunt. Perhaps Visot's great moment lay in a more distant future. His whole life was a preparation for some great act of calculated defiance. A secular martyr. To men of my kind, a constant discomfiting challenge.

"Where are we going?" I asked Roger.

"Thought we could just drop in on old Eddie." Roger spoke casually. "He lives out this way. No harm in trying him just once again."

Did he hope having me with him would help him to gain a foothold in the house? Had he gone there alone Edward would have merely told him plainly to go away.

"I'm interested in Howard's future too. I honestly don't think they ought to send him back to that loony bin, do you?"

I needed to be cautious. Roger would make use of anything I said if it suited his purpose.

"It didn't seem to suit him. But I don't know enough about the place, or about the boy really."

"Oh! The place is an absolute racket." Roger lifted one hand from the wheel illustratively. Racket, I thought, you can certainly speak with authority on rackets. "Anyone with half an eye can see that. That chap Templeton is walking out. He's made all he can out of it and now he's in hot pursuit of another profitable fad. The place will just quietly fall apart. I see no point at all in Howard's going back. Do you?"

I maintained a cautious silence.

"I've got a good plan if Edward will listen. I just mentioned it *en passant* to Janet last night. I'm going to Spain next week. Collecting material for a series of articles—*Spain Today*—for an American syndicate. Why couldn't Howard come with me? I'll be there until about the middle of June. Then I intend going to Austria and if possible putting my nose into Yugoslavia to see how the Jug-Jugs are getting on."

What was I supposed to say? 'What a chance for a fifteen year old boy!' How educative. Not to be missed. An enlightened parent's dream.

"That's the best kind of education, I think. Don't you agree?"

"Depends a lot on the boy," I said.

"I wonder if they are at home?"

The gates were open. Roger drove in. The garage was empty. I hoped there might be no one in. We got out of the car and walked to the front door. Roger rang the bell. We heard no one approaching to answer the door. Roger rang again and I waited until I would be able to say 'Well. There's no one at home.' Then we heard the sound of rapid footsteps coming downstairs. Howard opened the door. I glimpsed at the misery on his face before his expression changed at the sight of his uncle.

"Hello!" Roger said. Antipathetic as I was, I could sense

the warmth the man radiated enveloping the boy, bringing a new smile to his face. "Where are the old folks?"

"They're out. Mummy's at the B.B.C. and my father has a committee. They should be back by nine." The boy gave me a puzzled hostile glance. Obviously he wished Roger had come alone. "Won't you come in?"

I felt like an intruder. I had never considered the house without Allenside before. I saw it now, through the boy's eyes and it was too large too deserted and too gloomy: something of a prison, not enough of a home. I wondered what he had been doing alone upstairs when we called. He looked all the misery of fifteen: as if the world was a bitter disappointment. He didn't even seem to have the desperate hope that would allow him to try to run away. As if he had made one mistake and didn't know what to do next. It depressed me to think how very long it would take him to learn, although I could not say exactly what it was he had to learn, perhaps because I had not learnt it myself.

"There it is." They were talking about Roger's new car. Roger had taken him to the window in order to see it. I tried to understand the boy's wordless admiration; his lips were parted and twisted slightly by an arrested smile, as if the sight had inspired and excited him with new dreams of greatness. It stood on the gravel like an enormous toy, a red glittering plaything of the gods. They talked about it in garage jargon that I could barely follow and which did not interest me.

We went up to it, so that Howard could examine it himself. In no time his head was underneath the bonnet. Roger switched on the engine so that Howard could see and listen. Flatteringly, he asked the boy's advice about a non-existent noise in the cylinder-head.

When he switched off Roger said,

"I'm taking her to France next week. I'll drive down to Spain. Barcelona first, I think." He waited until the lad was suitably impressed. "How would you like to come?"

The boy's eyes grew round with wonder. It was cruel how easily he was impressed.

"Spain," he breathed the word as if it were sacred. "Spain."

Roger laughed delightedly. I could not believe he knew how cruel he was being, raising the boy's hopes. His father would never let him go.

"I'd like you to come. I shall probably need a second driver. Doesn't matter about your being only fifteen over there. He looks more than fifteen, doesn't he, David?"

Actually he looked a lot less, trying to control the excitement that was rising within him. Why didn't he dance about wildly and be his age?

A car hooted in the roadway. It was Janet wanting to get in. Roger nodded cheerfully and moved his car up closer to the house. Janet drove straight through into the garage.

"Shall I mention it to your mother?" They were conspirators. Howard nodded. He pinned what was left of his hopes in his uncle's powers of persuasion not in his parents' resonableness.

"Is this yours Roger?" Janet pointed to the car.

"All mine. Howard's made me an offer though. What was your figure Howard; two thousand?"

She greeted me with nicely-judged luke-warmth. Her ideas about Roger seemed to have changed radically. Her attitude to him was respectfully polite. To others she seemed to say, after all, for all his faults, he is a success. And after all, he is one of us, he is an Allenside. Perhaps because of her ill-disguised view of my comparative unimportance, I found it impossible to think of anything to Janet's credit. Now, she seemed to be a bigger fool than ever. It maddened me to think what a useless wife she was to Allenside. She imagined herself to be propelling him forward, forcing his boat into mid-stream: whereas in fact she was leaden ballast that continually threatened to submerge the boat, and made him work with fiendish energy baling out water that need never have been there. I wished I could tell him to push her overboard.

"About this Spanish trip of mine, Janet. I told you about it last night, didn't I? Do you think Howard could come?"

She glanced at her son and looked away quickly.

"I won't be gone more than five or six weeks. I shall probably go to Austria and Yugoslavia as well, other things being equal. Education and a holiday rolled into one. It would give you all time to think over his future. It looks as though Bearings is about to go bust anyway."

"It's rather sudden," Janet said slowly.

"I only settled the contract yesterday morning."

"You'll have to ask his father." Janet was on the defensive. "I can't say anything until I've discussed it with Edward." Roger was undaunted.

"You'll agree it's a good idea?" Roger said winningly.

"Umm. It certainly sounds interesting." Janet was playing for time. She did not want to offend Roger by an outright refusal, but she knew well enough that Edward would not be inclined to approve. Her reasons for her new-found respect for her brother-in-law were not reasons that her husband would be likely to share. She did not understand Edward's principles, but she was well aware they existed.

"Ah well. We can but hope." Roger looked at the boy. Could he not see the unhappy conflict of hope and misery in the pitifully open face? I wished I could say to the boy, '*Look here, put the whole thing out of your mind. It's phoney. You can't go. There is no hope. Your uncle is phoney too. Forget about it. And listen to your father. He's a man worth listening to.*' But I could not speak. It was not my place to speak. And if I had spoken, it would have made no difference.

On our way back to town, Roger enlarged on his nephew's good qualities. He seemed unaware of having brought more discord to an already divided house. I wondered whether the boy would plead with his mother, or just go upstairs and lie upon his bed torn with apprehension, making violent and fruitless vows. It appeared that in Roger's view the boy was a combination of the best in Edward and himself. Howard had Edward's steadiness and Roger's flair for adventure. He was clever too in an unconventional way, like Roger. He could see through the sham of a place like Bearings. He had his head screwed on the right way. A genuine Allenside. I listened gloomily. There didn't seem any limit to Roger's illusions. They were so big, he couldn't see anything else. The whole world was out of sight.

"It's early," Roger protested when I said I wanted to get back. "The night is young."

I insisted that I had some work to do before going to bed. When he saw I was not to be persuaded, he asked how Helen was. I was annoyed with him. His impudence was beginning to irritate me.

"She's very well," I said curtly.

"I'm afraid she didn't take to me," Roger said. "My stupid

sense of humour didn't appeal to her. She's a very serious-minded girl, I should say, isn't she?"

I fumed inwardly. That he should have the nerve to discuss her with me! I ransacked my mind for some crushing sarcasm. But none I found would do, because each one revealed too clearly what I thought of him: that he was a fraud and a crook.

We pulled up at the entrance to the block. In the twilight I did not at first notice two tall men standing apparently engaged in conversation. As I got out they approached the car. I heard the elder of the two address Roger.

"Mr. Allenside? Mr. Roger Allenside?" A deep voice with a faintly colonial accent.

"Yes." Roger did not seem at all put out.

"I am Detective Inspector Mervill. This is my colleague Detective Sergeant James. We are making inquiries about a Bedford truck that appears to have belonged to the Atalanta Garage, Shepherd's Bush. Would you be so kind as to come along to Shepherd's Bush, in order to look at the lorry and certain other documents, and answer one or two questions? We would appreciate your help."

"Certainly. Anything I can do to help. Care to come David? Good material. See the police at work."

"No thanks. I've got too much work waiting me upstairs."

"Perhaps you would drive Detective Sergeant James along, Mr. Allenside? I'll bring up the rear with the Wolsey."

He pointed to a large black car, parked unobtrusively across the road.

"O.K. Jump in."

The younger man got in alongside Roger and the red car drove away.

"Mr. David Flint?" The Inspector's deep voice sounded at my ear.

"Yes."

"Could I ask you one or two questions?"

"Of course." I shook my head nervously. "Won't you come upstairs?"

"Well just for a moment or two." It might have been a social invitation.

As we stepped into the lift the light went on and I saw the Inspector clearly, for the first time. He wore a light brown suit and a black homburg hat that rested on his large ears. His trousers were held up by a belt, in the American way. His bulky figure seemed to make room scarce for me in the narrow lift. His face was long and serious, except when you noticed his large humorous brown eyes.

When he took off his hat his head became grey and professional, the full extent of his forehead coming into view. A scholarly looking man who would exercise authority with gentle politeness.

"I take it you are a friend of Mr. Allenside's?"

"We are on friendly terms. Actually I would prefer to call myself a friend of his brother's."

"Who would he be, may I ask?"

"My headmaster."

The inspector made a note of the name of the school and of Edward's private address.

"What subjects do you teach, Mr. Flint?"

"Scripture mostly, and some history."

"How interesting." The Inspector rose to his feet and glanced around the bookshelves. "I'm particularly interested in Comparative Religion myself. Do you tell your boys anything about other religions apart from Christianity?"

"There isn't time for much else."

"I suppose I'm cursed with an Open Mind." He examined the titles of Helen's father's books very closely. "There's only one thing I'm sure about; Corruption. It's a corrupt world, Mr. Flint."

"I call it sin," I said.

He returned to his chair.

"Maybe it is sin. But I don't like the word myself. It seems to suggest that man has the power to hurt God. I can't believe that is so. All this mess of misery and suffering people inflict on each other, I can't see that it affects God, even supposing it concerns him. It's all too aimless, too inconsequential, 'birth copulation and death' with 'getting and spending' in between. All so aimless. What's it got to do with God? He's locked us up in the Universe and thrown away the key. Maybe he's just hidden it. And it can only be found by those who are detached from worldly pursuits. . . . But I can tell by the way you're looking you don't agree with me."

I found the self-deprecatory smile and the musical unfamiliar accent most winning.

"It isn't often in the course of duty one gets a chance for this kind of conversation. I am much obliged to you."

His charm was great. I toyed with the notion of inviting him to my sherry party. He would be something of a find; he would add colour to the catholicity of my reputation. He was both 'real', and 'amusing'.

"Do you happen to know a Mr. Rufus Wod?" The question was unexpected, and I made haste to answer.

"Yes. I met him once at a party. A friend of Roger's."

"Or an accomplice." The Inspector added softly.

"Have they . . . been up to something?"

"Quite a lot. Rufus Wod has a phoney House and Flat Agency. Then there's this Atalanta Garage in Shepherd's Bush. Who does that belong to?"

I said hastily, "I don't know. But I believe Roger tried to persuade Helen to put money into it."

"Would that be Miss Helen Brown the tenant of this flat?"

For some reason I felt guilty as if my conscience was under cross-examination. He was watching me closely and I was blushing.

"I borrow the flat while she is away."

"I see." I wondered how much he saw. I wish he knew I was a novelist as well as a teacher of Scripture.

"Is she a friend of Mr. Allenside's too?"

"Good Lord, no! She hates the sight of him."

"Why?"

"He annoys her."

"How?" What was he after?

"Oh! Imposes on her. Tries to impose upon her."

"I see." Why did I not say that he had been blackmailing Helen? What a chance this was to avenge her. But I couldn't. He seemed to be in enough trouble already. I didn't want to get dragged into it farther. If anything went to court I would be a witness. That wasn't the kind of publicity I wanted.

The Inspector got to his feet.

"Thank you Mr. Flint. Here's my card in case you want to get in touch with me."

I took it without looking at it. I wanted him to go. He was no longer amusing. His old colonial charm was just a convenient mask. Did the man think I had something to do with Roger's activities? He was making my whole life seem suspect.

"Corruption," the Inspector said as he was leaving. "Policemen have to keep it from overflowing its banks. Teachers of religion try to tame it. We have something in common." Ready to close the door, I did not think so. I was one of the hunted not one of the hunters. His way wasn't mine. "Good night Mr. Flint. You have my number if you feel you need me. Good night."

XXII

Was my way of living actually as suspect as it must have appeared to the Detective Inspector? A teacher of Scripture living in a woman's flat; obviously living with the woman. A teacher of Scripture who had a wife and child elsewhere, living with a wealthy woman in a comfortable Kensington flat. A teacher of Scripture having dealings with a black marketing swindler. A poor sort of life to be dragged into the lurid black and white of the evening papers. I felt as if I were threatened with exposure, as if I were being forced to regard my life as someone else's, told in columns of suggestive print and read by everyone; by Allenside, my friend; by Janet, who always thought there was something fishy about me; by Cloudspeake who would suddenly decline the invitation owing to a previous engagement he had overlooked; by Phyllis who would be ashamed to face her neighbours; by Eglinton who would bring the wretched paper into the staff-room crying joyfully, "I say, you chaps, just look at this!"; by Brunt who would lift his eyebrows; by Visot who would sadly shake his head; by Hawkes who would grin "the deep old devil"; by them all, by them all.

Roger was in for serious trouble. It was the kind of case that would feed the evening papers for days. WELL-KNOWN JOURNALIST UNMASKED. RESPECTED WRITER RUNS BLACK MARKET. The headlines jerked before my eyes in a monotonous dance of accusation. The façade he had put up was about to topple over. He was on the verge of exposure. His position could no longer be held. And neither could mine. The game of a double-life was up. Helen was right. When she told me, I should have made my choice. Well, I could do it now. Resign. Stop being a teacher of Scripture. Become just a poor weak antinomian novelist.

It seemed a solution. It certainly released the exultation a solution is supposed to give. Eureka! I drank my own health in gin and water and sat down to compose a letter to Helen that would warm her heart. A full generous declaration of dependence and love. It did not bear re-reading. Nothing is more injurious to style than the first flush of unwarranted enthusiasm. It sounded gauche and too sycophantic. It revealed too much of what I felt instead of what I believed I ought to be feeling.

Far better a sudden descent upon Boscombe, announced barely by a suitably inscribed postcard. "*You were right, darling, David.*" We could go abroad while Roger's case was being dealt with; while waiting for my divorce to come through. I imagined Helen and myself in Florence. Perhaps we could tour the Dalmatian coast. I would show her the places I knew. It seemed absurd and incredible that I had been unwilling to travel before. A lack of trust in Helen and myself? It was time to take the plunge. I should have done it before. Marriage presupposes absolute trust in each other. Texts sprang to mind. It was all due to lack of faith.

For the sake of my writing, I had gone to work each day to maintain contact with people on a basis of everyday reality; to preserve my independence of judgement and observation; to earn an honest living; to think with a mercilessly unclouded mind. For the sake of writing, I had pursued a mixed existence; and now it threatened to kill my writing with fear and worry and guilt. My life was like a house condemned as unsafe, liable at any moment to collapse and bury my writing talent for ever. A fortress become a tomb.

It did not take me very long to cancel out my obligation to the school. The boys had a right to a better teacher and a better witness of the faith than myself. My righteousness was a long long way from exceeding that of the Pharisees. Allenside had a right to a better colleague, and a more steadfast friend. When I had gained my freedom in the future, we could re-establish our friendship on a firmer basis.

By the morning, my mind was so firmly settled on the question that the only remaining concern was how Allenside could best be told and how soon I could get away. My first impulse was to go down to Boscombe and resign from there by letter. But that was too shabby, even for me. On the underground a notion presented itself which made an instant appeal: to combine pleasure with business. Robinson and I, the deputation, were to see the Governors that afternoon. Why not take the chance to tell them the outrageous truth about themselves, and then, with a final flourish, hand in my resignation? It was the kind of opportunity that many timorous men dream about. Why not take it?

As the train rattled on, I saw myself point an eloquent finger at Lord Whiteway, who shrank before the blaze of truth that poured from my lips. Alderman Caffey nursed his head in his hands, guilt-stricken by my exposure. Mrs. Treadle, a former Mayoress of the Borough, pale with anger, but too interested in the Alderman's secret history to interrupt. The H.M.I. trying to creep quietly out of the room but caught by Allenside and Robinson, and compelled to wait his turn. How I would wag my tongue! How my flashing ruthless phrases would win my colleagues' applause! No restraint left, no limit except the exhaustion of my art. The hooves of my steel-shod words would thunder over their heads. All day I would parade about in the glittering uniform of my integrity. My presence would be a visitation, a day of truth; my coming the coming of the oracle, the messenger, the prophet.

The train was delayed for almost five minutes outside the terminus. I could not prevent myself from becoming anxious. Other passengers rose from their seats, poked their heads through windows and frowned impatiently down the line, as if the Railway Executive, at the sight of their displeasure, would fly, terror-stricken, to tear away the offending obstacle. I looked fussily at my watch. I put away my Review, fastened up my bag, took out my season ticket, ready to dash out as the doors opened and race up the broad flight of stairs, dodging and bobbing among the people descending.

Outside the station, in the High Street, I caught up with Eglinton.

"Damn train," I puffed. "Outside the station for nearly five minutes."

"Made your speech?" Eglinton asked. He carried a neat brief-case. He seemed more like a lawyer than a teacher: he was neatly turned out.

I remembered my silent orations on the train. At least I could amuse my colleagues. Say daring things and never mind if Briarman or anyone else is listening.

"I'm going to tell Whiteway what I think of him," I said. "Then I'm going to resign."

Eglinton laughed. He assumed at once I was joking. Which was, of course, correct. I couldn't even begin to deceive him. I would never do it. The absurdity was that I had entertained the notion, had embroidered upon it. Fantasy. Escapism. I would not be able to summon up enough courage and determination to tell Allenside I was leaving. I would carry my desire around with me for days like a guilty secret until some desperation like a gust of wind would blow me into his room.

Throughout first lesson I was occupied with deciding my approach. While the children did written work, I sat motionless at my desk as if waiting for inspiration. The important thing was to avoid any suggestion that the school was of no significance compared with my career, that his work was only of secondary value compared with mine, that our friendship was something to be easily sacrificed for the sake of my art. When teaching I was irritable and unsympathetic; I snapped at the slow-witted, barked at the innocent enquirers and the eager to please, and cowed all but the boldest into timid silence. It was time I left the class-room; a source of escapist fantasy second only to strap-hanging.

I needed direct communication with Nature. Solitude. A Retreat. The life of a hermit in which to accumulate spiritual resources that would allow me to face the rough world with a purposeful courage. Meditation. Secluded Study. The Pursuit of the Word. Patient groping for the pulse of the Absolute. Waiting upon God. Learning the alphabet of Prayer. Acts of Submission and Contrition; acts of Renunciation and Humility.

Boscombe did not seem the right place for my withdrawal. But Boscombe would only be a beginning, a starting-point. Helen would need to be informed—instructed in almost—of my new point of view; the latest stage in the emergence of my vocation. Some village in Dorset, or in the Ligurian Alps. Some quiet spot was awaiting my coming with eternal patience. Journeying that way, bound for another destination, I would pause suddenly and say, 'This is it. This is the place. Here I shall stay.' A withdrawal in which to accumulate a new rare power, to absorb spiritual strength as a sheltered sensitive plant draws life from the distant sun.

In the staff-room everyone was making an effort to be cool

and self-possessed, as if this day was in no sense an occasion. It was Robinson who broke the artificial calm. During the break, he entered the room flourishing a letter. He held up his hand for silence and quoted:

> . . . I am directed by the Governors to thank you for your letter in which you outline the sentiments of the staff regarding the inquiry the Governors propose to make into Mr. Visot's alleged political activities in school. The Governors consider that the views of the staff have been amply expressed in your valued letter, and they are of the opinion that listening to a deputation of the kind you suggest would be an unreasonable trespass on your time and on theirs, serving no useful purpose. . . .
>
> Arnold C. Pluminer,
>
> Clerk to the Governors.

Immediately the room was filled with indignant comment. Impatiently Robinson waved his hand, shouting, "Order! Quiet! There isn't much time. What are we going to do?"

"It's deliberate," Hawkes insisted on saying. "They've delayed sending their reply to the last minute so that we won't have time to take action."

"All right." Robinson posed the problem. "What action *are* we going to take?"

We were silent. At such short notice everyone was prepared to wait for suggestions from someone else.

Brunt said carefully: "I hesitate to suggest this. It has been mentioned before actually. But I think it is worth considering. I mean we can't just force ourselves in can we, if they refuse to hear us."

"I'd bloody well like to," Hawkes said belligerently. "But seriously, that wouldn't do any good. We need a constructive proposal, don't we?"

We listened to Brunt more willingly than usual. I thought as hard as I could, but no idea presented itself that was not impractical or phantastic.

"You remember Robby, I think it was, pointed out that Jack was under no obligation to attend their meeting."

"Who's Jack?" Eglinton murmured unhelpfully. He knew very well it was Visot.

"Why not reconsider that course now?" Brunt's voice was

never more sweetly reasonable. Visot had become red in the face. "Of course," Brunt added hastily, "it's a matter that only he can decide. But my feeling is we've reached a stage at which actions would speak louder than words."

Visot cleared his throat and said loudly: "I have already made my position clear. I intend to go."

"Time for the bell," Briarman pointed to the clock.

"To hell with the bell!" Hawkes said. "This is more important."

There was a chorus of noisy agreement. Briarman was not the man to go across such a strong current of feeling. He went out and told the prefect on duty to delay ringing the bell for another two minutes. He hurried back like a boy eager not to miss the details of a dormitory conspiracy. It appeared unseemly in a man of his age. He was too patently anxious to be accepted as "one of the boys". Now he had power, he yearned for popularity.

"You are under no obligation to go, I think that's clear enough," Dell said, looking at Visot and drawing at his pipe. It seemed to suit everyone that he should not go. For once I saw the point of the newspaper phrase about opinion 'hardening.'

Robinson said: "Hawkes and I have already brought the case to the notice of the Union. You would be quite justified, Visot, in saying the Union was behind you if you refused to go. You should treat this summons as an invitation and decline it. The less you say the less you are committed, and the stronger is the Union's case for saying that there was no *prima facie* case to warrant the Governors taking this kind of action. Your position is all the stronger and all the safer because the Headmaster has told us that he is in full agreement with our point of view."

"I'm sorry." Visot rose to his feet, tugging down his buttoned-up jacket. "I've made up my mind. I'm going."

He walked out of the room.

"Martyr complex," Eglinton said. "He wants to be canonised. Hero of the Soviet Union."

Brunt, concentrating on the grave problem before us pretended not to hear.

"Lock him up!" Hawkes smacked his knee with the palm of his hand. "I've got it. Where's the Time Table?"

He ran his finger down the columns of letters and figures on the wall.

"Where is the first lesson this afternoon? He's in the Demonstration Room. We could lock him in the store cupboard for a couple of hours."

Eglinton at once supported the suggestion. He was all for making the affair as ridiculous as possible. Brunt shook his head and went on thinking deeply. Robinson smiled tolerantly. The rest of us were amused by the idea. Briarman said, "Sorry, gentlemen," and pointed to the clock as if he were a bar-tender.

Hawkes took his idea seriously. By the lunch hour he had evolved a complete plan of action. Four men would force Visot into the store-room and not only lock that door, but the Demonstration Room door as well. Mitchley, who was free first period, would take Visot's form in another class-room. As for the rest of the afternoon, arrangements had already been made in any case for other men to take Visot's classes.

By quiet pressure and humorous persuasion Hawkes enrolled three of us to assist him, Eglinton, Thorpe and myself. Hawkes had ample physical strength to carry out the business by himself; we were needed more for moral support than anything else.

Immediately before lunch, Allenside came to the staff-room. He asked us for our attention. The whole staff was present except Briarman, Downs and Visot who were on dinner duty in the boys' canteen.

"I understand," he said seriously, "how concerned you must be at what is to happen this afternoon. We all of us share a real affection and respect for Mr. Visot. I may say how warmed I am by the friendly unity you are showing. It does you all great honour, and I feel privileged to be associated with you."

Unity of friendship! I knew a little better. But that wasn't the point. As I watched him speak, I was deeply moved. His integrity compelled us to conform with the nobility of his vision. He had something of that quality of leadership which inspires men not only to excel themselves but to burn out a lifetime's unworthiness in one reckless act of atonement.

Allenside said, "I would like you to know that I have made it clear to the Governors that I have the fullest confidence in

Mr. Visot, that I share the sentiments expressed in your letter, and that if they persist in harrying Mr. Visot in spite of my reassurances I will consider it a sign of no confidence in myself and my administration of the school."

We realised that we were hearing a considered statement of policy. Allenside had made up his mind, chosen his course. Although his voice was serious and his language slow, heavy, and over-measured, Allenside looked happier than I had seen him for some time. Whatever had passed between Whiteway and himself, he had enjoyed it. His confidence in himself was re-established. He was able to take the initiative in his own way, and not wait, with uncharacteristic nervousness upon events.

"It is my hope that the Governors will be satisfied with a formal denial by Mr. Visot of the accusations that have been made against him."

We were all moved and inspired by the view that Allenside took of the affair and of ourselves. Everyone felt he could approach his neighbour in a spirit of honourable fraternity. No doubt at the end of the afternoon someone would propose we had a celebration. Mitchley probably. It was his hobby to organise informal social occasions: 'staff and wives'.

None of the Governors came to lunch, not even Mr. Frazer-Bouquet an octogenarian clergyman of the Established Church whose appetite was always a source of amused admiration. Dell murmured to his neighbour at table that he suspected the Bilateral would not be the darling of the Education Authority for much longer. He thought Allenside would need to look very far afield for promotion now. The idea pleased him. Allenside's wrong would add permanent lustre to his own.

Hawkes and Eglinton sat on either side of Visot. They treated him with a humorous affection that obviously puzzled him. Later, in the staff-room, over coffee, Thorpe and I demanded his company. Rather obviously I felt, I opened an argument on the nature of Reality; but Visot suspected nothing, and in a short time we were well under way impatiently waiting for each other to finish, clawing as we believed at each other's arguments to demolish them, but all the time jumping at the sheer walls of separate prisons.

Five minutes before the first bell, I walked out, making conscientious noises about preparing my first lesson. I wanted to giggle with excitement; it seemed such a glorious lark. Visot, not to be outdone, went up to the Demonstration Room.

When we four entered the empty room Visot was setting up some illustrative apparatus. He looked up at us with surprise. My heart was beating fast. To my unaccustomed palate this seemed daringly like an act of violence. Was I enjoying a guilty pleasure? Or was it good clean well-meaning fun?

We had agreed to say nothing. The longer we kept him guessing the easier he would be to handle. It was my job to open the store-room door. There was a chair there for him and electric light. We had even left him a book to read. That was Eglinton's idea. It was by some Russian who had escaped to America to write books.

We just pushed him in. It was surprisingly easy.

"For your own good, Vizzy old boy," Hawkes said as he locked the door. We smiled at each other. The most difficult job was over. It remained to keep the Demonstration Room empty for the afternoon. With Mitchley's help, we could cope quite easily with Visot's classes. We had violated the sacred law of the Time Table, and so far it had been surprisingly easy.

"There's just one point," Hawkes said, rubbing his chin thoughtfully, as we stood together at the top of the stairs, "the Governors ought to be informed that Visot will not be appearing. I'll just pop in there as soon as they start, if you'll keep an eye on my class, Flint. They're next door to yours, first lesson."

"What will you say?" Eglinton giggled nervously. I wondered whether he was beginning to regret the escapade.

"Mr. Visot has bowed to the opinion of his colleagues. On their advice and insistence he will not appear before you this afternoon. He apologises for not having let you know sooner. Something like that?" Hawkes made a comic gesture with his hands. He seemed the only one among us who was not worried. "We can say he's put his case in the hands of the Union."

"But he hasn't," Thorpe said quietly.

"No, but he will." Hawkes swept his own misgivings aside, but not ours. We had committed ourselves. A lot depended now on Visot.

Quite suddenly I remembered my resolutions of the morning; how I had intended to harangue the Governors and then resign. I wanted to laugh at my nervousness. I longed to show the others how devil-may-care I really was. I spoke up boldly.

"Don't worry chaps. If there are any repercussions, I'll be responsible. I'll probably be leaving before the end of this term."

They seemed uncertain whether or not to believe me. Hawkes smiled as if I was joking. As if to make my position clearer, I said, "Better let me pop in and tell them Mr. Visot regrets he's unable to come today."

I did not really want to go. It alarmed me to think of facing the Governors to make such a misleading statement. But some obscure sense of obligation led me on. It was time I dared.

"Listen!" Eglinton raised his finger. We heard a faint banging. Visot was hammering the door of the store-room. It wasn't likely that anyone would hear him. He was boxed in a top corner of the building. The room beneath him was also a store-room, adjoining the chemistry lab, full of bottles and damaged equipment. So long as he did nothing wildly foolish, such as breaking the door down, he was safe.

The bell rang and the school was filled with the clamour of the boys going to their class-rooms. Eglinton and Thorpe left Hawkes and myself to settle between us who would interrupt the Governors' meeting. We were teaching in adjoining rooms and as soon as our classes were settled down to work we met in the corridor outside.

From a corridor window we were able to obtain a partial view across the small quadrangle of the Assembly Hall in which the Governors were meeting.

The meeting had not yet started. We could see a corner of the polished table around which they would sit, and Lord Whiteway in conversation with Mrs. Treadle and two others whom we could not identify.

"Look at 'em!" Hawkes said with quiet ferocity. "Vultures! Bloody bourgeois vultures. Authority! There's the kind of people who run Education in this country."

A noise of unrest sounded from his room. He strode back to the open door, and stood scowling at some invisible offender. The Governors began to take their places at the table. I saw Allenside bend over old Frazer-Bouquet's chair. The old man held his hand behind his ear to listen. It was time I went down. The sooner the apologies for Visot's absence were made the better.

"I'm off," I said to Hawkes. I might have been jumping over the side of a ship. "Keep an eye on my class till I get back."

I breathed deeply several times outside the closed doors of the Assembly Hall, in order to gain some control over myself. When I felt as confident as I ever would be, I knocked the door lightly and went in.

All the Governors turned their heads, surprised at the intrusion. A moment's cowardice made me go up to Allenside as if I had a message for him instead of addressing the whole meeting. He sat next to Whiteway, whose bushy eyebrows were raised enquiringly, his mouth still open as if I had interrupted him in the middle of a sentence.

"Mr. Visot will not be able to attend. The Union have advised him not to come. He apologises for not having informed you before this."

I tried to make my voice sound as amiable as I could. The situation was more absurd and at the same time more dangerous than I had imagined. Already Whiteway was frowning.

"Where is he?" Allenside was puzzled. "Isn't he in the building? He gave me to understand he would be here at half past two."

All I wanted now was to get away as quickly as possible. The more I said the more I committed myself.

"This is a strange way to behave." Whiteway's voice boomed like an angry deity. "Most irregular, if I may say so, Mr. Headmaster."

I did not know what to say. Should I nod and smile and say, "excuse me," and hurry away? A noise outside the door was a welcome diversion. The Governors turned again to see who was there. The doors flew open and Visot walked in.

Behind him I caught a glimpse of Sergeant Plum, the caretaker, holding his immense bunch of keys. Plum closed the doors softly behind Visot who stood glaring short-sightedly at the meeting. He had broken his glasses. He held them dangling in one hand while he pushed back his hair with the other. By some unhappy accident the caretaker must have heard him and let him out.

"Would someone kindly explain what exactly is happening?" Whiteway said. "Am I to understand Mr. Visot that you are complying with our request to attend this meeting?"

"That is correct." Visot's voice was loud and harsh. "I am perfectly prepared to answer any of the accusations brought against me."

"But Mr. Flint here has just told us that you were not coming. Are you quite certain you know what you are doing?"

"Perfectly." They had declared war on each other already. "I am not prepared to answer for Mr. Flint's actions." He stared grimly at me. "They are quite irrelevant."

"I am bound to say Mr. Headmaster that all this does no credit to the school's good name. None at all. Since Mr. Visot is here, perhaps the meeting would like to proceed straight to his case. It may afterwards like to inquire into Mr. Flint's behaviour."

XXIII

W<small>HAT HAD SEEMED</small> rather smart and witty had turned
very sour. I spent a miserable afternoon exploring the extent
of the damage we had done. We had made matters rather more
than worse. We had helped to divert the displeasure of the
Governors from a member of staff to the headmaster himself.
We had played into Whiteway's hands.

Whiteway had swung violently away from his former high
regard for Allenside and his abilities. Defending Visot and
insisting on Brunt's merits so stubbornly—or unreasonably as
Whiteway would say—had made Allenside himself suspect.
Was he, Lord Whiteway must have asked himself heavily and
frequently as he fished the depths of his mind for the most
conveniently comprehensive answer that would closely
entwine what he wanted with what he could believe was
right, was he, this Allenside, really reliable himself? From his
brother Roger he had learnt, to his dismay, that Allenside's
political sympathies had always been very Left. It was
disagreeable to learn this after cherishing the idea that
Allenside had the *Times*-like 'independence' that Lord
Whiteway expected of every decent educationalist. Allenside
was suspect; Allenside dared to defy Lord Whiteway's
declared wishes, to ignore Lord Whiteway's advice.

A man like Whiteway never found it difficult to change from
high regard to deep displeasure, or from amity to enmity.
There was always more sincere feeling in his hatred than in
his admiration, and since education was his hobby, Whiteway
could give free rein to extremes of temperament he could never
have afforded to deploy in the serious world of business. If
Allenside had gained too much credit for having created a
model Bilateral, he could now collect the full blame for
harbouring a nest of sedition and misrule. It was difficult to
estimate the limit of the harm that Whiteway could do to
Allenside. His disinterested righteousness was something that
Whiteway, who thought in terms of interest and influence,

could not begin to understand. Impelled only by the determination to win at all cost, there were no consequences he needed to reckon with in the unlikely event of his losing. Safe from any danger of retaliation, he could indulge in saturation bombing to make his victory absolutely certain.

The least thing, the only thing, I could do now, was to resign. Make myself into some sort of scapegoat. But that would not be easy because Whiteway had some knowledge of the friendship between Allenside and myself. There was a limit to the amount of blame I could usefully take. All that afternoon I taught with surprising energy and steadiness, not once tempted to steal a further view of the Assembly Hall or to communicate with my colleagues. As for Hawkes, next door, the occasional sound of his raised voice got on my nerves. I felt as if I had been taken in by him and I was in no mood to forgive him any more than myself.

At the end of the afternoon the staff-room buzzed with excited chatter. I only stayed long enough to give the briefest account of my own actions. Eglinton grinned as he listened in a way that made me want to hit him. Visot, it seemed, had gone straight home without saying anything to anyone—not even Brunt. Rumour flew about the room. What Eglinton wanted was to know whether it was true that the Head had resigned. Had I heard anything? I found their unrestrained curiosity distasteful and ugly: it was like some catalyst that threatened the whole set up of the school with dissolution. The idea that Allenside might have resigned opened such vistas in their minds, that acquired habits of loyalty and respect seemed to be set aside in order to give them greater freedom in discussing the intriguing shapes the future was likely to take and the particular place it held for their greater comfort and glory. But their disloyalties were petty compared with mine. They had never been bound to him by ties of personal friendship. In my self-centred thoughtlessness I had done him more harm than anyone else.

The Governors had mostly departed. A last group stood at the head of the stone staircase that led down to the main door. I went to the Assembly Hall. It seemed like a deserted battlefield; the chairs had been pushed back carelessly; abandoned positions. Only the large padded chair in which Whiteway had sat was neatly in its place, a vacated throne.

I wanted to be with Allenside; to explain and excuse myself; to help; to comfort; to salvage something from a situation that had suddenly gone to pieces. There was someone with him in his room. I climbed the stairs that led to the second floor in order to gain a view through the top half of his window. Allenside was seated at his desk and someone, a figure I knew I should know yet could not immediately identify, leaned across the desk talking to him earnestly, a black homburg hat at his elbow. That earnest grey head? Inspector Mervill.

Nothing was more imperative now than helping Allenside. I was not romantic enough to imagine I could rescue him from the rising flood of his troubles, but it seemed the least I could do to attempt to share his fate. To be hurt myself as much as he was being hurt. If somehow I could atone not only for this afternoon's rash folly, but for the whole of my deception, my masquerade of virtue and friendship, perhaps I would re-establish some form of self-respect. It was intolerable to continue thinking so badly of myself for such a length of time.

I waited about the corridor while the Inspector talked with Allenside. It was a long talk. It might have been myself they were discussing their conclave affected me so acutely. For that matter, what was the Inspector telling him about me? Did he give him his opinion of the relationship between myself and Helen Brown? Did he know I was married? Policemen checked up on such things. Would he tell Allenside I had a wife and child? How I wished I had told Allenside the truth long ago. How I hated the hypocritical self-regard that had kept me silent. Behaviour not in keeping with the nature of my work. I should have told him long ago. I could have taught some other subject. Even if I gave up teaching altogether I could still pursue my study of Scripture in the harmless seclusion of my own room.

They emerged at last. I walked quickly down the corridor to meet them. Allenside looked tired.

"Hello David," he said. As if to relieve the worried look on my face, he smiled. "Mr. Flint, Inspector Mervill."

"We have met." The Inspector smiled and bowed slightly. "Last night we had a little discussion on Comparative Religion. A favourite study of mine, Mr. Allenside."

I said nothing. The Inspector's charm bore no effect. All

I wanted was to see him going, so that I could do something to help Allenside.

"Well, you mustn't let me detain you any longer. We must have another talk on the nature of sin, sometime, Mr. Flint." He walked off jauntily, turning back to add, "Don't bother to see me off. I know my way out. Good night to you both."

I spoke as soon as he was out of earshot.

"I can't tell you how sorry I am about this afternoon. I was an utter fool. It was an idea we had to keep Visot out. But it only made matters worse. I'm desperately sorry."

"Visot took care of himself quite well. You needn't have worried. They have broadened the basis of their investigation now. They intend making an inquiry into the general administration of the school. They didn't like the sound of the School Council by the way—especially the chairman. Whiteway thinks you are too irresponsible. Those are the key words, unreliable and irresponsible. It's absurd really. If there are two things I've always tried hard to cultivate they are being reliable and responsible."

I said I was sorry again.

"I don't think your escapade made much difference. I insisted on giving the S.R. to Brunt: that was the real bone of contention. All the rest were trimmings. They have decided to ask for a special inspection. I think Whiteway rather hoped I would indignantly resign. Well I didn't. I just dug in my heels."

"I'm resigning," I said. "It's the least I can do."

"Don't be silly." For the first time he sounded annoyed with me.

"I've made up my mind," I said with miserable determination. "I'm not fit to be a teacher of Scripture. My life doesn't stand close examination."

"Whose life does?" We went back into his room. He packed his case ready go to home and took his hat off the peg.

"You don't know," I said quietly. "I'm married. I have a wife and a son." It was more than I could manage to say I had been living with someone else.

Allenside looked at me. "I knew that," he said. "As a matter of fact I've met your wife. She called here a few days ago to see you."

He had not only forgiven me; he was taking pity on me and giving me comfort. Had I been so eager to help him in order to hook this sympathy for myself? I was a parasite that drew on other people's goodness. Was my condition so much worse than his?

"Come home with me for tea," he said. "We need to hurry. It's getting late."

He made me go. My spirits rose in his company; as if I borrowed strength by proximity. As usual we studied the cricket scores. For a while everything seemed deliciously normal. I enjoyed sitting beside him in the swaying tube and on the bus. The occasion seemed safe, it had the attracted virtue of having been done many times before.

As he walked to his house, he said:

"The Inspector had been to see you about Roger?"

"Last night."

"After he had been here?"

"Yes. As a matter of fact he wanted me to help him persuade you to give way to Whiteway. That is, in order to make sure of the Directorate."

"He believes there are wires to be pulled for everything, doesn't he?"

I remained silent.

"He's booked two passages to Spain. The police are keeping an eye on his every move. The Inspector thought I could tell him who his companion was to be." Allenside pressed his lips together firmly. "I told him there wasn't going to be any companion."

I thought for a second of the disappointed boy.

"It's about the worst thing Roger has ever done." Allenside seemed to know what I was thinking. "To raise the boy's hopes—upset him completely."

I imagined the difficult scene that must have taken place in the Allensides' drawing-room the previous evening. Tears, misunderstandings, recriminations, bitter feelings. Scars that would take so long to heal.

Inside the gates we saw Roger's red sports car parked confidently in front of the house. Voices came from the direction of the small terrace that overlooked the triangular lawn. We found Roger accepting a cup of tea from Janet. "No sugar!" he said and lifted a cheery hand to us in greeting.

Howard was withdrawn in his large basket chair moodily munching his cake.

Janet looked at Edward anxiously. "Well, darling, how did it go?"

He ignored her question. He was gazing grimly at his brother who was struggling amiably to his feet, a plate in one hand and cup and saucer in the other.

"Did you handle the old war-horse gently?" Roger said pleasantly.

He was one of the family, sharing the family's sympathies, a sympathetic brother come to give valuable help.

"The police are interested in your movements, Roger," Allenside said.

Roger smiled and shrank away in mock fear as though his brother was joking.

"You're not going to dodge the consequences so easily this time. I knew you had no respect for any kind of law but I never imagined you had become a professional criminal."

Roger put down the crockery. The balancing of them no longer amused.

"I came here to try and help you," Roger said with surprising dignity. "I am sorry you choose to say these things."

"I find it quite loathsome to have to mention them. The trouble is that they are true. The police fancy that you control quite a traffic in new cars diverted from export, and cars sold out of covenant and even stolen cars. They also imagine that you hire lorries to other criminals for the transport of black market commodities. One of your lorries was ditched near Chelmsford last week with a load of sugar in it."

"You seem very ready to believe such nonsense. I don't own any lorries. I'm not a haulage contractor. Being shut up with boys in school all day doesn't give you much chance to learn about the world outside does it? With a little effort the police could pin a story like that on almost any garage in the country. . . ."

"Excuses won't do Roger," Allenside said. "It's too late for excuses. They know you've booked a passage for Spain. You booked two passages. Who was the other one for?"

Janet made a shocked noise. It was almost possible to see

her changing her attitude, a hasty undignified scramble out of one carriage into another.

"Not for Howard, do you understand?" Allenside turned to look at his son. Fright exposed the bewildered pain the boy was feeling. "I hope you see now Howard why I could never allow you to accompany your uncle. He would teach you that being crooked was being clever. He would have you believe there was no rule except being smarter than the other fellow. He may not know he's a cheat and a swindler, but you must."

Roger frowned, as if his brother spoke of someone they both knew in a way he could not recognise.

"You're trying to poison the boy's mind against me," Roger protested. "Why should you want to poison his mind against me?"

"I'm sorry Roger, I want you to get out now and stay away, for good. I don't want to see you here again. You've done too much harm already."

"You're jealous," Roger said suddenly as if he had hit on an explanation. "You've always been jealous."

He barely heard Allenside's accusations, made no attempt to consider them. He was too busily occupied trying to explain what he imagined was his brother's antipathy towards him.

"I've asked you to go," Allenside said wearily.

"I came here to help you. You've handled Whiteway the wrong way Edward. I could have fixed the whole thing for you quite easily."

"Don't you even hear what I'm saying?" Allenside shouted. "I don't want your help. Can't you bring yourself to see things as they are, not just as you want them to be?"

The boy jumped up from his chair suddenly, as if he could bear it no longer.

"Stop. Why can't you stop . . ?" But as soon as he began to speak he lost control of his mouth; it became distorted with the tears he could no longer hold back. He pushed his way past his father and rushed indoors.

"Poor kid's upset," said Roger. "Doesn't like to see us quarrelling. He thinks the world of you really you know Eddie. He's a good kid."

"I'm not quarrelling with you. I'm trying to make you understand that the way you live is wrong, and I can't stand by and let you influence Howard in any way. You must keep away. Go and face up to the consequences of what you've done."

"I thought blood was thicker than water."

"The way you are living is criminal, it's wrong. Can't you see that?"

Roger turned away, pushing his hands deep into his trouser pockets. "Uncle James. Uncle James," was all he said.

Allenside said quietly, "You'd better go now."

Without another word, Roger picked up his cap and left the house.

XXIV

SCHOOL THE NEXT DAY was hateful. I held the whole place responsible for Allenside's suffering. I saw little of him in the course of the day, but I thought of him constantly, confined as he was in the solitude of his unhappiness. The school, upon which he had lavished so much of his creative power, I knew with prophetic certainty, would lapse into a below the average Secondary School, an outcast languishing in shabby anonymity and permanent unimportance among a network of insignificant side-streets. The hope of new buildings had gone for ever. The Authority like a capricious prince would seek a new favourite on which to lavish its favours. Allenside had lost more than the hope of promotion. The plans he had made for the future of the school would never be completed. Men change rapidly when their dreams come to nothing. I did not doubt that he would fight. Everything would not be lost. But when the fight was over and the issue settled, would he suddenly discover he no longer cared? He would never degenerate into a premature pensioner or a sour cynic. His devotion to righteousness would alone save him from that. But without the compulsion of ambitious dreams, he would become a victim of jog-trot routine, a devotee of a steady watch-like precision. Intellectual middle-age would set in.

His dreams and ambitions he would transfer to an increasing concern for the welfare of his son. Upon Howard he would spend a treasure-house of thought and feeling with the wise budgeting of total devotion. At least he had won the first battle. But it would be a very long war. Concerning their son he would maintain rigid control over his wife, compensating her with greater freedom to nag against himself. And until he could be sure of Howard there would always be the threat of Roger upon the home's horizon.

I hoped Roger would be caught and sent to prison. I toyed with the idea of helping the police in some obscure way to complete their evidence. It would be a way of helping Allenside. I would offer the Inspector my services; contact Roger and lure him into a police trap. He would be put away and Howard would be safe from his influence. It was an absurd impractical notion. My urge to help Allenside was completely frustrated. I could only relieve him for a while of the additional burden of my clutching friendship. Even if I prayed for him what value were my prayers? Wishing Allenside well always ended in wishing myself better.

Unrest was already rife among the staff. I listened to Dell advising Eglinton and Thorpe as men still young with excellent qualifications to seek posts elsewhere, to bale out while there was still time, before they became stigmatised by too long service at an unsuccessful school. Brunt was angry because his special responsibility allowance had been awarded him 'subject to annual review'. He said it was an insult and Hawkes asked him if that meant he would be refusing the money? Mitchley, during my free period, took the opportunity to launch an outburst against the injustice inflicted upon him by Allenside. Visot, in whose reactions I was most interested, to my shocked surprise, refused to speak to me. This I considered especially mortifying, since I had already seen him in civil enough conversation with Eglinton and Thorpe. He seemed to consider me a particularly despicable type of traitor.

Four o'clock was a blessed release. I had already packed a bag and I took the underground direct to Waterloo to catch a Bournemouth train. I barely had time to dispatch a wire to Helen, worded "*How right you were. See you tonight. David.*"

I was escaping from a web of living that had threatened to entangle me. I had spread my consciousness like a membrane across the street for too many feet to trample on. An artist requires privacy as much as a tree needs its bark or a snail its shell: a prerequisite of existence. If life threatened to overwhelm me a law of self-preservation compelled me to retreat. The rhythm of the train speeding southwards seemed to induce a lyric of self-regard which I sang to myself with unashamed abandon. Off to somewhere better from what seemed worse and worse. Congratulatory, laudatory; the song of the blissful haven, the song of holiday safety. Freedom spread out like a sunset waiting to receive me; and at my back the shadows gathered over the city of Despair.

I hired a taxi to carry me from Boscombe to Helen's house. I resisted an impulse to buy an evening paper in case of any developments in the police's attempt to catch up with Roger. With mounting excitement I devoted myself to sorting out the stories I would soon be relating to Helen: my meeting with Phyllis; Peter Bayley's visit to the flat: Roger and Howard and the progressive school; the troubles at the Bilateral. It all needed editing and sub-editing to suit Helen and my new resolve to resign and follow her advice. During the last week I had not written and naturally enough I had received no postcards in reply. In the taxi, I reminded myself it could be possible that Helen would not be at home. I had forgotten the address of the children's new school, but I had a vague idea it was in Devon. Perhaps Helen had gone down to see them. I prepared myself for such a disappointment. I was intensely eager to see her now; to explain how my mind had changed to a complete acceptance of her point of view. There was no barrier now to our happy union. The last barrier was down. The taxi swept down the drive and pulled up outside the front door. I paid the driver and waited on the steps as he turned round and set off again the way we had come.

In the music room someone was playing the piano. Not Helen. She did not play. Was it Nurse Jones revealing an unexpected grace beneath her starchy exterior? It was very pleasant. It cast a warm glow about a house in which I was after all, a stranger. I pushed open the door and walked into the hall. There was no one about. A light from upstairs merged half-way up the broad staircase into the indoor gloom. Outside the twilight was gradually deepening into darkness. It was a warm night. I listened to the music, not disposed to interrupt, the notes fell so delightfully on to the still night air. I rejoiced in the spaciousness of the house, all the evidence of elegance about me. Through the open window in the deserted drawing-room, I could discern across the cobbled yard the pale white face of the stable clock.

The music had stopped. I caught the scent of the flowers outside the window. A strand of ivy hung down above the window shaped like a question mark. Someone switched on the light. I turned to face a man of my own age, wearing a double-breasted dinner jacket. He held a freshly lit cigarette. He had a wide intelligent face. He was threatened with premature baldness. His composure suggested effortless self-control.

"Hello!" I smiled, trying not to look like an intruder. "Where's Helen?"

"She's upstairs, resting. She's not very well."

"Oh!" My mouth opened inanely. It was something I had not prepared for.

"You are David Flint I presume?"

"Yes."

"My name is Reis. I'm a doctor. I'm attending Miss Brown."

"I see." As a matter of fact I saw nothing. I was acutely puzzled. "What exactly is the matter?"

"A form of neurosis that needs lengthy treatment. She is making good progress."

His air of calm authority irritated me. Who did he think he was? I resented the way in which he seemed to be in charge of everything. It did not seem like Helen to lapse into the feather-bed of valetudinarianism.

"Would you care for something to eat? Nurse Jones could get you something?"

I refused, although I was hungry. It would have been too much like a capitulation.

"Helen knew I was coming? She got my telegram?"

"Yes. I'm afraid it upset her a little." He stubbed out his cigarette thoughtfully in an ash-tray balanced on the arm of a settee.

" 'Upset' her? What exactly do you mean?"

"It would take rather long to explain in technically accurate terms. Miss Brown is suffering from a profound mental upheaval which will take some time to resolve itself. Indeed might never resolve itself unless it is correctly treated, and the correct treatment is begun at once."

"You are a psycho-analyst?" I said rather accusingly.

Reis smiled. "That is one of my qualifications. I'm glad you've come Mr. Flint. But I must warn you that your coming has precipitated something like a crisis. Her relationship with you is one of the deepest causes of Miss Brown's unrest. There are many ways in which you can help, if you will. Perhaps we can have a talk tomorrow morning. A room has been prepared for you. The blue guest room. You know where it is?"

I said yes although I did not know. I wasn't going to betray my ignorance to this fellow at any cost.

"I'd like to see Helen," I said. "I'll see her first."

"You mustn't get annoyed with me." Reis said in a calm voice that suggested it wouldn't make the slightest difference if I did. "But I think it would be wiser to put that off until tomorrow."

"I don't agree. I shall see her tonight. It's a ridiculous notion to put off seeing her until tomorrow. You don't seem to understand we are going to be married very soon."

Reis nodded his head patiently.

"She has told me a good deal about your life together and the plans you had."

"Did she say she did not wish to see me tonight? In so many words?"

"As a matter of fact she agreed it would be wiser."

To have rushed upstairs under such circumstances would have been boorish and ignorant. Inaction left me full of the sour ill-temper of defeat.

"I am spending the night here myself," Reis explained. "Would you like something to drink?"

"I'll help myself, thank you." I sounded petulant and sulky. I could not bear the suavity of his professional approach.

"Helen tells me you are a teacher of Scripture as well as a novelist."

"Yes."

"What does teaching Religion entail?" he said. I resented the tone of his question. "What text-books do you use?"

"The Bible," I said. "The New Testament and the Old Testament. That's what I teach."

"Have you read *Moses and Monotheism*?" He sat now very much at ease in the corner of the settee.

"Yes," I said, prepared to gamble on a second-hand knowledge of its contents. "All about the Hebrews killing Moses. Interesting guess-work. I prefer William James."

Reis nodded understandingly. "I grant you James is a good starting-off point for the intelligent layman."

I yawned with polite rudeness. "Excuse me," I said. "I've had rather a long day. I think I'll turn in."

"Good idea. I'll do the same."

We walked upstairs together. The door of Helen's room was

222

closed but I thought I saw a light under the door. Reis's bedroom was nearer Helen's than mine. The air of mystery about the place infuriated me. I could not sleep. What exactly was happening. Was Helen really ill? It seemed a bogus sort of illness to me. Was it some elaborate way of concealing that she had changed her mind about me? A way of getting rid of me. I could not dismiss the notion as ridiculous. In the darkness, suspicion festered in my mind until I stuffed my mouth with a blanket and dug my teeth into the fluffy stuff to stop myself from groaning and crying aloud. Was this doctor chap her new lover? Or merely an additional apparatus to assist her lawyers in protecting her from the less pleasant facts of existence? All the new fund of love that had accumulated in the course of our time apart was evaporated by the scorching heat of jealousy and suspicion. My mind was prepared to believe anything about her. The trust and faith which I longed for simply did not exist in practice. Nothing restrained me from thinking the worst of Helen as I lay biting a blanket, rigid with savage angry pain.

I was tempted to get up and go to her room. I actually got as far as putting on a dressing-gown that hung behind the door, and standing in the corridor. A lamp still burnt in Helen's room, pale and shaded, judging by the light that filtered under her door. Nothing disturbed the utter silence of the sleeping night. Occasional sounds in the trees behind the stables sounded as loud as small explosions. Fear of making myself ridiculous turned me back. Or fear of a situation which I did not understand except that vaguely it seemed to threaten me. A decisive crisis was at hand, and yet I had no idea of its nature, no plan or principle with which to meet it, no idea how to behave. As I lay in bed again the night beat against my head in warm overpowering waves of darkness.

I slept late. My situation fastened itself upon me before I had properly opened my eyes. The blue light caused by the drawn curtains was repugnant to me. I was a patient whose conscious will was submerged, anaesthetised, and I was at the mercy of the smiling omniscient physician who tilted the hypodermic needle delicately towards my white helpless arm. I pulled the curtains furiously apart, as if committing an act of rebellion.

My window overlooked a pleasant expanse of sloping lawn

and trees into which paths disappeared. Each leaf and flower seemed stretched to suck some white secret life from the full morning sunlight. It was a warm and golden morning, ready to extinguish the smouldering ends of my misery, ready to give, if not content, the thin serenity of forgetfulness.

But I saw Helen and Doctor Reis walking slowly, absorbed in conversation, away from the house. Eagerly I pushed the window and placing my hands on the sill outside, I thrust out the top part of my body and loudly called her name. They turned about. She was wearing a white blouse and a flowered skirt. Her skin was deeply tanned and she looked extremely well. With an absurd gaiety completely contrary to what I was feeling, I waved to her. She spoke quickly to Reis and walked rapidly away by herself in the direction of the trees. Reis looked after her, as if he were considering calling her back. Then he calmly lit a cigarette and walked back towards the house.

To my annoyance, in spite of my misery, I found I was acutely hungry. I could not resist the breakfast laid out for me on the terrace. The coffee was still warm and under the cover I found appetising eggs and bacon. When I was well immersed in the business of eating, with calculated premeditation, Reis joined me.

"Good morning," he said pleasantly. "You had a good night?"

My mouth was full. I nodded ungraciously. Chewing as fast as I could in my haste to speak, when my mouth was free I said, "What's the matter with Helen?"

"I began to explain last night." Reis crossed his legs patiently. "She isn't well. Disturbances of the psyche often . . ."

"Never mind about that. Where has she gone now? Why is she trying to avoid me now?"

"I was hoping," Reis said, "you would be intelligent enough to discuss the case in an enlightened and detached manner."

"I presume you yourself are entirely enlightened and utterly detached?" My tone was offensive.

"You won't gain anything by being rude," Reis said.

"I don't want to gain anything," I said. "I want to be enlightened and detached. Why can't I speak to Helen?" My voice rose in spite of my efforts to control it. "Why all this damned nonsense?"

"Because she does not want to speak to you."

Was that the horrifying truth?

"She is very conscious of a sense of obligation towards you. She feels she has led you to expect so much, she cannot face telling you that she can no longer face the idea of marrying you, and she no longer wishes to continue living with you. You may know yourself that her sexual life has never been satisfactory. The fault I would say was on both sides in each case. You will have observed a tendency to swing from frigidity to an artificial warmth mostly grounded on fear-neurosis. It is extremely doubtful whether she has ever experienced an orgasm which may be. . . ."

"There she is!" I caught a glimpse of her hurrying quietly along the path leading to the rear entrance. "I'm going to get to the bottom of this."

"It won't do any good Flint." I shook off his restraining arm. He followed me as I marched through the drawing-room into the hall. Helen was half-way upstairs.

"Helen!" She stopped as I shouted. She glanced at me quickly and looked away again. In that glance I understood that what Reis said was true. She looked at me as if I was an object rather than a person. It hurt and infuriated me. I just wouldn't go quietly to oblige her. I would kick up all the fuss I could. If she thought she could fix everything with money and doctors and money and lawyers, she was damn well wrong. Like a man carried away by force, who still kicks and screams, I had to assert myself.

"Helen!" I shouted so loudly, I arrested her flight upstairs. "Is this fellow telling the truth? Is it true everything is over between us? No! Don't move! Answer me! I demand an answer!"

"Yes." She did not look at me as she spoke. "I'm sorry David. It is true. You mustn't be too upset. You can have the flat. Carl knows all the arrangements. Discuss it with Carl please, will you?"

"No! Stay there! Don't run away! So you've got a doctor to hide behind now as well as a lawyer. I am going to be crude and vulgar and common, and you are going to listen. You are going to pin your hopes in this chap: he is going to provide you with everything you need. You ought to let me tell you a few things, Reis. You don't quite know what you're in for, old chap."

Reis said: "Cut it out Flint. This kind of raving doesn't help."

"Don't you believe it, Doctor. Raving helps like anything. Gets it off your chest, empties the slops. Wonderful thing to do. I'll tell you what's the matter with Helen. You can work out the technical terms yourself. She was a spoilt child. Papa's girlie pet. Papa was naughty and got sent to prison. She wouldn't forgive him for getting himself caught. He settled things comfortable for her, but she left him in clink and never went near him. She let her father die in prison completely alone. She was monstrously selfish; but that doesn't fit in with her idealised picture of herself as an angel of mercy and a benefactor of the weak and the needy. She's sweet and pure and good; never sour or lustfully barren or selfishly evil. She helps people; a dabbler in other people's lives; a damager of children's souls; a self-indulgent female with the cunning of a cheap-jack and the curiosity of a whore, and all the money to satisfy her whims.

"Look out Doctor Reis! She'll have her own way with you in the end. You may give her children, and orgasms and soothing psycho-analysis, but she won't be happy until she has control of you. She's bound to win. She's got the money and the determination. She'll go on until she's tired and then she'll find something new and you'll go the way I'm going now."

Helen had run upstairs, slamming the door of her bedroom behind her.

"Listen Helen. You can still hear me!" I shouted louder than I ever imagined was possible. I was in the grip of some horrid ecstasy which used me as an instrument and would not let me go until I had finished. "You will never love and never be loved. You are damned to a cold isolation which nobody will touch. Take all your money Helen and give it away. All of it. There may be a chance then. Just a chance. But you can't part with the power it gives you: you can't do without the means to procure satisfaction for your enormous lonely vice—which your whole being lives to feed and never satisfies. Pray Helen! Pray. Do you hear me? Never mind about your refined doubts and fashionable hesitations any more. Pray until you scream!" I stopped suddenly as if the flood of words had been exhausted.

Reis was watching with interest and without any obvious embarrassment.

"How do you feel?" he asked with professional concern.

"Fine!" I said defiantly. "Absolutely fine! Never felt better in my life."

"No distasteful reactions yet?"

He was right. It was all hateful. But I spoke calmly enough.

"Not yet, Doctor. But I feel no urge at all to start again. I am replete with satisfaction and too disgusted to worry."

"Disgusted?"

We walked back to the drawing-room.

"You find my case interesting?" I said. He offered me a cigarette. I had misjudged him. His passion for his science was disinterested enough. He still did not realise how deeply he had walked into Helen's web.

"There was an undertone of self-disgust in your outburst," Reis said. "As if you felt that what you were saying was also a condemnation of yourself."

"It was." I was prepared to speak with utter frankness. "But you didn't feel it applied in any way to you?"

He ignored my question.

"I had hoped to achieve a situation in which you and Helen would part amicably after coming to some reasonable objective arrangement. That would have been the most beneficial course for you both. What you have done this morning will make my work very much more difficult."

I did not trouble to conceal my pleasure.

"You have strong destructive impulses Flint," Reis said.

"What do you suggest?" I said flippantly. "A course of crockery breaking, a fortnight's smashing-up therapy?"

"Your behaviour certainly suggests mal-adjustment of a profound nature."

Depression in an ever deepening fog gathered about me. It seemed such a futile occasion, so absurd a quarrel to end so meaningless a relationship. This bland young man was beginning to get on my nerves. If he was clever, his cleverness would get him nowhere. Intelligence was a sharp tool that dug the deepest grave.

" 'If we say we have no sin,' " I did not care whether Reis was listening or not, " 'we deceive ourselves and the truth is

227

not in us.' Self-knowledge cannot be true unless it also induces self-disgust."

I lapsed into a gloomy silence, uncertain what to do next.

"What you were saying about Helen's father," Reis said carefully. "About his having been in prison, was all that true?"

"Quite easy to verify. For further notes on Helen's behaviour you could consult one Peter Bayly, her former husband; a harmless young man who would probably regard you with the greatest distaste and suspicion."

I was eager to leave, but I had no idea where to go. I felt like the lonely survivor of some defeated force. The greater part of the justification for my existence had been wiped out. The marriage, the one far off event towards which my whole life had been moving, would not take place. Not only would not take place. Not only would nothing be the same again; but nothing was what it had seemed. My life appeared to have been so empty that to recall it resembled sweeping up the dust.

I rose to my feet. "I'm going," I said. It was possible to leave without knowing where to go. I had some money in my pocket. The wind could blow whither it listed. My own will seemed beaten into a softness that was only a willingness to be used, to be driven on without knowledge or desire of any destination.

"There was no need for it to end like this." Reis sounded rather annoyed. "Helen was fully aware of her responsibilities towards you. She wanted you to continue in possession of her London flat. She also had plans for a financial settlement. . . ."

"I prefer not to be pensioned off," I said. Arrangements I seemed to have acquiesced in for so long, now seemed monstrous and intolerably degrading.

"I was practically certain an amicable arrangement was possible," Reis said. "It may not be too late yet."

I gazed at him with vague stirrings of curiosity. How had Helen picked him up? Attending the children perhaps? He was a promising young something just as I had been a promising young something. She was demonstrating a deep disinterested concern for the great work he could do for humanity. She believed in her talent for piloting genius to the harbour of achievement. Reis seemed a decent fellow. Too cocky perhaps, too assured of the panacea he peddled. I bore him no ill-will.

More astonishing, I no longer bore Helen ill-will either. Helen and all her works; her men-servants and her maid-servants; her oxen and her asses; Helen Brown Purposes, Projects and Paraphernalia; yesterday's Mecca, today's mirage: I didn't give a weak damn for the whole bang-shoot. My outburst seemed to have drained me dry.

I said: "There's one thing I'd like to ask you."

"Well?"

"I'm not trying to be spiteful. I'm just curious that's all. Would you have the same concern for Helen's mental welfare if she did not command an income of eight thousand pounds a year."

To my delight Reis began to blush.

"Well," I said, "I wish you joy. I do indeed. Say good-bye to Helen for me."

I had lunch in a café in Bournemouth. I spent the first part of the afternoon on the beach, as aimless as a soldier given a brief unexpected leave. But Bournemouth got on my nerves. It was the kind of sea-side resort with unhappy associations I would avoid visiting again.

I hung about the bus-station for quite a time, toying with the notion of going out into the country. But clouds were gathering in the sky and I did not wish to add to my discomfort by getting caught in the rain. There was nothing for it but to take the next train back to London.

XXV

THE KNOWLEDGE OF complete isolation was not acutely
unpleasant. I will not pretend I was not sore, and angry
with Helen for the way she had treated me. My pride was
bitterly wounded. No one likes to be discarded. The real wasp
sting that pierced my sensitive flesh was the thought that she
had summed me up, judged me and written me off as second-
class, or a failure—which was just the same. I was possessed
with a burning desire to avenge myself by the magical composition of some masterpiece which would prove her eternally
wrong. Why not compose some grotesque portrait of a selfish
woman having all the money she needed to gratify all her
whims and fancies? A fat jagged-haired woman enduring
monolithic loneliness in a mansion stinking with the filth of
cats. But Helen didn't keep cats. And as for selfishness it was
not as crude as my own.

Some scruple held me from returning to the flat. As if to
make up for my former lack of dignity and pride, I vowed
never to set foot in the place again. Someone would be sent
to collect my things. It was humiliating to realise that the
only things belonging to me in the place were personal clothes
the best of which had been presents from Helen. Those I
would not touch; not even the evening dress, or the warm
dressing-gown or the fur-lined slipper. My attitude was rigid:
to hell with Helen. It seemed fantastic to imagine that I was
looking forward to marrying her less than twenty-four hours
ago. The cold truth was, it seemed so simple and obvious as I
walked down Victoria Street, I had never loved her. It was
possible that at one time she had loved me. But I had never
loved her. The thought brought me some consolation. Our
community of interest had been temporary and fortuitous—
the friendliness between two travellers accidentally sharing
the same compartment on a long distance train. Now the
journey was over.

The end of a journey meant a destination, but I had arrived

nowhere, shop-window gazing in Victoria Street. There had been no one to meet me at the station, and I had nowhere to go. I had arrived alone between the high purposeful buildings where policemen stood on duty, buses ran to schedule, and taxis, released by the traffic lights, bowled along on urgent private errands. I was unnoticed among a sea of others, barely aware of my own existence, a small anonymous worn engine of habit, coated with a sameness that saved me from falling quietly apart.

It was not unpleasant. A sort of painless melancholy I enjoyed as I drifted along. My 'ego' was an idiotic swollen shadow I could send out to stop the wave of traffic by raising a great shadowy hand and declaiming in a voiceless stretching of gigantic jaws *I am David Flint, the novelist. Look on my works ye Mighty, and despair*; and to my amusement the traffic would drive through him as if he was not there, and the shadow would shrink to a dark rim around my eyes.

Depression came only when I was tired, foot-sore and hungry. I had not escaped from anything, since no one wanted to capture me. Freud or somebody said that the writing of novels arose from the urge to escape from the unpalatable realities of life. If the unpalatable realities escaped from me would I no longer wish to write? Have nothing to write about? Queuing up in a Corner House for a cheap dinner was not an unpalatable reality. It was nothing. Nobody gave a damn whether I queued up or not. If the chattering line of people on the steps above me suddenly decided to move one forward and trample upon me as if I were a vacant space, it would be of no consequence to anyone. I was on the verge of not existing.

"Four." The brown clad commissionaire gazed at me with stern concern. "Room for one single, sir." I was in. My feet moved over the thick carpet. The small orchestra infused the conditioned air with musical trimmings to the great buzz of conversations. Diners leaned forward in the flattering light. With a sigh of comfort I sank into the comfortable chair.

Eating, I re-enacted the morning scene at Boscombe, this time improving my own part, lending more bite and edge, more dignity and refinement to my words. I preached Helen and Reis a frightening sermon: an oration that conjured up Hell until they were pale with fright, and frantic with repentance, begging to be forgiven. They begged me to stay, implored me for my mercy; went on all fours to pick up crumbs from the table of my all embracing love. The people about were my congregation, listening with approval, their presence a silent applause. O diners, fugitives from loneliness, O little people who mean well; simple and honest, weak and faithful, pursuing your daily tasks, short of money but infinite in patience, observe the lump of sympathy in my throat the loving tear in my eye, come near to my table, share out my crumb of pity.

Among all these no one was smaller, more lonely, more weak and faithless, more worthless than myself.

"It's very rude." I did not hear the woman at first. "Do you hear me young man. It's very rude!"

A large red face with glowing protruding eyes filled with rage against me. An absurd red hat like an upturned flower pot, embellished with a curved feather.

"It's very rude," she repeated furiously. Her voice ululated with indignation. Her feather wagged in the conditioned air. "Staring at me all this time. Upset me proper. Who do you think you are?"

"I'm sorry." I hadn't seen the woman. I must have been staring right through her.

"Sorry! What's the use of saying sorry can't you see how you've upset me. It's wicked, that's what it is!"

Her great eyes became watery with tears. Her self-pity was as great as mine. A head waiter appeared at her elbow. He gazed at us both with impartial concern.

"He stared at me. Rudely. As if I was dirt. I won't be stared at. It isn't right. I'm a decent hard-working woman . . ."

Soothing her, he led her away. People began to look at me. I left my vanilla ice unfinished.

It was worse in the street. As if I had just come up from the country, Leicester Square and Piccadilly overwhelmed me. The hard, brassy, loud, brutally confident crowd, mingling like innumerable shining snooker balls in endless small collisions on a dark table. I was too uneasy even to go into a News Theatre. There on the pallid screen, with tough music and breathing darkness, life would seem even worse. I had not the confident drive for Power that make mobs contemptible raw material to be moulded into patterns of determined dreams. I had nothing of the awful love of martyrs who see God smiling in the jeers and jostlings of the herd demanding blood. I had nothing but pity and fear and a whining desire to be loved.

The bus took me to the bottom of Gower Street. The street-lamps were lighting up. Birds twittered in the trees of Bedford Square. I wondered if Phyllis would still be at the boarding-house. At least she would be someone who valued my existence. I walked slowly up the street, passing the door, perhaps hoping for a casual meeting that would appear accidental, and would not commit me to accounting for my actions. Why not, I told myself, take another look at her? A revaluation in the light of changed circumstances. It was possible that she was not as hopeless as my previous desires had insisted she was. I would discover redeeming features that could be built about the unquestionable sweetness of her parting kiss. Compared with Helen now, Phyllis seemed superior. But compared with Helen, almost any woman would appear superior.

I had walked into Gordon Square and I found myself sitting on a bench among the trees, thinking of Marian. Six years ago she and I had sat talking beneath the same trees. I could not remember what we talked about, and Marian seemed only the ghostly centre of a glowing aura of remembered love. Love had escaped me. I was too mean a man to experience the supreme joy. Few people ever knew it. It was something not to be found by pursuing romantic illusions. All that was left to me was the common ability to search my conscience and discover my duty, and having discovered it, to carry it out.

I rang the bell of the boarding-house in Gower Street. A stern looking woman in her fifties answered the door. An air of confident possession told me she was the landlady.

"Good evening," I said politely. "Is Mrs. Flint still staying here?"

"She went home two days back." The landlady folded her arms and fixed me with a hostile stare. Her accent was un-pleasantly familiar. She was a native of my part of the country. "You her husband?"

I could not deny it.

"Well you ought to be ashamed of yourself. If I had my way the likes of you would be clapped in jail. Every man jack. Breaking the poor girl's heart."

She stepped back and slammed the door in my face.

The voice of public opinion and the monstrous regiment of interfering women. Phyllis had confided in her. With horrifying clarity I could see them at it, in the kitchen. The older woman nominally caring for the gas stove that could perfectly well look after itself, greedily gobbling from the sobbing younger woman the details of my iniquity. Phyllis's love for me was a limited affair; it did not restrain her from discussing me unfavourably with a casual acquaintance. She was lonely in a strange city, tormented with disappointment and worry, at a loss what to do next. I should sympathise with her; but I could only contemplate what I considered her betrayal of me.

If I went back to Phyllis, I was not to imagine it would be a honeyed happy-ending. She had some kind of love but it wasn't the love I needed. She would never understand me. If I went back, my only motive would be—what would it be? Duty. An unpleasant unfashionable word. Doing what my conscience clearly declared to be right. I was being driven back to what I had hoped to escape from by a conscience that insisted on operating of its own volition according to its own laws, even when they were countermanded and suppressed by my dictatorial will. Throughout the long servitude of absolute obedience to my chief desires, my conscience had its shadow government working underground. Now by a palace revolution, conscience had gained the ascendancy.

Like a sunflower in darkness my Will had wilted from lack of something to wish for. Its persistent nagging voice had been, for a while, silenced. The voices of other people went on outside like traffic in a distant street. I had nothing to listen to except my conscience, because my conscience alone kept at bay the vast sea of silence.

I never liked Euston Station. All the trains that pulled in from the north-west carried with them smoke and grime to maintain the great smudge of polluted air that overhung the place. To pass through the great arch was to enter the mouth of a street that led to all the industrial towns of the North, among others the area I had escaped from. I made enquiries about the times of trains but I hesitated long before buying my ticket. Was it really necessary to go to such lengths to obey my conscience? Could it not be satisfied with something less drastic? (I had been wrong to imagine my Will with its retinue of desires had abdicated all its powers.) Why not stay in London? Ring up some neglected friend and ask for a bed for the night. Pursue a literary career with single-minded devotion. Lavish upon your art the whole force of your desire to love. Renounce your half-hearted allegiance to dogmatic details of your religion. Enjoy the relaxation of an open mind. Embrace a vague agnosticism that would leave you to adopt an attitude of melancholy indecision more becoming to your nature. Develop the broad-minded sadness of an Anglo-Saxon who lives in exile on a southern shore, a connoisseur of living who does not pretend to know why living should be.

To call up a neglected friend would demand a degree of warm interest in his welfare I had not the energy to simulate. If I rang Allenside, what right had I to add the burden of my worry to the load he already carried? His voice would be an uncomfortable reminder of the unquestioning devotion with which he pursued the paths of righteousness without any reward except the welfare of others. I could not even go back to work at school until my life had been arranged more to my satisfaction. Later perhaps I would have some comfort for Allenside. I had to get myself straight first.

If it was salvation I so earnestly yearned for, was it absolutely necessary to travel home to find it? Stay here, said the voice of my Will, rapidly gaining strength, stay here. You have never been clear about the link between Religion and Morality, why should you stress it now? Become a great sinner, and enjoy the complete abandon of throwing yourself on God's mercy. Put the whole story in memorable prose. Travel like a war correspondent through the fires of damnation to collect despatches the whole world can read with profit and admiration.

With an effort I dismissed these worn enticements that still had power to charm. Words of one syllable, I told myself, sitting in the great waiting-room, my chin on my chest, among a throng of people. Within even so bad and weak a man as myself there were urges to goodness and a longing to be right and not bad and weak. It was necessary to be good, to do what was right and shun what was wrong. I had known all this since I was a boy in Sunday School. What had it got to do with my present situation?

The moment had come when I was to obey God. If he existed the time had come for him to speak to me. I had reached the edge of being. I was to listen for a voice, watch for a falling star across the dark silence: some message to come to me out of vast Nothing, some wordless vision, some blinding flash of light. And meanwhile I should obey my conscience, not to start winning points in my own favour, or even to work out my salvation. In order to learn how to find pleasure in living to please God. One cycle of vicious weakness had come to an end. I could not begin another and continue my lip-service to God. This miserable occasion was my chance. If I did not take it I would have to abandon my religion, my pretended worship of God in Christ. Even to have intellectual doubts was no longer an excuse, faced as I was with so simple a choice. It was time for me to become the victim of my own propaganda.

I bought my ticket. A single. In any case I would not have had enough money on me to buy a return. It was an uncomfortable journey. I shared a third class carriage with two railwaymen in their working clothes and an Irish priest who muttered over his breviary all the way to Crewe. I wanted to ask him if he had a Testament I could borrow. The two railwaymen were discussing a mutual acquaintance who had committed suicide by throwing himself under a train. They resented his lack of consideration for others. It was such a mess, one said in an habitually reasonable voice. There were neater ways of doing it. He was sorry for old Ben, mind, but there was water in the harbour, or the gas-oven. The compartment was badly lit. The priest held his book close to his nose, darting occasional shocked glances at the two railwaymen. The English, I imagined him thinking, a godless people, cold-blooded, hard and pagan. Old Ben was fed-up with living, they said, that was all, just fed-up. Sixty-five years of living—childhood, the sunshine of so many summers, first love, fatherhood, home-making, the whole white working body, sixty-five years of living thrown under a train. I never felt more eager to attach value and significance to mere living of the barest simplest kind.

At Crewe, at half past one in the morning, I had an hour to wait for my connection. I sat in the waiting-room, with a man with a bronchial cough, who smoked and wheezed and coughed and spat with a regularity that was harrowing to hear in the silent station at that time of night. He was a fitter. He travelled about the Midlands attending to faults in anthracite stoves.

"Seem to spend most of me time in waiting-rooms and refreshment-rooms," he said. "But I blow my own trumpet that in thirty-one years of this game I've never touched a drop." His missus was in a bad way. His daughter and her husband looked after her. I marvelled at the objective view he was able to take of his own life, until I wearied of listening to his story punctuated by bouts of coughing. If I were alone here with my thoughts it would be an ideal place for a dark night of the soul. But I was only asked to endure the company of a coughing man. God wasn't expecting too much from me. *If a man say, I love God, and hates his wife he is a liar: for he that loves not his wife whom he has seen, how can he love God whom he has not seen?* It was as simple as that. I had to go back.

The place frightened me more than I expected. Especially the High Street. I stole past *Rayment's General Ironmonger* as if the old man's ghost was watching me behind the lowered blinds. Sinister closed up shops, secret-concealing, living to buy and sell, like their owner's minds, closed and sunless. Instinctively I made for the only part of the town I had ever liked, the small Public Park. The four swans still moved elegantly about the ornamental lake. I bought some Sunday papers and took shelter in a wooden covered seat from a shower of rain. I expected to find some mention of Roger's garage—of his arrest even. But there was none. It looked as if he was going to get away. I was sorry. I had no strong feelings about the man, but if there was a crime, it should not go unpunished. And Allenside's boy would need to be carefully protected.

I had a foul lunch in a cheap café that smelt of frying fat. My distaste for the place was growing hour by hour. These people were alien to me. They lived on a different plane of existence. They were a community that would never accept me as I was. A Christian looks for a church: what church would I find here? My church should be a community of David Flints, me multiplied and reflected, like light in a heap of broken glass. Fragments of Flint. My protestantism was the extreme of the centrifugal tendency in historical reform. This was a new danger I had still to face, isolated individualism among an alien people. How much of my spirit was still to be broken?

It was seven o'clock in the evening when I walked down Warrington Avenue. It could not be far off Stanley's bed-time. I needed time to come to terms with Phyllis first before attempting anything with my son. I closed the garden gate as softly as I could, and walked round to the back door. I could see them through the window. The wireless was on. The boy was playing with a Meccano set on the table and listening to what sounded like Radio Luxembourg. His mother was darning socks, a pinafore over her black frock. Stanley was pretty obviously the master of the house. The puritanical Sunday of the old man's day would be something preferable to this.

Suppressing the last flicker of impulse to turn back, resolutely, I knocked; and opening the door myself, I walked in.

THE END